TWELVE DAYS
_of_
CHRISTMAS

Also by Stephanie Barron

BEING THE JANE AUSTEN MYSTERIES

Jane and the Unpleasantness at Scargrave Manor
Jane and the Man of the Cloth
Jane and the Wandering Eye
Jane and the Genius of the Place
Jane and the Stillroom Maid
Jane and the Prisoner of Wool House
Jane and the Ghosts of Netley
Jane and His Lordship's Legacy
Jane and the Barque of Frailty
Jane and the Madness of Lord Byron
Jane and the Canterbury Tale

OTHER NOVELS

A Flaw in the Blood
The White Garden

Jane *and the* TWELVE DAYS *of* CHRISTMAS

✦✦✦✦✦✦✦✦✦✦✦
BEING A JANE AUSTEN *MYSTERY*
✦✦✦✦✦✦✦✦✦✦✦

Stephanie Barron

SOHO
CRIME

Copyright © 2014 by Stephanie Barron

Published by
Soho Press, Inc.
853 Broadway
New York, NY 10003

Library of Congress Cataloging-in-Publication Data

Barron, Stephanie.
Jane and the twelve days of Christmas : being a Jane Austen mystery /
Stephanie Barron.
pages cm—(Being a Jane Austen mystery)

ISBN: 978-1-61695-423-9
eISBN: 978-1-61695-424-6
1. Austen, Jane, 1775-1817—Fiction. 2. Women novelists—Fiction.
3. Murder—Fiction. 4. Suspicion—Fiction.
5. Upper class—England—Fiction.
6. Christmas stories. I. Title.
PS3563.A8357J339 2014
813'.54—dc23 2014013493

Interior design by Janine Agro, Soho Press, Inc.

Printed in the United States of America

10 9 8 7 6 5 4 3 2 1

Jane
and the
TWELVE DAYS
_of_
CHRISTMAS

PROLOGUE:
CHRISTMAS EVE, 1814

1

ENCOUNTER IN A STORM

Saturday, 24th December 1814
Steventon Parsonage, Hampshire

"Jane," said my mother over the lolling head of the parson slumbering beside her, "be so good as to shift your bandbox and secure my reticule. I cannot manage the hamper with one hand, to be sure."

"No, indeed." I pressed my bandbox—already crushed from the confines of the stage, which was crowded beyond bearing—into my friend Martha's lap, and seized my mother's purse. She had netted it from silk, an effort demanding considerable invention and time; none of us should hear the end of it if Mrs. Austen's work were ruined, well before it could be universally admired. I braced my booted feet against the unsteady coach's floor and cradled the reticule as tenderly as a newborn babe.

My mother's hamper was a sturdy article, its contents swaddled in linen. She had provided herself with a nuncheon of cold brawn, cheese, and bread, and was determined to partake of it when we quitted the coach at Basingstoke. I doubt that any of our party had the stomach for brawn—which is invariably strong in both taste and smell—after swaying together for more than fifteen miles. Martha appeared faint and my sister, Cassandra, has never borne well with publick conveyances since the overturning of our chaise a decade ago in Lyme. For my own part, a medicinal glass of mulled wine seemed in order: my feet were become as insensible as ice, for the interior of the carriage was almost as frigid as the air without.

The odour of pickled boar's head wafted to my nostrils; Mamma had determined to inspect the hamper's contents. She was inordinately fond of brawn; it was just such a dish as recalled the festivities of her girlhood, when meals were less elegant and more English. I reflected that the increase in the numbers of French among us—due to the horrors of the guillotine and Buonaparte—has done much to improve the British palate in recent years.

"Lord," whispered Cassandra hurriedly, one gloved hand over her pinched nostrils. She was seated on my left, closer to the hamper than Martha or I.

"Never fear," I murmured. "A quarter-mile at most shall end the agony."

We wallowed through the rutted outskirts of Basingstoke, the stage lurching as though at sea. We ought to have been six within, but the coachman's avarice had persuaded him to add two more to his complement, burly fellows of the prosperous yeoman class. These were snoring within moments of our departure. Their personal cleanliness did not appear remarkable. Martha huddled against my right shoulder, Cassandra my left; and in short, we were quite crushed from the moment of quitting Alton.

The coach windows were fogged with damp, and a light snow had begun to fall; but if I narrowed my eyes and peered over my sister's shoulder I could just discern a pair of ostlers, poised at the entrance of the Angel's coaching yard with a fresh change of horses.

Happy release!

With a harsh halloo and a blare of his horn, the coachman turned into the yard and pulled up his strengthy beasts. The ostlers were at their heads in a moment. The coach door was pulled open, admitting a welcome blast of air, icy and tinged with the smell of horses. I drew a shuddering breath and waited for the burlier folk to quit their seats. Next to me, Martha heaved an unhappy sigh.

"I cannot bear the thought of continuing on alone to Bath," she said. "Perhaps I ought to have accepted my sister's invitation, and passed the Christmastide with all of you at Steventon."

Martha's sister, Mary, is my brother James's wife. It was to spend Christmas among our friends and relations in Steventon that we had ascended the stage this morning. Martha, however, was fortunate in a pressing invitation to Bath—and must bear all the indignities of a publick conveyance until well past nightfall. We were to transfer to private accommodation here in Basingstoke for the final four miles of our journey. James had promised to send a man for us. I glanced at the lowering sky—the fall of flakes only increasing—and fervently hoped that my brother had elected a closed carriage over his usual donkey cart.

"Pray take the hamper, Jane," said my mother briskly, holding out her hand for her reticule. "I am sure the good man at the Angel will overlook our nuncheon, provided we offer custom in another quarter. I shall order hot lemonade, to throw off the cold."

At a few pence per draught, this should hardly supply the loss of a fine dinner in a private parlour—but Mr. Fitch, the Angel's publican, was unlikely to expect much from us in any case. Four ladies of shabby-genteel appearance, ranging in age from thirty-nine to seventy-five and travelling upon the common stage, are unlikely to loosen their purse-strings. Even if the purse is netted of silk.

Martha was already supplied with a steaming mug of what I

suspected to be mulled wine; as the coachman would stay only for the change of horses, she could not spare a moment for the Angel's interior. I gave her a swift hug and wished her joy of the Christmas season in Bath, which was likely to be far more festive than our own; considered briefly the madcap notion of abandoning the brawn in the stableyard and stowing away in the coach with my friend; then turned resolutely and trudged after my family.

Novelists, I reflected, are rather apt to pass in silence over the rigours of travel. Our heroines are generally accommodated in private carriages, complete with fur lap robes, enormous muffs, and hot bricks to their feet; they travel post, with private teams of horses at every stage; and invariably are pursued by a rogue so handsome and dangerous as to render them insensible for the better part of the journey. I should dearly wish to be insensible for the remainder of mine.

"Miss Austen, ma'am?"

I glanced up from the muddy ruts, already turning grey with snow. A man in nankeen breeches, heavy boots, and a worn sailor's jacket: James's man, no doubt.

"Jem Harley, ma'am," he said. "Rector sent me to fetch you. I've stowed the cart in the stables so's to keep the nag warm."

The cart. My heart sank.

Four miles through open country at a snail's pace. In snow.

Having been pretty well-acquainted with James for nearly forty years, I ought not to have hoped for much else.

The man was holding out his hand for the hamper.

"Pray partake of the contents," I urged as I handed him the basket. "I am sure you will need fortifying for the journey ahead."

DUSK COMES SWIFTLY IN late December, particularly when the sun is obscured by a heavy layer of cloud. Now that the snow was falling in earnest, the roads out of Basingstoke were grown deserted as more sensible people sought safety within doors. I am sure that our driver, Jem, could hardly see beyond the nose of his nag. He did not complain or mutter oaths, however; indeed, he uttered not a syllable, his shoulders hunched and his gaze fixed on the road.

The unfortunate horse moved at a walk. Given the weight of our baggage and ourselves, I was surprized that it moved at all. It was nearly four o'clock, and growing dark. More prosperous travellers would have lit their carriage lamps before departing the Angel. But we had none to light.

"Ought not we to turn back, Jane?" Cassandra asked in a lowered tone. "James and Mary expect us every moment—they shall be in considerable suspense—and James has already laid out good money for the services of this man—but surely our present attempt is out of all proportion to what is required?"

She was huddled beneath one edge of the lap robe, which was so narrow as to prevent its being tucked beneath her; we had decided without comment to place our mother as warmly and securely as possible between us. Both Mamma and Cass kept their heads bowed, as though at Divine Service, to prevent the snow from stinging their cheeks. Cassandra's feathers—so proudly set to trim her Christmas bonnet a few days ago—were sodden and draggling by the tip of her nose.

"James may lament the loss of his coin when he has sense enough to hire a closed carriage," I retorted crossly. "His parsimony has long been cause for ridicule, but I refuse to allow it to finish us. Jem! Jem!"

Our driver turned his head.

"Pray pull up your horse. We—"

I broke off, mouth agape in dread, my eyes fixed upon the luminous spheres wavering over Jem's shoulder. Carriage lanterns! At the same instant I caught the muffled beat of hooves, deadened by snow. The oncoming coachman could not perceive us for the whirl of flakes; our paltry conveyance was unlit, and moreover, should afford not the slightest protection from the impact of a coach and four. I rose from my seat, waving my arms in panic. Jem turned, espied the danger, and attempted too late to haul his nag into the hedge at the side of the road. He achieved only the most awkward of situations, his front wheels canted into the ditch, and the rear ones rising at an angle from the roadbed.

"Jane!" Cassandra cried. Her right arm clasped our mother to her bosom, her left braced them both against the mad tilt of the cart. Placed as we were, full against the hedge, it must be impossible to escape. We should all be killed

The crash, when it came, threw me violently on top of my relations and brought my face into abrupt contact with the hedgerow. The nag was screaming in alarm and the neighs of other horses were strident in my ears; a gout of snow had fallen from the hedge full on my bonnet. There was snow in the neck of my pelisse. But my throat was open in protest, which suggested I was not quite dead—nor did I appear to have suffered any broken bones. I struggled to right myself against the yielding stuff that was Cassandra, and found purchase on my knees in the body of the cart.

The coach had come to a swaying halt some twenty yards further down the road. I could hear the coachman's curses as he struggled to control his team; he must be driving four in hand, a remarkable feat in such weather. That augured a private conveyance. I glanced about—saw Cassandra drawing breath, her eyes wide with shock, and my mother's eyes tightly closed, her lips moving in prayer.

"Are you hurt, ma'am?"

The hoarse enquiry was Jem's. He had jumped down from the box and gone to his horse's head; the beast was shuddering, but no longer attempting to throw over the traces.

"I shall do." I gathered myself in a huddle on the canted seat beside my mother and observed that the rear corner of the cart had carried away, leaving only a splintered gap. The wheel, too, was a bent misery of iron on that side. We should go no further this e'en.

"Halloo-o there! Are you injured? Is your equipage damaged?"

A deep voice, crackling with annoyance and leashed anger—but the voice of a gentleman, all the same. Its owner remained obscured by the storm.

"Nag's all right," Jem called, "but the cart's done for. You'm torn the wheel right off."

"Blast. What in the hell were you thinking, pulled up in the road without a spark of light?" The voice was approaching; I heard the quick sound of booted feet, careless of the slippery roadbed beneath them. "I'd have been damned well within my rights if I'd killed you."

"Sir!" my mother cried in outrage. I doubt she had heard so many oaths uttered in a single sentence before. "Pray consider where you are!"

There was a groan, half exasperation, half amusement. "I fear I am in the middle of a frozen wilderness, madam, with a party of Amazons I have vastly incommoded." A shape loomed out of the whirling snow: a tall beaver and a greatcoat sporting numerous capes. A gloved hand swept his hat from his head, and the tall figure bowed low. "Mr. West at your service. May I implore you to seek shelter in the far warmer interior of my carriage?"

I SUSPECT THAT IT shall be long, indeed, before I cease to think of the exquisite relief of that carriage—how opulent the dark blue velvet squabs and cushions appeared, after the careworn benches of Jem's cart, and how loath my sister and I were to spoil its beauty with our dripping pelisses. Once the coach doors were closed, the warmth of several hot bricks was palpable at our feet; my mother uttered a deep sigh of relief.

"I have no notion whom that fellow may be, Jane—he is most vulgar in his expressions, to be sure, and where the tongue goes, the mind undoubtedly follows—but I cannot think death preferable to this brush with iniquity; and I confess I felt myself to be within mere moments of expiring, so frozen as my limbs were become. I could not bear to think of my dear girls cast alone into—what did he call it? A frozen wilderness?—and thus if your brother James showers us with reproaches when he learns all, I shall take the burden of blame upon myself, as a mother and a Christian."

"Blast James," I said crossly. "He is a damned fool. You see, Mamma? I have profited by my brief association with Mr. West, in the enlargement of my vocabulary."

"You have been acquainted with such words this age, Jane," my parent retorted sharply, "so do not attempt to bamboozle me. What are those men about, with all this to-ing and fro-ing? It grows excessively late, and I want my dinner."

The brawn.

I surveyed the interior of the carriage, but no hamper betrayed its existence. The air was markedly devoid of odour, as well. The basket and its contents were vanished into a snowdrift.

"I believe," Cassandra said hastily, "the men are determining what is to be done with the damaged cart."

"Drive it entirely through the hedge," I suggested, "so that it may do no harm to any unsuspecting person on Christmas Eve. The villagers might make merry with it, in the form of kindling."

At that moment, the door nearest me was wrenched open and a dark head was thrust inside.

"Madam," he said.

I found myself confronting Mr. West. His eyes were dark brown and capable of great expression—amusement, exasperation, and weariness evident in their depths. His countenance was hardly youthful—he might claim roughly my own years, indeed—but his features were fine-boned and beautifully proportioned. Something else I detected, however, as my cheeks warmed—the gentleman seemed accustomed to study the human form, and quite intently, as though it were in his charge to record every visible detail of those he surveyed. Mr. West appraised me with an attitude both intimate and detached. He anatomised me at a glance.

"Mr. West?" I said faintly.

His gaze broke from mine and travelled over my companions.

"I understand I have the pleasure of addressing a family party, by the name of Austen, and that you are bound for the parsonage in a village called Steventon."

"Yes, indeed. My brother, Mr. James Austen, is rector of St. Nicholas church there."

"How appropriate."

I must have looked my confusion.

"It is, after all, the season of St. Nicholas. My own road, unfortunately, lies elsewhere—as you must have divined, at perceiving my approach from the opposite direction to your own. I have come, indeed, from Bath . . ."

His position in the open doorway must be growing excessively uncomfortable, as the snow was driving harder than ever; certainly the draughts were no pleasure to those within.

". . . and I am expected this evening at The Vyne."

"The Vyne!" Cassandra exclaimed. "Are you acquainted, then, with Mr. and Mrs. William Chute?"

"In a manner of speaking." He inclined his head to her. "We have maintained a voluminous correspondence, but have yet to meet in the flesh. If I hope to do so before another twenty-four hours have passed, I must conclude our conversation and send you on your way."

"You do not accompany us?" I said hurriedly.

A flicker of interest from those brown depths; and then their light was shrouded by half-closed lids. "I entrust you, rather, to my coachman. Tower is, as his name suggests, the epitome of strength. He has obtained the parsonage's direction from your carter and has unharnessed two of my team. I shall take one horse and ride onwards to The Vyne; your carter shall take the other, and lead his poor nag home. She has gone lame in her off rear."

"But what of your baggage, sir?" my mother demanded. "What of your safety? We cannot possibly exile you from your own equipage, and in such weather! That is to be doing too much!"

"Not at all, ma'am. I shall regard it as a trifle."

If I detected further amusement in his countenance, I did not betray him. I could well imagine that any man should prefer a brisk trot towards dinner and a fire, to a tedious seven-mile journey through snow seated on the box next to his own coachman. That Mr. West did not wish to embarrass us with his presence inside the carriage, I ascribed to an unexpected delicacy.

"Tower shall join me once he has set you safely down at Steventon parsonage, madam," he informed Mamma. "It is only a matter of three miles, and the road to The Vyne not much longer again than that. The horses were changed at Reading, and may easily stand the distance."

"You are very good, sir."

He smiled wryly. "Having been nearly the death of you, I cannot be too solicitous of your security." A last quicksilver glance at me, the ghost of a nod, and his head was withdrawn from the body of the coach. The door slammed to, and we heard the rap of his knuckles without; the wheels began to turn.

"Happy Christmas!" he shouted.

I peered through the sidelight. But it was already fogged with moisture, and the darkness obscured every outline; he was an indistinct figure bracketed by horses, with a whirlwind descending.

Happy Christmas, Mr. West, I mentally returned; and wondered what might bring a stranger to so wild a place as The Vyne at such a frigid time of year.

2

CHRISTMAS SPIRITS

Saturday, 24th December 1814
Steventon Parsonage, cont'd.

" A nd so you are come at last." Mary groaned as she lifted her
head from the sopha cushions. "I declare I had quite given
you up! The children have been asking for you since breakfast—
and you know how their teazing makes my head ache. But you did
not consider of me, I suppose, as you dawdled along the lanes. I
am the very last creature alive, however, to complain of ill-usage at
the hands of those I love."

"You can have no idea what we endured," my sister, Cassandra,
protested indignantly. "The conveyance James elected to despatch—I
cannot in conscience call it a carriage—"

"Poor Mary," my mother broke in briskly. "Are you unwell? That
will be very trying for James, with the Christmas service to manage."

"James!" she retorted with deepest loathing. "He has not been near
me all week! It does not suit the rector of Steventon to nurse the sick.
He is far too busy hunting!"

We remained awkwardly in the parsonage's central hall, our
clothing sodden and our tempers frayed. Despite the coldness of
our welcome, we were anything but strangers to this house—fully

half my life was lived within these walls, and I might find my way from kitchen to garret in pitch darkness without a single misstep. Judged by worldly eyes, Steventon parsonage is little more than a cottage—the front entry a latticed door, flanked by double windows to right and left. It was never an elegant abode, tho' my father sheltered eight children and generations of pupils here. Ten bedchambers above-stairs, three of them in the garrets; two wings at the back of the house, where Cassandra and I shared a bedchamber and a small dressing room we dignified with the name of boudoir. Our father, I recollect, was so good as to purchase matching tented beds for his daughters, swathed in blue-and-white-check dimity, from Ring Brothers' establishment, in Basingstoke; years later, my brother spent the giddy sum of two hundred pounds to new-furnish the parsonage for his bride—the sum being a wedding gift from Anne Mathew's father, old General Sir Mathew. He cannot have spent a tenth of such riches since.[1]

But that is to be digging up matters better left buried. Anne was James's first wife, a mild and sweet-faced creature who expired a few years after acquiring the pretty mahogany table and dozen matching chairs. They have grown worn and neglected under Mary's authority.

There are other ghosts than Anne, however, in this dearest of childhood homes. I glanced around the low-ceilinged front hall with an aching heart, half-expecting my beloved father to emerge from his study, white head bent in amusement to the piping voice of a young scholar struggling with his Latin; but such fancies are in

[1] For more information regarding the Austen family accounts at Ring Brothers, see "*Persuasion:* The Jane Austen Consumer's Guide," by Edward Copeland, in Persuasions, No. 15, pp.111–123, The Jane Austen Society of North America, 1993.—Editor's note.

vain. Papa died years ago in Bath, far from Steventon, and there he remains—solitary in the churchyard.

When my mother was mistress of the parsonage, it was filled with candlelight and warmth. We were buried in the north Hampshire country each winter, to be sure, the village boasting but a string of cottages and its twelfth-century church—but Mamma did not stop to consider of her dignity, nor pine for the brilliance of Society. She cultivated such acquaintance as she found, among Great and lowly alike, from Lord Bolton at Hackwood Park to the meanest villager in his hovel. I know for a certainty that funds were scarce, but we rarely wanted for much. The parsonage was inveterately cheerful. Curtains of cherry red hung from the windows, and the low beams echoed with myriad voices.

Mary had wrapt herself in shawls and was propped among her cushions by a churlish fire. She had not troubled herself to stir the coals, nor had she unwrapt a languid hand in welcome. Impatient with such die-away airs, I tore at my bonnet strings and discarded the offending object on the flagstone floor, unwilling to dampen the seat of a hallway chair.

"We were overturned, Mary," I said as I strode into the room, "and but for the kind offices of a complete stranger, should be frozen stiff, somewhere between the Winchester and Andover roads. If Mamma has not caught her death, it will be the wonder of the season—and we are all sorely in want of our dinners. Happy Christmas."

She shifted round slightly so as to face me, her wan face expressionless. "Your dinners? How extraordinary. I have no appetite at all. The slightest morsel is as ashes in my mouth. James has a little gruel, to be sure, when he comes in at this hour—you will observe how late it has grown whilst you idled in Basingstoke! But perhaps Cook has considered of you. A cold collation, left out on the sideboard."

Impossible that she should grasp the severity of our ordeal; it should be left to Cassandra or me to chivy the housemaid into preparing hot coals for the warming pans and hot bricks to the feet, when once we made our cheerless way to bed. Not for the first time did I wish myself wedged back into the publick stage with Martha, still swaying towards Bath!

My mother had disappeared into the dining parlour in search of sustenance; she had long known what Mary was. Cassandra, being more selfless than Mamma and more charitable than I, attempted once more to move the poor sufferer before us.

"You know we always make you better once we are come." She crossed the room and perched herself upon the sopha's creaking arm. A few drops of melting snow fell from her bonnet to Mary's faded hair, drawn back in a makeshift knot at her nape. But Mary persisted in staring bleakly at the leaded casement, like a child in a fit of the sullens.

"Such gaieties as we shall have," Cassandra attempted, hastening to remove her gloves, the better to wrestle with her bonnet, "now that Christmas is upon us."

"Twelve days entire of rank frivolity," I agreed sardonically.

"We shall call upon the Terrys, and the Harwoods, and the Bramstons at Oakley Hall," Cassandra enumerated, more for the benefit of ourselves than the listless Mary. "And we may claim a new acquaintance at The Vyne! A Mr.—West, was it not, Jane? Our deliverer from the snowbank. I have not seen Mr. and Mrs. Chute this age. What a delight it shall be to meet once more!"

"Then you are more easily pleased than I," Mary retorted spitefully. But her attention was reclaimed, and she forced herself upright against the sopha cushions. Her form emerged from the shawls; a drift of Paisley slid down her shoulders. "Mrs. Chute is an excessively vulgar woman, I believe, who presumes to comment upon those above her station. Only think, Cassandra—she deigned to give me what she termed a ha'porth of advice. Utterly unsolicited, I assure you. 'If Mrs. James Austen were only to undertake some useful employment'—careening about the country on horseback with that wretched Vyne Hunt, no doubt—'she should be much improved for it, and throw off these airs and megrims.' Mrs. Chute shall think better of her insolence, I suppose, when she sees me in my grave."

"Now, Mary," my mother interjected as she reentered the parlour bearing a platter in both hands, "here is a fine bit of ham and a round of Stilton. I declare I have not seen such a Stilton in many a year!"

"A gift to James from the parish, I suppose," his wife noted indifferently.

"Should you like a morsel?"

"Of so strong a cheese! No, indeed. I should fall ill directly."

We had risen at cock-crow to prepare for the long journey from Chawton Cottage to my brother's house—all of seventeen miles— and even without the chaos of recent hours, should have dearly loved a little consideration. But it was ever thus, in James's household: the invited guests must immediately minister to the desperate heroine who commanded the scene, and no concerns but hers were broached. I might happily have strangled Mary many years since, so poor a patience do I possess for nerves; and therefore cannot trust myself to cross her doorstep unattended.

She hunched one shoulder at Mamma and returned her gaze to the blank windowpane; my mother sank down into a chair and threw up her hands.

I seized a knife and cut into the ham with heartless industry.

Pray apprehend: Mary is not ill, exactly; she merely fancies herself so. She quacks and physicks herself, and announces portentously that the End is Near; she lies upon the sopha the better part of the day and laments the coldness of a world indifferent to her dying. She refers to her grave with all the consideration of an old friend; but where it may lie, and what may drive her into it, remains a subject of conjecture among her intimates. Tho' a trifle thin, Mary possesses as sound a body as the rest of us. It is her mind that is ill. A want of energy and interest are the chief evils—although I suspect that Mary secretly revels in the distinction her humours give her. Her portion in life is meagre, her social ambitions constrained; but as an invalid, her stile is equal to the greatest duchess's in the Kingdom.

"I daresay you wish to know how we left Martha." Cassandra had succeeded in removing her bonnet and was smoothing her disarranged hair. Our dearest Martha may be Mary's sister, but there cannot be two more dissimilar women in the Kingdom; where one is indolent, the other is active; one self-absorbed, the other benevolently inclined towards all the world. I carried my plate of ham as close as possible to the fire, too chilled to remove my pelisse, and took up the tongs. Once stirred, the embers glowed with faint life; I tossed some kindling upon them and was rewarded with a flame.

"Pray do not trouble, Jane," Mary said sharply. "For what do we possess a parlour maid?"

"Merest show, apparently." I grasped a log in my gloved hands. "Draw your chair nearer to the hearth, Mamma, and allow me to take your wrap."

"Martha," Cassandra persisted a shade more loudly, "was excessively well. We saw her safely onto the stage at Basingstoke, and have every expectation she will reach her friends in Bath by nightfall. She begged that I wish you all the joy of the season."

"Martha does not know what it is to be ill," Mary said fretfully. "She has no compassion for those who suffer."

Thus she despatched her sister, whilst I despatched the ham.

It is a pity, indeed, that James's choice did not light upon Martha when he went looking for a wife among the Lloyds of Ibthorpe. It is many years since I ceased to regard Martha as an acquaintance, and embraced her wholeheartedly as a relation. A friend of the bosom in my distant girlhood—a companion in wet country walks and overheated Assembly-Room balls—she is become as much a sister to me as Cassandra. Since her mother's death, indeed, she has made her home with us at Chawton. Martha should never have met us with gloom, or served my mother's parsonage with neglect. But it is probable the high spirits and excellent sense of my dearest friend should have been entirely thrown away upon my eldest brother. The loss of his Anne, a mere eighteen months after the birth of their only child, seems to have turned his heart queerly—tho' I do say it of a clergyman, whose solace ought to be in the prospect of Better Things.

Certainly James did not attempt to supply Anne's gentle place in his second attachment; his union with Mary might best be regarded as a marriage of convenience, undertaken by a gentleman perplexed with the care of managing a parish and raising a female child entirely alone. If there was an initial liking in James's choice—if indeed there was even love—it has long since gone off, like a beauty's brief and early bloom. Such an unhappy situation cannot be without its ill effects upon every member of the household.

Mary consented to raise little Anna, James's child; but what maternal love she claims is reserved, in rare moments, for her own progeny: James-Edward, a youth of sixteen who spends the better part of his year at Winchester School, and Caroline, a young miss of nine years who wanders the hedgerows in summer and hides in the garrets with stolen books during the long winter months. It was the "teazing" of these two that had set our Mary's head to aching; but as I had heard not a peep from the adjoining rooms in the interval following our arrival, I concluded both children were gone out—Caroline to visit her pony in the stables, perhaps, and James-Edward to one of the happier households of Dummer or Sherborne St. John. After the bustle of Winchester, I should imagine the poor boy was desperate for any amusement that might offer, for certainly none was to be found within the parsonage.

As for Anna—she is now grown and married a month to her improvident curate, Ben Lefroy, the youngest son of my own dear departed friend, Madam Lefroy. Ben is indolent and barely inclined to shift for himself, much less a wife; to unite their fortunes must be regarded as one of the worst decisions either party ever made; but as a certain release from the household at Steventon, Anna's match may be credited a success.

I was summoned from my ruminations—and my enjoyment of the ham—by all the noise of arrival emanating from the rear of the house.

"James!" Mary said with a curious air of satisfaction. She drew her draperies once more to her chin, cast her head languidly on the sopha pillow, and stared fixedly into the blank windowpane—the very image of one sunk in suffering.

The heavy tread of booted feet sounded in the passage. There was a flicker as James paused to light a wall sconce with his taper, the only light in the parsonage save the glow from the hearth.

"Pray secure an oil lamp, dearest, whilst you are about it," my mother called out. "Else you are likely to trample us in all this gloom."

"Mama!" James hastened through the parlour doorway, his hands outstretched in welcome; one of them still clutched the burning taper. I slipped it from his fingers as he embraced our parent, and tossed it into the fire.

"Jane! And Cass! Welcome, welcome! I trust you arrived safely before the snowfall?"

"We arrived safely," Cassandra replied, with a hint of unaccustomed irritation. "Happy Christmas, James. You look very well."

And naturally she was correct—I have never had a glimpse of my eldest brother when he is not beaming with the most sanguine self-satisfaction. It need not concern us that his pate has suffered a diminution in its luxurious hair, or that his figure has increased beyond what is strictly acceptable in a man of Fashion, or that he is buried in the country with only four-and-twenty families to admire his sermons of a Sunday morning. James is above such worldly concerns. He inhabits the realm of the Spirit; and those of us required to ascend to its heights in his train, may only congratulate ourselves.

If we did not, we might be tempted to seek our beds with as much lassitude as the unfortunate Mary.

"My dear," he said sternly to his wife the instant my thoughts chanced to light upon her, "do not alarm me with this attitude of dejection. Say not that you have suffered a relapse of your habitual complaint!"

Mary merely sighed, her shoulders drooping. Being lost in contemplation of the grave, she could not lift her head.

James knelt by the sopha and secured her hand. "You must endeavour to overcome your worse self, my dear. You must pray to our Lord to arm you against the Devil—who comes in the form of an oppression of spirits, and wrestles for your soul!"

My eyes met Cassandra's over our brother's bowed head. He was murmuring words of scripture into Mary's palm. It was as I had foreseen: our lighthearted Christmas season was at an end before it had begun.

My mother quitted her chair and gathered us up, linking an arm through each of ours. "I should enjoy spirits of an entirely different order, girls. I am sure that sherry will accompany this Stilton delightfully—and I know exactly where James hides it!"

THE FIRST DAY

3

A SUMMONS TO THE VYNE

Sunday, 25th December 1814
Steventon Parsonage

The snow ceased to fall during the night, and it was a sparkling world that greeted us this Christmas morning. The verger had swept the churchyard pavings, despite James's prohibition against any form of labour on so sacred a day, and thus we were able to walk in a sedate file from the parsonage to St. Nicholas's. Cassandra's bonnet feathers were past repair, but Mamma exhibited her reticule with modest pride.

Mary was markedly pale, the consequence of having refused all sustenance in the past four-and-twenty hours. How interesting we may make ourselves, through the conscious mortification of the flesh!

The local farmwives had festooned the stone interior of the old Norman church with green boughs of fir and holly, a ritual dear enough to the villagers that James must have submitted to the practise with grudging grace. I know him to regard such decoration as thoroughly pagan—as he does most of the gaieties of the Christmas season—and would never allow it to be attempted at home. And indeed, as he mounted the rostrum to deliver his Nativity sermon, my brother's brow was lowering and his aspect melancholic. How strange this seems! Our dear father was joyous in his offerings of mistletoe to every lady of his acquaintance, however seriously he regarded his duties as a clergyman. James's repugnance for worldly happiness must be viewed, then, as the determined rebellion of a disaffected son. We Austens were not reared to be cheerless and disdainful; on James's part, this is a conscious choice. I must assume, therefore, that having been treated to a childhood of strictest sobriety, young James-Edward shall take the shortest road to ruin—through a gaming hell and a brothel—and that little Caroline will be a heedless madcap, wanton in every material display, when once she attains her freedom.

Caroline is approaching her tenth year, a slip of a girl with waves of chestnut hair pulled painfully into a knot at her neck. Clear grey eyes—Austen eyes—and a rose complexion bode well for her looks; she requires only time and care to bloom. I should like to carry her off to Godmersham, my brother Edward's estate in Kent, where young ladies are allowed to be foolish and silly, and to dance in the nursery wing long before they are permitted to waltz in publick. But lacking all authority, I must content myself with the early presentation of Caroline's Christmas gift—which by rights should wait for Twelfth Night, when all our presents, trivial though they may be, are exchanged. I believe I shall steal into Caroline's room and leave my token on her pillow without a word, as tho' some good faerie had bestowed it. Caroline will delight in the game of discovering her benefactress, which will increase the gift's value threefold.

She was sitting between The Aunts, as she calls Cassandra and me, profiting from our collective warmth. James abhors the waste of fuel in a church stove, believing that discomfort is conducive to spiritual fervour. Caroline's eyes were fixed steadily upon her father as he spoke, but her fingers beat the faintest of patterns upon her knee.

She was, I collected, humming a secret song in her head. With very little encouragement her toes should soon be tapping too.

James was delighting us on this splendid Christmas morn with a grave reminder that the Christ Child's birth was but a Prelude—Necessary, and therefore Joyous—to the Solemn Mystery of the Cross. The Virgin Birth in the stable must end with the Sacred Sacrifice at Calvary; the veneration of the angels, with the violent pounding of nails through flesh.

It occurred to me that this trend in James's speech, being riddled with both Mysticism and Gore, was very nearly as pagan as the festooning of the church with holly boughs; and that perhaps I might twit him on couching his spiritual instruction in such crude and vivid terms as his villagers must relish.

But why bait a bull, Jane? He would only chide me for having missed the sacred point.

I glanced aside at Caroline; her eyelids drooped. She, too, had heard this sombre profession of Crucifix-in-the-Cradle from the time she could speak. Beyond her head, James-Edward was frankly nodding. He had been late abed after a stolen night of revels among his cronies at Ashe Park. He is a handsome lad, at just the age to reject his boyish pursuits and ape his elder heroes. The points of his collar are ridiculously high, his mop of brown hair is fashionably tousled, his cravat exceedingly ill-tied. From what little conversation we shared this morning, I should judge him to be torn between two modes of life: that of the Byronic Aesthete and that of the Corinthian Set. He wastes what free hours he may claim in scribbling poetry, or riding a borrowed hunter to hounds.

His father intends him for Oxford, and Holy Orders; I wonder very much what James-Edward intends?

I was recalled to virtue by the uncertain lifting of voices under the stone architraves. James had concluded his edifying words, and the congregation was on its feet. There might be no more than fifty parishioners in St. Nicholas church, but on this cold, clear Christmas morn they were united in wavering song.

Blessed be that lady bright,
That bare a child of great might,
Withouten pain, as it was right,
Maid mother Mary.

AN HOUR LATER, WE had endured the well-wishes of the villagers and tramped home, chilled to the bone, to partake of an indifferent breakfast. I consumed a modest portion of buttered toast, washed down with tea, being disinclined to sample the congealing eggs on the sideboard. James regaled himself on cold beef and ale. His wife had returned to her bed after Divine Service; she was firmly attached to her indisposition, and might not be seen again for the duration of our visit, tho' we intended to remain a fortnight. Cassandra had already quitted the table; James-Edward was engrossed in a London newspaper several days old; and my mother was smiling benignly into the middle distance. I hoped she was revolving memories of happy seasons past, when my father was alive and all her children gathered in this breakfast-parlour.

Into this scene of hectic pleasure burst little Caroline, with shining eyes. "Papa!" she cried. "Look what the faeries have left upon my pillow!"

She held up a winsome-faced doll arrayed in the very latest mode, with hair of gold and a painted bisque face. Caroline had glimpsed just such a doll, in the possession of her younger Knight cousins, whilst my brother Edward and his household were on a protracted visit to Chawton Great House the previous summer. I had suspected how her young heart yearned for such a treasure—an intimate friend for confidences at bedtime; a silent audience for the stories she read aloud in her snug attic. I purchased the doll whilst visiting my brother Henry in London last month—but Cassandra and I had fashioned her clothes with our needles, from scraps of finery we had to hand. Her ball gown was dark green silk trimmed with gold floss; her headdress was fashioned of tiny crimson flowers and paste emeralds; and her tiny china hands were sunk in a pillow-muff of swansdown. There were additional costumes, as befit a dashing lady of the *ton*: morning dresses, walking dresses, carriage dresses, opera cloaks, and even a riding habit. But Caroline had not yet glimpsed these delights—they were to be doled out, piecemeal, over each of the season's twelve days.

"That's a very fine doll," James-Edward told his sister as he set down his paper. "But she seems far too substantial for faeries. I reckon The Aunts had something to do with it."

"The Aunts are faeries," Caroline retorted snubbingly.

"That will do, Caroline," James said. He glanced quellingly at me. "I could have wished that my permission had been sought before such an extravagant gift was bestowed upon the child. It is unlikely that her behaviour merits it."

Caroline looked stricken, and clutched the doll to her bosom. "If you would refer," she said with awful dignity, "to the untidiness of my lessons yesterday, I assure you, Papa, that I shall endeavour to write more legibly. I shall contrive to leave off blots. Only James did not mend my pen properly."

"Nonsense," my mother declared, in her son's general direction. "The child is good as gold. Come here, Caroline, and let me have a look at your treasure!"

Caroline obeyed her grandmamma with alacrity.

"What is to be her name?"

"Jemima!" Caroline breathed.

"Pray present us," my mother said. It was exactly the sort of formal nonsense in which Caroline should delight; she forced the doll to curtsey. They would be trading teacups in a very little while.

"I must suppose," James said to me in a lowered tone, "that I have you to thank for this . . . gross indulgence. This is the result, I presume, of a lady's having come into her own funds. An independence that must be deplored, when it is allied with lightness of mind."

James has long despised my habit of penning novels, and regards my forays into authorship with an alarm that increases as my fame widens. It is unseemly, he believes, for a spinster of middle years to engage in such a display of intellectual arrogance. It is unseemly, as well, for a lady to earn her own money—and control its disposition herself. James should like to intervene on my behalf, and is jealous of my brother Henry's influence, Henry being a banker well-established in London and a knowledgeable man of the world.

The secret of my authorship having unfortunately got out, through the offices of that same Henry—whose pride in my accomplishments cannot be contained, any more than his delight in sharing news—I am now known to be the Lady lately hidden behind the covers of *Sense and Sensibility* as well as *Pride and Prejudice*. I had thought that my third novel—*Mansfield Park*—might mollify James, as one of its principal subjects is Ordination; and aside from a minor portrait of a gluttonous Canon, there can be nothing improper in my depiction of the clergy from beginning to end. But having secured his set of my presentation volumes, James was subdued in his praise; it was "commendably less vulgar in stile," and my insipid mouse, Fanny, "admirable in her contemplation of Duty." I valued Henry's delight in the witticisms of Mr. Crawford, and the viciousness of Mrs. Norris, infinitely more. As I have not the slightest hope that James will approve of my newest heroine, as yet unrevealed to the world's censorious eye—for a sillier, more indulged child than Emma Woodhouse never existed—I must accept his disapprobation of my life and character as the cost of pursuing Art.

"My dear James," I said as I rose from the table, "I am sorry to prove such a perpetual disappointment. You may have the satisfaction, perhaps, of viewing my torment in the Afterlife—when my portion shall be so much smaller than yours."

He opened his mouth to respond—shall I admit that I had not the slightest interest in what my brother had to say?—but was forestalled by the sudden appearance of his housemaid, bearing a missive upon a silver tray. She bobbed a curtsey and extended the tray to me.

"Thank you, Sarah." I took up the folded square of hot-pressed paper, sealed with bright blue wax in a design I did not recognise, and tore it open.

The Vyne
Sherborne St. John
25 December 1814

My dear Jane,
You will forgive me the liberty of addressing you, and not the good Rector and his wife, when you know the delight that news of your presence in the neighbourhood has afforded me! When Mr. West revealed his precipitate introduction with all your party upon his arrival last e'en, I was fit to be tied— for berating his stupidity in not having conveyed you here! What fun we should have had, Jane, had your overturned

carriage led you to harbour for the season at The Vyne! But Mr. West was too circumspect; too much the gentleman in his consideration; too good, indeed, to be worth bearing! He repents of his virtue even now, and adds his pleas to mine. If you and yours—the Parsonage Party, as we have taken to calling you—do not take pity upon us, and dine here this evening, we shall positively murder one another out of sheer boredom. Pray do not protest, but come to us as soon as you have received this missive. We shall not be happy unless you consent to remain our guests for several nights, at least.

I have required John Coachman to wait upon the pleasure of all your party, not excepting the children.

Yours ever,
Elizabeth Chute

4

A - WASSAILING WE WILL GO

Sunday, 25th December 1814
Steventon Parsonage, cont'd.

"And so Mrs. Chute would have us fill out her numbers," Mary said waspishly. She was propped up in her bed, a quantity of pillows disposed behind her back. "James will be wild to go, of course—The Vyne Hunt invariably meets on St. Stephen's Day, the men being fretful after a protracted period within doors. Trust a gentleman to leave his lady to bestow the servants' Christmas boxes, while he dashes about on horseback!—And then demand a cold collation and mulled wine upon his return, I daresay, once all the servants have gone off on their holiday. Only consider, Jane, how much work that will mean tomorrow, if we accede to Mrs. Chute's inordinate pleas, and drag ourselves to The Vyne! It is such a great, old, draughty place—and without servants it shall be a veritable Purgatory."

Just so did James's wife greet the happy news that we were bid to join the Christmas gaieties at one of the first houses of the neighbourhood—with all the promise of informed and intelligent conversation! Heaven forbid we should stir ourselves to partake of such delights; better to wander forlornly through the stuffy rooms of the parsonage and sigh over the world's neglect.

"Depend upon it," Mary added as she reached for her smelling-salts, "that is Elizabeth Chute's object in offering her pressing invitation. She requires more hands in the absence of her staff tomorrow."

I had expected perversity from Mary, and her very predictability now suggested a method of persuasion. She should always be inclined to do exactly the opposite of what was desired.

"James never intended to go," I said with a casual air. "He declared your Spiritual Crisis to be at such a critical point that he means to remain in prayer with you for the rest of the day. On his knees. Before the altar of St. Nicholas's. Hunting would be sheer misery, he says, when a Tormented Soul languishes for want of aid. He appears to believe that you harbour a Devil, Mary, that must be cast out. He bade me tell you to dress yourself very warmly, as you know the church is both damp and freezing."

She stared at me, her vinaigrette suspended. "Why cannot James comprehend that mine is a bodily wasting? There is nothing spiritual in the matter at all."

"Indeed, I urged him to reconsider, for I cannot think the atmosphere of St. Nicholas's to be salutary for one in your dangerous condition."

"No, indeed! He cannot be so cruel! So lost to all humanity!"

"I'm afraid he regards it as a kindness," I said solemnly. "Only think. He has sacrificed his chance at sport with Mr. Chute—to ensure the salvation of your soul."

"Abominable cheek!" Mary said contemptuously. "I will rise this instant. Send Sarah to me, Jane—for your brother shall never contrive to work his tricks upon me at The Vyne!"

THE UNFORTUNATE JOHN COACHMAN had been walking his horses up and down the lane before the parsonage for nearly an hour by the time we were collected upon the doorstep with our satchels. James-Edward was to ride up beside the coachman on the box, while the rest of our party were arranged three to a side within the closed carriage. It was not a fashionable conveyance, being an old travel-ling chariot that had probably been procured on the occasion of the Chutes' marriage, some twenty years before—but it would serve. The lanes about The Vyne, and indeed throughout all of northern Hampshire, are notoriously bad in winter, and the fresh fall of snow should have made them impassable to a hired cart or James's gig, the latter being a one-horse conveyance employed for his visits to the sick and dying among the parish. I blessed Elizabeth Chute's kindness in having provided for her guests so well.

John Coachman had warmed his bricks in our kitchen while we busied ourselves, and these greeted our feet as the carriage door was shut. Caroline wriggled excitedly between her parents, Jemima resplendent upon her lap. "Shall they have a Yule log?" she enquired. "And shall we play at Snapdragon?"

The very word recalled a memory of hilarity: a darkened Godmer-sham withdrawing-room; a bowl aflame with lighted brandy, glowing eerily blue among the shadows; and eager hands reaching into the bowl, for raisins snapping with brandy and flames!

"You most certainly shall not," Mary sniffed. "You are far too young to put your fingers into fire."

"Then I shall snatch the raisins for you, Caroline," my mother interjected.

And so, between scolds and caresses, we made our stately progress towards The Vyne. The house sits some three miles north of Basing-stoke, and Steventon is at least another mile further west—we should be full an hour upon the road at our present pace.

How shall I describe The Vyne? I suppose from its initial aspect, as one turns off the Sherborne St. John road half a mile past the village, into the long expanse of lane leading to the house. On every side are groupings of copses surrounded by empty meadows, the very sort of ground a man like William Chute must value for sport. He is Master of The Vyne Hunt, a distinction accorded him by his neighbours, in recognition of the fact that he has bred and maintained the best pack of foxhounds known in the entire country. But I was speaking of the great house—which deserves to be as admired as Hatfield or Stratfield Saye, both its neighbours. The Vyne has presided over this part of Hampshire since medieval times; sheltered Anne Boleyn and Henry VIII under its roof; holds the tomb of the first Speaker of Parliament; and gave up a Recusant traitor to execution in Queen Elizabeth's Tower. The present family have no direct claim upon this illustrious history, The Vyne having passed through more ancient hands to modern cousins. But the house itself recalls vanished dignities. Its south front, complete with sweep and porch and flanking towers, is mellow Tudor brick; its north front is a Neoclassical dream, rising from a lake, with specimen trees dotted across its lawn. There is even a portico, all columns and pediment, designed by a disciple of Inigo Jones.

John Coachman pulled up his horses before the south porch and immediately two liveried footmen helped us from the carriage. In the interval required for our journey, the weak Christmas sun had vanished, and tho' the hour was not much past two o'clock, a determined dusk appeared to be falling. The temperature had also plummeted. I placed an arm around Caroline's shoulders and hurried her inside.

The entrance hall of The Vyne is one of the most remarkable sights in Hampshire, being deeper than it is wide, and almost entirely filled with an Adamesque staircase designed in the last century by the late John Chute—an aesthete, world traveller, sometime-architect, and bosom friend of Horace Walpole. As a member of the Strawberry

Hill Set (named for Walpole's Gothick home), the vanished Chute placed Taste above everything—even the continuation of his family line. He spent his hours collecting antiquities and designing monuments for The Vyne's famous chapel; and tho' his fanciful fretwork of white-panelled steps still rises triumphantly at the centre of the house, the estate passed to a secondary line at John Chute's death.

Caroline was staring open-mouthed at the staircase; the pillars and railings that defined it were wrapt with heavy garlands of holly and bay, tied up with gold silk ribbon. The scent of greens mingled with the smell of beeswax and clove. Having been treated to the delights of The Vyne these twenty years at least, I occupied myself in drawing off my gloves while the child stared.

"Is that a Yule log, Aunt Jane?" she enquired, pointing at the great oak trunk, twice Caroline's girth, smouldering on the hearth.

"It is, my sweet. They will have lighted it last evening, I daresay. You may watch it burn down slowly whilst you are here."

"Too slowly." Beside me, Cassandra shivered; the heat provided by the log was prevented from reaching us by the quantity of architecture filling the middle of the room.

"Mrs. Austen! And all the Austens, exactly as I had hoped and desired! It is too good of you to travel across the country like this. I hope you find that our Christmas cheer is equal to expectation."

Elizabeth Chute is a handsome lady some five years older than I, whose snapping dark eyes and carefully arranged toilette proclaim the lady of Fashion. Today she wore cherry-red sarcenet, with a braided trim of chocolate, and a figured turban becomingly set in her dark hair. I first dined with the Chutes, some fifteen years since, and have danced in Eliza's drawing-room—and I may say that on this occasion she appeared in as admirable looks, and as high a flow of spirits, as she had when a young bride in the full bloom of youth.

"Mrs. Chute," I said warmly as she grasped my hands in both of hers. "A very happy Christmas."

"Jane," she murmured. "Do not affect formality with me, I beg, tho' it has been an age since we met! Caroline, my dear, is that beautiful creature your very own? She is so cunningly turned out, I declare she shall throw all the other ladies into the shade! And now let us repair to a better fire—for the chill in this hall is impossible to dispel!"

We gave up our wraps to the footmen and followed our hostess down a panelled passage. The Vyne's remarkable reception rooms are very little altered from Tudor times, however much the Strawberry Hill Set might have wished otherwise. As I made my way through the large drawing-room, however, I saw it was filled with a colourful array of strangers—something our Steventon family could not have anticipated from Eliza's missive. But there could be no turning back now; I must endure the gauntlet of critical eyes, with chin raised high.

My brother James, who led our parade, halted before William Chute, Eliza's husband, and bowed; the two are old cronies these many years, their friendship having to do entirely with dogs, horses, and guns. Mr. Chute married his Eliza when she was three-and-twenty, a lady reared in comfortable circumstances and considerable elegance; he was four-and thirty, a trifling disparity at the time, and only lately come into his inheritance. Twenty years on, Elizabeth still appears to considerable advantage, enjoying all the blessings of health, prosperity, and high spirits—while William looks the full weight of his years, being much weathered from his persistent exposure to the out-of-doors. Tho' he has spent the better part of the past two decades in Parliament, his acquaintance with London has given him no town bronze; he remains the affable and unaffected country gentleman he ever was.

The Chutes make an enviable picture: the lady so charming and gay, the master so mild and easy; it is a pity that they have no houseful of children to support them. But for all their good fortune, they were denied this single material blessing, and chose instead to adopt a distant relation—much as my own brother Edward was adopted by Sir Thomas Knight and his lady.² In the Chutes' case, however, the choice fell upon a girl—one Caroline Wiggett, who came to The Vyne at the age of four. She is now a shy, blushing miss of fifteen, who retires with relief from her elders to the schoolroom whenever possible. She stepped forward on this occasion, however, and bobbed a curtsey to our Caroline in welcome. James-Edward hovered near the two, uncertain whether to treat Miss Wiggett as child or young lady.

"Let me make you known to each other," Eliza declared in a ringing tone. "How ever am I to accomplish such a task, Mr. Chute, when we are so bewildered by numbers?"

"Leave 'em to present themselves," he suggested.

She scowled at him in mock annoyance. "That should never do. Pray attend, dear friends! You have before you Mr. James Austen, rector of Steventon and vicar, I might add, of our own Sherborne St. John—we hope very much, Mr. Austen, that you will favour us with a short service of Evensong tonight, in the Chapel, in respect of the season."

"I should be delighted, ma'am," James said.

"Next to him is his excellent wife, Mrs. James Austen; his mother, Mrs. George Austen; and his sisters, Miss Austen and Miss Jane

---

² Jane's elder brother, Edward, was adopted by wealthy cousins at the age of twelve, and subsequently named the heir to their estates in Hampshire and Kent. Edward Austen Knight's good fortune in becoming a landed gentleman was shared to some extent by his family; it was in one of Edward's cottages in Chawton that the Austen ladies lived out their days.—Editor's note

Austen. The young people are Master James-Edward and Miss Caroline Austen." Eliza drew breath. "I am afraid, Caroline, that I cannot present your doll."

"Jemima," she piped, and held up her treasure.

"Jemima," Eliza repeated. "Allow me to make Lady Gambier known to your acquaintance—"

An aging woman, of considerable magnificence in dress, who inclined her head coldly at little Caroline.

"Her niece, Miss Gambier—"

A Fashionable miss in her late twenties, I should judge, and approaching the years of Danger. Tho' fair-haired and blue-eyed, she was possessed of a something forbidding in her countenance.

"—and her nephew, Mr. Edward Gambier."

The gentleman was just enough James-Edward's senior, to figure as a possible hero: his curling locks guinea-gold, and his address assured.

"Gambier!" my mother cried. "But surely you must be connexions of our dear Admiral?"

"I am his wife," Lady Gambier replied.

Admiral Gambier is known far beyond the Service, for he is called upon, from time to time, to intercede on such delicate matters as the Government has in train. Even now he is absent from England about the business of the American War—in parley at Ghent over the cessation of hostilities between the Crown and that upstart nation. But we have nearer reasons to regard him: my brother Frank has twice served under the Admiral's flag, and Gambier's favour has advanced Frank's career. Indeed, all the Gambiers must be of consuming interest to our party, for Lady Gambier was born a Mathew—first cousin to poor Anne, James's late lamented wife.

Beside me, James's second wife was all alertness, quivering like a tightly-strung bow.

"I have two sons, both Post Captains, in the Royal Navy," my mother said warmly, "and the elder has excellent cause to be grateful to the Admiral."

"So kind," Lady Gambier murmured indifferently.

Mrs. Chute had turned already to a handsome gentleman of perhaps thirty, whose dress and looks proclaimed him a prosperous man of Town. A gentleman of independent fortune—perhaps a political crony of William Chute's, I thought; and was thus surprized to learn that "Mr. L'Anglois is my husband's confidential secretary."

Eliza pronounced the name *Langles*, but I guessed it was properly *Langwah*, in the French stile—which explained the man's air of elegance. The French carry refinement in their veins.

"Mr. Raphael West," Eliza said, "I know you have already met."

Raphael West? I performed my curtsey to the gentleman, who had hung back throughout the introductions. His right hand clasped a book, its place marked with one finger; his expression was all wearied tolerance. I noticed that he was dressed in deepest mourning. A near loss, then, and a recent one.

"We are entirely indebted to Mr. West, indeed," my mother said. "You will know, Lady Gambier, that we suffered an accident in our equipage yesterday—and Mr. West sacrificed his own comfort, that we might be conveyed safely to the parsonage."

"I beg your pardon, Mamma," I broke in. "Mr. West we may have encountered—but to meet Mr. Raphael West is something else entirely! Am I correct, sir, that you an artist—and the son of Mr. Benjamin West?"

"You have found me out, Miss Austen," he replied with a bow.

"I was privileged to see your father's *Christ Rejected* by the Elders while in Town this past September. It is the only representation of our Saviour that has ever contented me."

"My father shall be honoured to hear it." Again I was conscious of that too-close scrutiny from Mr. West's eyes; I understood, now, the discipline that authorised it. He was trained to look past one's countenance, and take the measure of muscle and bone.

"Raphael West?" Mary edged forward, her right hand dramatically at her throat. She slipped her left arm around young Caroline's shoulders, a tender gesture I had never witnessed before, and pulled the child close in a melting maternal pose. "It is an honour to meet you, sir. I have long admired your father's portrait of you as an infant—held in the arms of your mother! Can there be anything more eternal than the bond between a woman and her child?"

"If so, ma'am, I have yet to encounter it," he said; but I detected a satiric glint in his eye. Who knew, indeed, the nature of his relations with his parents? The assumptions of the world are rife with hypocrisy.

"Pish!" The voice was high-pitched and verging on the hysteric; the comment was accompanied by a snapping of the fingers. "If we are to talk of fame, West, we have to look no further than Miss Austen herself! Dear Lady, where have you been hiding yourself this age? In a garret, the better to scribble your outrageous nonsense?"

It must, it could only be, Mr. Thomas-Vere Chute, William's brother. I had but to revolve the thought, and the creature was upon me. He availed himself of my hand and bent low, his lips almost grazing my skin.

A vanished age might have called Thomas-Vere a Macaroni. Ours contents itself with the term *dandy*. Tho' a recipient of Holy Orders and ostensibly dedicated to the Church, Thomas-Vere is more properly known as an Aesthete. He is an enthusiast of opera, an ardent follower of Kean and Siddons, and a devotée of Dress in all its extremes of Fashion. When he bows, a quantity of fobs and seals jingle at his waistcoat; the shoulders of his jacket are padded with buckram; and it is whispered that he even pads his hose—the better to fill out his spindly shanks. The most severe of his afflictions is a quizzing-glass, which he thinks to employ to devastating effect, putting all his acquaintance out of countenance. Add to this a penchant for wigs, and a valet who delights in arranging them, and you have a picture of the man.

As he murmured over my hand, I observed Cassandra to roll her eyes; Mr. West's lips quirked ironically.

"Look to your secrets, West," Thomas-Vere declared in an exaggerated whisper as he straightened from his caresses. "We have admitted a Celebrated Authoress into our midst, and before her penetrating eye all is revealed. We owe the very novel you hold to Miss Austen's pen. Set it down immediately, I beg! The lady's wit is more dangerous than a basketful of adders!"

My eyes strayed to the book in Mr. West's hand and the gold lettering on its spine. It was the second volume of *Mansfield Park*—and he had read fully half of it. I flushed. If the Chutes' guests were formerly ignorant of my secret, they were now all alive to its possibilities. A novelist, scrutinising their every word and gesture, in order to ape them! It was not to be borne. No one should dare to come near me for the remainder of the holiday.

"I look forward to discussing literature with you, Miss Austen," Mr. West said with equanimity.

I was released from his probing gaze and commanded to accept a glass of punch, William Chute being just the sort of man to welcome his neighbours with a steaming bowl of brandy and lemon. We seated ourselves in little groups about the room as a parlour maid appeared with sweetmeats and cakes, a swell of incidental chatter rising now the introductions were done. The adventure of the carriage accident must be canvassed again, for the eager amusement of The Vyne party; the prospect of hunting on the morrow debated, as well as the general trend in the weather; and intelligence of family events shared to the full.

Mary, I observed, was still attempting to pose with Caroline for the benefit of Mr. West. No doubt she hoped that he might immortalise her in his sketchbook—or capture her in oils for the next Academy exhibition! Caroline was fidgeting under the iron hold of her mother's hand, and James-Edward took care to go nowhere near the parental end of the room.

Neither, I observed, did Raphael West. He had resumed the perusal of his book.

"Condolences are due to you, I understand, Mrs. Austen," Eliza said in a lowered tone as she settled herself beside us. Mamma and I were seated next to one another on a comfortable settee, and Eliza had crossed the room in her desire to convey her sympathy.

"If you would speak of the lost hamper of brawn," Mamma replied, "I assure you I do not think of it above once a day."

Eliza's brow furrowed in bewilderment and she glanced at me. "I meant to refer to Captain Charles Austen's wife. I am correct in thinking she passed away this autumn? She was quite young, was she not?"

"Sadly so," I supplied. We had never loved Fanny Palmer as well as we ought, because we had so little known her—being a child of Bermuda, she married my younger brother Charles while he served on the Atlantic station, when she was but eighteen. Seven years later, she was dead—of the birth of her fourth daughter, who survived her only a fortnight.

"How does the Captain bear it? He was very much attached to her, I believe?"

"I have rarely known any man more sincerely grieved," I said. "He has lately quitted us for active service on the Mediterranean Station; it is to be hoped that duty and command will recover him, in time."

Of the little girls, the eldest barely six, who had been left to the care of their grandmamma Palmer in Keppel Street, I said nothing. Tho' we were fond of these nieces, we knew them hardly at all—the bulk of their young lives having been spent abroad or at sea. Fanny herself had died aboard Charles's ship, the *Namur*, as it lay off Sheerness. Indeed, I suspect that Charles blamed himself for keeping her too long aboard, as tho' the ship had proved pestilential. He resigned his command almost immediately after his wife's death, and sought a posting into the *Phoenix*.

My brother Edward, who lost his Elizabeth a few years since in similar circumstances, posted to Sheerness to comfort his brother; but Charles was not to be consoled. He could not quit England soon enough. I believe that all our thoughts have turned to him, alone upon the seas at Christmas-tide. My mother's countenance was troubled; she held a scrap of lace to her lips.

"How do you come to be acquainted with Mr. West?" I enquired of Eliza, in an effort to turn the conversation. "Are you intimate with his family when in London?"

"Not at all." She adjusted the ruby bracelet at her wrist. "He is come to The Vyne in support of his father, who is to attempt a large historical painting, I believe, on the subject of Parliament. Something to do with the end to our European wars, and the exile of Napoleon; I do not pretend to know what it is."

The Monster who had so determined our nation's fears, for the better part of my adult life—whose military adventures on land and sea had shaped the destinies of my brothers—whose intrigues against the Kingdom had required the subtle employment of such men of parts as my late esteemed Rogue, Lord Harold Trowbridge—Napoleon—was defeated. His fall was declared complete but six months ago, and his exile to Elba engineered by the British government. Henceforth his guard was to be kept by officers of our Army appointed to the task. The celebrations in London that greeted this monumental coup, and the return to the Throne of France of the Bourbon kings, occupied most of the summer. Publick fêtes and displays of fireworks, publick parties in the streets, appearances by the Prince Regent, and a gala party at White's Club—which our own brother Henry was privileged to attend—had helped to relieve the high spirits and exultation all England must feel.

I wondered, from time to time, how Lord Harold should have greeted such a spectacle; and heard his wry voice in my mind. *Exclaim over your sudden access of safety if you must, Jane—but do not believe in it, until Buonaparte is dead.*

"I can easily credit that the Regent would commission a great work on such a subject," I said—for the Prince is nothing if not a squanderer of coin and a promoter of Self. "I am relieved that he chose Mr. West to accomplish it. The commission might have gone to Sir Thomas Lawrence—and tho' he is a fine painter of faces, he lacks Mr. West's sweeping grandeur."

"If Parliament were filled with women," Eliza returned, "Lawrence should be our man."

"What does Mr. Raphael West find to occupy him in Hampshire?"

"His father requires studies, as he calls them, of the various Members. The son is arrived to make sketches of poor William. Only think how droll, Jane! My shabby hound, to figure among the Lofty in a picture of State!"

I invariably forgot that William Chute had served most of his life among the Tory party; he was so obviously the sporting fellow, rather than the sage of Government. Eliza looked with such affection at her husband, in his leather breeches buttoned at the knee, his rough top-boots, and his serviceable brown coat, that I collected William Chute's lack of elegance troubled her not at all. The Wests, one presumes, might supply a more proper costume, in paint.

"That explains a good deal," my mother interjected suddenly. "I thought the man impudent—for he possesses a most penetrating eye, and very nearly put me out of countenance. But if Mr. West is a painter, he was reared in insolence."

So Mamma had felt the weight of the gentleman's gaze as heavily as I had.

Eliza smiled at her. "It is said that Raphael West possesses a remarkable talent, but too little inclination. He appears content to serve as his father's amanuensis, rather than strive for fame himself. It is just as well—for his younger brother is a sad disappointment, and tho' his father's namesake, has nothing to do with the parent at all. Old Mrs. West—Raphael's mother—is very recently deceased of a long and wasting illness; you will observe he goes in black."

"Mr. West's family did not accompany him into Hampshire?" I asked.

"He has little family to speak of, Jane. Raphael West is a widower. His wife passed away some years ago, I believe. He never speaks of her. There was one child—a daughter. I understand that she is lately married."

I should have liked to continue the interesting conversation, but Eliza, after a pause, pressed my mother to partake of further refreshment.

A little later we were led to our bedchambers, while the gentlemen of the party braved the cold. William Chute can never bear to be long indoors when he might be tramping to the stables, to display his fine pack of hounds. As I followed Eliza up the celebrated staircase, past the Yule log burning brightly in the hall, I reflected that my Christmas should be far pleasanter than I had found reason to hope in yesterday's snow.

I ought never to have dared the thought.

THE SECOND DAY

5

A CHRISTMAS CHARADE

Monday, 26th December 1814
The Vyne

The housemaid, to my distinct pleasure, crept into the room I share with Cassandra this morning and swept the remains of last night's fire from the hearth. As she laid a new one, I raised myself on one elbow—Cassandra still slumbering in the neighbouring bed—and whispered, "What is the hour?"

"A little past seven by the hall clock," she replied. "Will you be wanting tea, ma'am?"

This is the dignity that age has conferred upon me: at nine-and-thirty, I am to be addressed as *ma'am*. Oh, for the *miss* of yesteryear!

I ordered tea, and sank back into my pillows.

I had assumed The Vyne's servants would already have quitted the place—it being customary to give them a free day in place of Christmas, when servants are expected to wait upon their masters and silently witness festivities they cannot enjoy. But perhaps they should leave us at midday, when the house party had thoroughly awakened and might be trusted to fend for themselves. When the maid reappeared with my tray I enquired as to her St. Stephen's Day plans, but her gaze fell as she answered.

"Indeed, and it is snowing that hard, ma'am, I should never try to walk the three miles home to my mother! Christmas shall have to bide for my next free day."

She bobbed and left me in possession of my tea. I did not venture out of bed to peek through the draped windows at the storm—I did not like a sudden white glare to disturb Cassandra. The quiet of the great house around me suggested that no one else was afoot. I sipped contentedly, therefore, conscious of an unaccustomed luxury in the crackling flames and the hot liquid. There was even a branch of holly bestowed on the tray. Nothing was wanting at The Vyne that might supply comfort; indeed, the memory of last evening's Christmas Feast is one I shall cherish for some time.

We assembled in all our finery at half after six o'clock last evening—neither so early as to embarrass our hosts before their fashionable London guests, nor so late as to offend country sensibilities. I wore my cobalt-blue silk—newly trimmed with gold spangles during my visit last month to Henry and my publishers in Town. I left off my usual lace cap in favour of a bewitching shako of gold and cobalt, perched on my curls, which were brushed and arranged by Eliza Chute's personal maid; beside me, Cassandra wore a gown of deep rose. For ladies of a certain age, like ourselves, who go abroad in society so seldom, dress is a matter of considerable anxiety. Our wardrobes are neither large, nor varied, nor costly; it would be as well if we curtailed the length of our stay at The Vyne to suit the breadth of our costumes. But for Christmas Night, at least, we appeared very well—and in the admiration of our friends, I must be easy.

"I suppose it is a commonplace for ladies who engage in commerce," Mary said in a lowered tone, "to waste their funds in lavish display."

"Indeed," James replied. "Would that poor Jane's thirty pieces of silver had been turned to charitable good. But a profit in novels must struggle to find a worthy use; the frivolity of impulse that inspires their creation, must also attend their earnings."

"What an extraordinary reticule, ma'am," Thomas-Vere broke in, his quizzing-glass held up before my mother. "I have never seen its equal."

"I netted it myself," Mamma replied proudly. "Dear Jane brought the silk from London last month—so good to me as she always is."

Our party was thirteen, almost evenly divided at Eliza's contrivance between the gentlemen and the ladies; the schoolroom set supplied three more, accommodated at the middle of the table, so that both the Chutes might have charming partners at their respective ends. The dining parlour at The Vyne is an intimate and cheerful chamber, lined with linenfold panelling nearly three hundred years old. The walls are hung with landscapes and portraits of Chutes long since dead; a fire crackles at one end of the room, and at the other, long windows draped in crimson damask give out onto the lake. The great mahogany board where Walpole once presided was laid tonight for sixteen, with a parade of beeswax candles held aloft in silver, crystal glasses and porcelain chargers, a quantity of greens festooned with silk ribbons, and an exotic faerie castle rising from the centre, carved entirely from a block of sugar. This confection resembled the Regent's summer pavilion at Brighton, but in better taste. I stole a glance at Caroline, and saw her mouth agape. Far more exciting than Snapdragon, to one raised on Evangelical principles.

William took in Lady Gambier; Eliza was escorted by Mr. West; Thomas-Vere gallantly claimed my mother; Mr. L'Anglois offered his arm to Miss Gambier, as should be correct, and James took in his wife. Young Mr. Gambier presented an arm each to Cassandra and me, and with perfect good humour we accepted his gallantry. He placed himself between us at table. Mr. West was at my right hand. I turned to converse with him first, as was customary.

"I trust you benefited from your rest, Miss Austen?" he enquired.

"—As I hope you did, from your glimpse of the stables and dogs. Do you intend to hunt on the morrow, Mr. West?"

"Undoubtedly. Tho' I am no sportsman, I will follow the pack—with a sketchbook in my saddlebag."

"Such colour and chaos as the scene presents must be tempting to one of your skill! I almost wish that I rode."

"You do not hunt?"

I shook my head regretfully. "I was denied the means, as a young girl—clergyman's households do not run to mounts for all and sundry, you know, and there were a healthy number of us."

"Your brother followed your father's profession, I collect," he said, with a glance at James.

"In the very same parish—and being the eldest, was also taught to ride when young. He and Mr. Chute are old friends these five-and-twenty years. James shall be hallooing with the rest of you on the morrow—as will dear Eliza." I nodded to where she sat at the table's foot, on Mr. West's right hand, in a daring gown of silver gauze. There must have been a wistful note in my voice—for I dearly love to be out-of-doors.

"Then I shall carry the better part of the hunt back in my sketches," Mr. West replied warmly, "so that we may enjoy it together, in comfortable chairs by the fire!"

From across the table, Mary cried, "I should dearly love to peruse your sketches, Mr. West! Of all things, I am most alive to Art! I daresay there is not another lady in the country with as fine an appreciation of line or colour as myself. As a young girl, I was always at my sketchbook—but one is forced to set such things aside, regardless of one's talent or the calling of the Muse, when one has attained the maternal state." A languishing glance at her children, happily chattering in the middle of the table and fortunately inattentive to their mother's gushes.

Mr. West inclined his head without a word.

"Do not be prating of your poor daubs, my dear," James hissed audibly at his wife. "Mr. West can have not the slightest interest in them."

Poor Mary set her lips in a sneering line and reached for her wineglass.

Is there any agony comparable to the self-exposure of family?

My cheeks reddening, I said, "Do you prefer to draw art from life, sir?"

"Is it possible to draw it any other way?"

"Your father appears to rely upon invention, for his religious themes; the power of imagination is everywhere evident in his work."

"True—but his figures are inspired by living models, his draperies limned from real cloth, thrown over an arm. He possesses the discipline I lack, Miss Austen, to study the smallest detail of his vast compositions, in order that the perfection of each part contributes to the whole. I am too hasty, too impatient, for meticulous study. I prefer to seize my subject with rapid strokes, a thing of the moment. What I lose in perfection, I gain in animation. My father's generation composes in the classical mode; mine, in the Romantic."

I felt my heart quicken. There was a passion to West's words that argued truth. I had been afforded a glimpse, if only fleetingly, of the man beneath the Fashionable mask.

"When you write," he continued intently, "you do much the same. Your Tom Bertram—your pert Maria—your venomous Mrs. Norris—all are sketched with a brevity and deftness that argues economy of effort."

"Perhaps," I said unwillingly, "they are mere caricatures, and thus demand nothing more."

"Your Darcy is no caricature," he retorted. "Nor is Willoughby. I have met that gentleman's like on countless occasions, in the gaming hells and ballrooms of London—petted, indulged, weak, and subtle. That is where you excel, Miss Austen—in the subtleties."

Our tête-à-tête was suspended by William Chute's raising of his glass, and the resounding chorus of "Happy Christmas" on every side.

It has been whispered in the parish that The Vyne has fallen into sad disrepair under William Chute's stewardship; and if one is to compare the house to what it was under its previous owner—when display took precedence over comfort, and Taste was preferred above human warmth, I daresay the whisperers are correct. But in one respect, at least, The Vyne is lavish—and that is in the enjoyment of food and drink among friends. William Chute was forever motioning to his footmen to replenish our glasses last night, first with champagne and Madeira, later with claret and hock; and every variety of dish was on offer. A handsome goose was set out, its skin crisply browned and smelling delightfully of onions and sage; half a dozen partridges accompanied it, as well as teal, and woodcocks; soles in béchamel sauce were at one end of the table, and a lobster cake at the other. I partook of saddle of venison, culled no doubt from The Vyne's own park. With all this there were French beans and Jerusalem artichokes, stewed celery and mushrooms.

After the first remove, the white and clear soups went round, with a choice of jellies and Naples biscuit. I turned, as was only correct, to converse with Mr. Edward Gambier, who sat on my left. He had survived his interrogation at my sister's hands.

"I understand your family has spent many years in this neighbourhood," he began, with becoming easiness, "and has been intimate with The Vyne family forever. Tho' your sister informs me you presently live in the southern part of Hampshire."

"Not far from Alton," I replied, giving the name of the principal town near Chawton. "Our brother commands an estate in that part of the world, and has been so kind as to afford us a cottage. How do you come to be acquainted with the Chutes, Mr. Gambier?"

"Through my great-uncle," he returned. "General Edward Mathew. My mother was his niece, you know, and spent much of her girlhood at Freefolk Priors, not far from here. The house, of course, is now pulled down—and another built in its place. Laverstoke House, I believe it is called."

"Our acquaintance William Portal owns it now—tho' the manor is far less homelike than when old General Mathew lived there." I set down my wineglass. "But this is wonderful! My brother James"—I nodded across the sugar sculpture in his direction—"was married to Anne Mathew, the General's daughter. They met while dancing at the Basingstoke Assemblies. Mr. Chute was their good angel, in making the introduction."

"That will be Mamma and Aunt Louisa's cousin," Gambier said shrewdly. "Miss Anne was a twin, I believe. She died while I was still in leading-strings. I see your brother succeeded in forming a second attachment."

"He had a young child to raise," I said shortly. "I confess to a little confusion, Mr. Gambier—how do you come to share your Aunt Louisa's name?"

He smiled broadly. "Because my father was brother to the Admiral, of course. The Gambiers didn't look far when it came to brides, but married two sisters. Mamma is several years younger than my aunt, and much in request—she chose to spend the holiday in Bath, among her acquaintance. But Aunt Louisa has become accustomed to my sister's company, lacking daughters of her own—and I should sooner spend the season in the country, with a prospect of good hunting, then in all the tedium of Bath."

"I could not agree more. I detest the insipidity of such towns, with their host of invalids, all taking their daily dose of water."

"And the provender!" Mr. Gambier cried with relish, as the second course was set down. "Bath can offer nothing like a suckling pig, with an apple in its mouth! And I never see such a dish in Town. Are you fond of crackling, Miss Austen?"

"Invariably," I said, "but my joy at the sight is entirely for my mother. She is partial to pork in any of its forms."

"She seems a grand old lady," Mr. Gambier said. "I wish Aunt Louisa might have half her energy."

"Mamma may give Lady Gambier fifteen years," I replied, somewhat startled.

"And that is exactly why I say it," the gentleman replied, as he was served with crackling. "Only observe how much enjoyment Mrs. Austen betrays, and she with one foot in her grave! Aunt Louisa might as well be at a tragedy-play, for all the animation she offers."

"Perhaps she is anxious for her husband," I suggested. "The Admiral has been absent some time in Ghent, I believe, about the American treaty?"

"That is true," he admitted, "but they never seemed particularly bosom-bows when Dismal Jimmy was in country."

"I beg your pardon?"

"Dismal Jimmy is my uncle's name in the Service," Mr. Gambier confided. "On account of he's so particular about Sunday Service, and no end pious when going into battle. He and my aunt never drove well in harness. A life spent at sea ain't conducive, you know, to a love-match, particularly when there are no children in the case.

That's why Mary and I"—this, with a nod to his sister, not my brother James's wife—"spend such a deal of time in Aunt Louisa's pocket. Cheers the Relation no end—and ensures we shan't be cut out of the Will by a hired companion. When my father stuck his spoon in the wall last year, he left more debts than funds. Family habit. Must look to the future, and provide."

Unblushing frankness appeared to be one of Mr. Gambier's gifts. After an interval for appreciation of the second course—which was comprised of a beef roast, cauliflower in orange sauce, veal ragout, a dish of macaronis, and a pasty filled with spinach—I managed a reply.

"Are you then the Admiral's heir?"

"Must suppose m'self to be," he replied. "Unless there's an inconvenient by-blow hiding in the wings. But I shouldn't think the Admiral much given to natural sons—too devout by half. They call him the Praying Captain, you know. Devilish bent on Divine Service in the Fleet, and not ashamed to flog all shirkers. No, I think he'll do the handsome—and remember his nephew, when Davy Jones calls him to the Deep."

I could not like the thought of burials at sea, with poor Charles presently aboard—and gave Mr. Gambier no answer. I consoled myself with mince pies and apricot tart.

AFTER NEARLY THREE HOURS of jollity and conversation, Eliza rose from her place and nodded to the ladies. We left the men to their privacy and their port. I little doubted, with a Member of Parliament passing the bottle, that talk should be of the American War; and dearly wished I might have overlistened the gentlemen's opinions. It is not often, living in retirement as we do, that the Austen ladies are treated to informed society; we rely upon the London newspapers for nearly all of our intelligence of Government events. But this evening I should have to contain my impatience a little longer. I congratulated myself, however, that Mr. Chute must receive his papers promptly, no matter the condition of the roads, owing to his position—and that I might have a comfortable coze with them in the library while the men were out hunting.

Dessert was sensibly arrayed in the drawing-room on the Chutes' massive sideboard, so that we might sample the brandied fruits and biscuits, the oranges and raisins, the wafers and sugared almonds at our leisure. Coffee was poured out, too, once the gentlemen joined us.

"I say," Edward Gambier cried as he entered the drawing-room before the others, "it is as well that none of us must depart The Vyne tonight—for there is a gale of snow falling! I'd lay odds we'll see no hunting."

"Then it will be the first St. Stephen's Day in memory that the pack lies in," William Chute growled. He looked most unhappy, and went immediately to the large French windows giving out onto the back garden. A bitter swirl of frozen air blew into the room as he opened one of them, and the flames in the great hearth darted and hissed.

"Lord, William, you will carry us all away," Eliza cried. "Shut the window and prepare to play at charades, like a gentle host."

I daresay each of us was so stupefied by food and drink, that we should gladly have sat in silence for an hour or so before toddling to our beds; but Eliza was determined to lead us all in merriment—and what is Christmas night without charades?

"I do relish a good riddle," my mother said brightly. She is inordinately proud of what she terms her "sprack wit," or deftness with rhyme.

"Then I propose, madam," said Mr. L'Anglois the secretary, "that you take up this pad and pen." He stood ready with a supply of each, and pressed them upon us.

"Are we to enter the lists singly," I queried, "or play in teams?"

"Let it be teams," muttered Lady Gambier, "lest we be tied here all night."

If Eliza heard this dispiriting remark, she chose to ignore it.

"James," Mary said quite audibly, "I have a fearful headache; and I am sure that Caroline must be nodding!"

Caroline had long ago disappeared with Miss Wiggett and James-Edward to the Chutes' nursery wing—she was to have a bed near the governess, with all the delights of warm milk by the schoolroom fire. I had an idea of her introducing fine Jemima to Miss Wiggett's dolls—no doubt long since outgrown—and talking over vanished modes. But James bowed to his wife with alacrity. "As you wish, my dear. You will always know what is best for the child." He showed no inclination to accompany her upstairs, however, and made his way to the sideboard groaning with sweetmeats.

With a tragic air, Mary swept from the room. No one appeared to remark her departure.

We formed ourselves into three teams. William Chute, Miss Gambier, Thomas-Vere, and I were the first; Mamma, Mr. West, Mr. Gambier, and Eliza the second; Cassandra, Lady Gambier, Mr. Langlois, and James the third. Mamma's team—to the surprize of none of us Austens—offered their clew before the rest of us; it was a foregone conclusion that in charades, sprack wit must carry off the laurels.

We were handed a few lines of verse in my mother's hand.

> *You may lie on my first by the side of a stream,*
> *And my second compose to the nymph you adore,*

But if, when you've none of my whole, her esteem
And affection diminish—think of her no more!

Our group of four consulted feverishly, and I observed sidelong that Cassandra's party was in vociferous debate.

"The first is quite obviously bed," William Chute declared. "Streambed, you know."

"That is under the stream, not beside it," I muttered.

"Surely it is grass, Mr. Chute? Or perhaps moss?" Miss Gambier suggested.

"Bracken?" Thomas-Vere chortled. "Couch? Why could not one recline on a couch by a stream as well as by a window, Miss Austen? You are a genius with the pen; pray tell us your solution to this riddle."

"And the second must be letter," Mr. Chute persisted doggedly. "Bed letter. If your lady does not like your bed-letters, why, give her prompt notice—what?!"

"No, no, William—it must be poem." Thomas-Vere raised his quizzing-glass and stared at our host satirically. "One never writes anything so prosaic as letters to a nymph. You forget your classical education."

"Never had one," Mr. Chute snorted.

"Couch poem?" Miss Gambier repeated in bewilderment. "Surely not."

"The answer is banknote," I interjected, raising my voice a trifle on the final word, so that Mamma might hear me. She waved her reticule in gleeful congratulation.

By my side, William Chute's lips were moving as he went over the slip of paper in his hand, brow furrowed. Gradually his confusion cleared, and he laughed heartily.

"Excellent, Mrs. Austen—excellent! If your lady spurns you for want of the Ready, why—turn her out-of-doors this instant! Take care, Eliza—you have been warned!"

We parsed five more charades—a total of two from each team—and were evenly scored. The hour grew late, and I believe most of us should have gone happily to bed without a murmur, but our hostess would have none of it. "One last attempt," Eliza cried, "to decide the whole! In fairness, any of us may submit a teazing rhyme." She glanced round the room and seized upon an empty porcelain bowl. "Place your folded clews anonymously here, and I shall chuse one. I shall read it aloud—and recuse myself from play."

Everyone on my team looked to me; with a sigh, I bent to my pad and pencil. Perhaps three minutes passed, during which only the soft hiss of settling embers in the drawing-room fire could be heard. My mother uttered a satisfied "Hah!" and tripped over to Eliza with her folded chit; James proffered another; I tossed mine into the bowl. No one else moved.

"Come, come!" I chided. "We cannot have only Austens. At least three more charades must make up Eliza's pot, or this shall be far too easy for some of us!"

Perhaps two more minutes passed. Mr. L'Anglois and Mr. Edward Gambier sheepishly dropped twists of paper into the bowl. Cassandra forbore to add to the Austen weight. Miss Gambier, however, valiantly delivered a clew; and so, eventually, did Raphael West.

Eliza twirled her fingers among the bits of paper and drew one forth. With a smile, she said, "This is one for the season! It is entitled 'A Virgin Birth.'"

> *My first is best seen in the Garden of Eden;*
> *My second will serve to bore holes in shoes.*

By the time my third has set, this e'en,
Then any old name will do, that you chuse.

From its halting phrases, this was no Austen effort. We never titled our charades, from fear of giving away the solution. "Pray read it again, Eliza," I begged. I was unaccountably stuck on the first word . . . best seen in the Garden of Eden . . .

"Snake?" Thomas-Vere suggested. "Apple? Or shall we plump for the more mellifluous name of Mephistopheles?"

"Too long," William Chute said seriously.

"Could it be tree?" I frowned. "Or perhaps Eve—with Eve being merely the first part of a longer word, such as . . ."

"Awl," Thomas-Vere mused. He tapped his pursed lips with his quizzing-glass, the picture of foppish distraction. "Eve-awl. Evil. It does give one to think. I had been wont to consider Eden as the absence of all evil."

"Surely that can have nothing to do with a Virgin Birth," Chute pointed out.

Miss Gambier cleared her throat. She was looking pallid; the lateness of the hour did not agree with her. "You are wrong, Miss Austen," she said. "The first is not Eve, but Nature. I believe awl is correct, however, for the second."

"Natur-al," William Chute pounced.

"Natural . . . sun?" I attempted, considering the third word's clew. "For the sun sets in the evening." I felt my cheeks warm suddenly, as I heard the sense of what I had said. Natural son. A polite term for bastard.

"Indeed," Miss Gambier said. "The thing for which any old name will do." She uttered the words with sharp bitterness, and rose abruptly from her chair.

"Miss Gambier—" Eliza was staring at her, open-mouthed.

"I have grown weary of this game," she said brusquely. "I beg your pardon, Mrs. Chute—but I must retire immediately."

"But we intended to close the night with Evensong in the Chapel," Eliza protested. "Mr. Austen has been so good as to say he will preside—"

"Aunt Louisa, may I escort you to your bedchamber?" Miss Gambier interrupted, ignoring the import of Eliza's speech.

"Thank you, my dear," Lady Gambier whispered, and pulled herself to her feet with obvious effort. Although her frame was stout enough, her voice and aspect were frail; like her niece, she seemed about to drop where she stood. Mr. West caught her as she swayed and said tersely, "Gambier—a glass of brandy for your aunt."

The good lady protested, but was persuaded to resume her seat for a little, and consume one or two sips of brandy; at which point, supported by her niece and nephew, she was led from the room. I observed Eliza's gaze to follow them, a little frown of puzzlement between her eyebrows, and all hint of gaiety fled from her countenance.

"Who among us," she said as the Gambiers' footsteps died away, "can have written that charade?"

There was silence for an instant. "I did not," I said.

"I should be ashamed to own it," my mother added. "To suggest that Eden and e'en rhyme—!"

"Perhaps," Raphael West broke in quietly, "it were as well to say nothing more of the matter, Mrs. Chute. Such a source of obvious discomfort cannot be too quickly forgotten."

Evensong was not broached again. I half-expected James to be jealous of his office, and of such a setting as The Vyne Chapel— which is renowned for its age and quiet beauty—but he refrained from herding us all into attendance; and I confess I could not be sorry.

We Austen ladies did not long succeed the Gambiers, but left the gentlemen to the enjoyment of the drawing-room and its fire. As I mounted the darkened stairs by the glow of my candle, the house wrapt in the quiet of falling snow, I thought I heard a muffled sob from somewhere in The Vyne. Perhaps it was merely the wind crying.

6

A MESSENGER FROM GHENT

Monday, 26th December 1814
The Vyne, cont'd.

I closed the leaves of my journal, set down my drained teacup, and reached for my dressing gown. Cassandra still slumbered, but I had a duty to fulfill—the delivery of Caroline's present for the second day of Christmas: one of Lady Jemima's delicious costumes. It must be laid on the child's coverlet in the nursery before she awoke, as an act of faerie mischief. Tho' the doll had made her debut in ball dress, as befitted a lady at her first coming-out, she could not always be wearing silk. Mindful that the Feast of St. Stephen—in addition to being a day of gifts to the poor—was generally celebrated with a Hunt, Cassandra and I had fashioned a riding habit. It was deep rose (the very same stuff as my sister had worn last night, in fact), severe in its lines and closely fitted, with a sweeping train. Cassandra had employed a tiny crochet hook—intended for making lace—to create black silk braid for the trim, and twirled it into loops and frogs at throat and bodice. I had contrived the hat, a dashing black topper garlanded with tiny red cherries.

All we needed was a horse.

I drew the costume from the bandbox in which we had hidden all Caroline's presents, and tiptoed to the door. But as I did, Cassandra sighed and turned in her sleep. Her eyelids drifted open.

"Stay a moment, Jane, and I shall come with you."

I did as she bade, and perched at the foot of her bed whilst she drank a cup of my cooling tea. Trust Cass never to disturb a servant twice, while tea remained in the pot—she has a horror of imperious women, who live to be waited upon hand and foot.

"You slept well, I trust?"

"Not at all," she replied. "See how heavy-eyed I am? I was restless all night. Miss Gambier figured heavily in my dreams."

"The matter of the charade," I guessed. "I have been puzzling over it, too—for Eliza's question is apt. Who can have composed it? And why? Was it done with the intent of embarrassing Miss Gambier—or was it a bow drawn at a venture?"

"She certainly quit the drawing-room hard upon solving the riddle. Whether intended or not, the arrow went home. Virgin Birth—of a natural son? Grossly improper."

"You observed her aunt's discomposure as well?"

Cassandra nodded. "What can it mean?"

"A family affair. Nothing we shall be privy to."

"Can it be possible that Miss Gambier . . . that at some unfortunate period in her past—"

"She had a child out of wedlock? But why should a stranger—any one of ourselves—be aware of her history? Or use that private knowledge to Miss Gambier's disadvantage?"

I had a sudden memory of Edward Gambier's careless reference to by-blows and inheritance at dinner last evening. Surely he should not venture the topic with such obvious unconcern, if it touched his sister so nearly?

"It felt, Jane," Cassandra said slowly, "like a clumsy attempt at blackmail."

I shivered, despite the new-laid fire. An ugly thought of Cassandra's, in the midst of a jolly Christmas party. It caused me to feel exposed—unsure of my friends, and of the temper of those who surrounded me at The Vyne. But perhaps we had made too much of a trifle last evening; perhaps Miss Gambier and her aunt had merely been over-tired.

"I daresay we all guard secrets we cannot wish to share," I told my sister briskly. "A house-party is only as successful as the goodwill and mutual tolerance of its members will allow; otherwise, our carriages should be ordered within hours. Now, if you are done with your tea, Cassandra, we have a gift to bestow."

She thrust her feet into her slippers and was with me in an instant.

WHEN WE CAME DOWN to breakfast an hour later, it was clear there should be no Hunt on St. Stephen's Day. Even the less fortunate in the parish were kept within-doors, and only those few servants with families hard by in Sherborne St. John seemed likely to quit The Vyne for their free day. Eliza assured them they should have their Christmas boxes regardless, and a bowl of punch to celebrate with, in the servants' hall.

Little Caroline danced in from the schoolroom with Miss Wiggett behind her, both girls smiling at Jemima's transformation. "Look, Papa," Caroline cried. "A riding habit! Is it not lovely? Another gift from the faerie Aunts!"

James glowered at me over his newspaper. "Do you mean to spoil the child, Jane?"

"Yes," I said.

"May I learn to ride one day, too, Papa, and hunt with The Vyne?"

Caroline continued, oblivious of disapproval. "Miss Wiggett intends to do so, when once she is Come Out. Mrs. Chute is most decided upon the point that every lady should be adept at riding to hounds."

"That is only Aunt Eliza's way, Caroline, because she is used to do it herself," Miss Wiggett said. She coloured as she spoke, and her voice trembled. "I confess I am afraid of horses, myself. They are so very large, are they not? But I must attempt to conquer my fears, for Aunt Eliza's sake."

"Poor Miss Wiggett," Caroline said kindly. "Perhaps after breakfast we might visit the stables."

"You shall do nothing of the sort!" James snapped. "Not only is it vulgar for young ladies to hobnob with grooms—it snows!"

The snowstorm was absolute—a whirl of white at every window, without respite—and as the hours wore on, we were all thankful to secure a chair tucked by a table or in a quiet bay of the great library upstairs, and take down a quarto volume for perusal or slumber. The ladies drew out their embroidery. The gentlemen played at billiards. Miss Gambier sat with a travelling writing desk on her lap, composing a letter. Mary had produced a large sketchbook over which she was ostentatiously working—where she had unearthed it, I could not imagine, and suspected a pilfering of Miss Wiggett's schoolroom. James was at one of the large tables, busy about a sermon, his back to all of us and his head drooping over a sheaf of foolscap.

Mr. West prevailed upon William Chute to retire to his book room, where the Master of Hounds posed in various attitudes for nearly an hour, while his lineaments were sketched. Chute calls this smallish chamber off the library his book room, but it is properly known at The Vyne as the Tapestry Room—with a splendid collection of chinoiserie and arras hangings. I envied Chute this charming closet for the conduct of his business; what words I should have put on paper there! The light, however, was hardly good for Raphael West's purposes. I should dearly have loved to observe the portrait session—but that part of Mr. West's sketchbook was closed to me; the elements of Art intended for his father's use were not for anyone else's delectation.

When I tired of Berlin work and reading, I found myself gazing absently at Miss Gambier's hand, moving fluently across her writing-paper. Her expression was hardly cheerful. Did the lady harbour a private sorrow? Her aunt had not come down to breakfast today, as tho' last evening's irritations had been too much for her. I glanced around the library, with its composition of idle and industrious faces. Who among us had written the offensive charade? And why had she or he delivered it? There was a puzzle, here, that all the good manners in the world could not entirely erase; and I could hardly put my questions to Miss Gambier herself. She was a reserved young woman.

What I had yesterday chosen to regard as haughtiness and Fashionable airs appeared in the light of morning to be mere shyness and diffidence. She was not the sort to chatter with strangers, or indulge in a comfortable coze with an intimate; confidences were probably reserved for her journal and pen, or the recipients of her letters. I should judge her to be in her late twenties—long since off the Marriage Mart—and yet her delicate features and trim figure were pleasing enough. A want of fortune, perhaps, had been the ruin of her hopes; or a Disappointment in a first attachment. I could easily fabricate an interesting past for Mary Gambier—her brushes with Naval personages, her intimacy with Government through the Admiral—but perhaps her life had lacked these dashing interludes.

"Miss Gambier!"

There was one among us who did not quail at approaching her. The secretary, Mr. L'Anglois, strode into the library with a sheaf of music in his hands. His usually sombre looks were smiling; he was transformed from a correct and self-effacing young man to a jaunty and charming companion. But Miss Gambier appeared unmoved. She lifted her head from her letter, and stared at him impassively.

"Mr. L'Anglois?"

"May I entreat you to delight us with a turn at the pianoforte? I had nearly forgot in all the bustle of Christmas—but I have lately received some new music from France. I know that you are a true proficient. If you would wish to peruse the selections—"

She lifted the writing desk from her lap and set it down, folding her letter. "Thank you, no. I must attend to my aunt, Mr. L'Anglois—she is most unwell today."

"I am sorry to hear it," he faltered. "Perhaps at another time—"

Miss Gambier ignored him, sweeping out of the room without another word. L'Anglois could not with propriety follow. But there was an interest, there, that Miss Gambier appeared determined to quell.

Eliza, too, had witnessed the secretary's rebuff. "Miss Jane Austen is a devoted player, I believe, Mr. Langles. Perhaps you might turn the pages for her this evening after dinner. The pianoforte, Jane, is in the Saloon, you know, and tho' we generally remove to the drawing-room after dinner, we might make a change tonight, if you wished to play."

Ah, the poor lady left with a house full of guests and a snowstorm out-of-doors! Such stratagems and tricks as she is forced to employ, to banish collective ennui! Mr. L'Anglois should be required to stand this evening, turning pages intended for another, while I dinned the ears of all and sundry with discordant keys. But I smiled at Eliza and submitted. I was charmed by the thought of compelling Mr. L'Anglois to unbend; he had not yet devoted his hours to the amusement of spinsters.

He betrayed his sense of propriety and good manners, however, by approaching me next and offering to show me his selections.

"Here is a new piano sonata in E minor, by Herr Beethoven—but that should require considerable hours to master, I think. I have also six polonaises, by Hummel, and some very pretty pieces by the Irishman, John Field, which he calls nocturnes."

"I do not know Field," I admitted. "He is at the Russian court, is he not?"

"A great favorite of the Czar's, indeed," L'Anglois replied.

I glanced at the Beethoven, a taxing swarm of black notes, and set it aside in favour of the polonaises. "Miss Gambier may attempt the sonata. I shall content myself with playing tunes you younger folk might wish to dance to."

The secretary smiled. "I shall hardly discourage you from that. I shall leave the Hummel in your hands, Miss Austen, in the event you wish to practise."

"Thank you. It has been many months since anything new has come in my way. You are fortunate in your friends, Mr. L'Anglois. I think you said they are presently in France?"

"Paris, to be exact. Have you chanced to visit there?"

"I have not been so fortunate," I replied regretfully. "I was reared in Hampshire, and am often in London and Kent—I have brothers resident in both places. But I have never crossed the Channel."

"Now that peace is returned, I hope you may."

I inclined my head. "Have you been very long acquainted with the Gambiers and the Chutes, sir?"

"Only ten months," he replied. "Mr. Chute was kind enough to employ me when my previous situation came to an end."

"You have generally served Members of Parliament, I collect?"

"For many years I was confidential secretary to a member of the

French royal family," he replied seriously. "That gentleman being recalled to France at the rout of Buonaparte, I had a lamentable amount of time upon my hands. I do not know what I should have done, had Mr. Chute not been kind enough to secure my services."

"Benedict is joking you, Jane," William Chute declared as he ambled into the library, Raphael West at his heels. "Never knew a fellow more sought after than Langles, once the Comte d'Artois was done with him! Had to put in my bid for preferment early and often—and I'm still damned if I know why he didn't accept Dalrymple's offer over mine."

"Sir Peter Dalrymple deals almost exclusively with land reform," L'Anglois riposted, "and I never come within a mile of the farmyard if I may avoid it."

"Aye, and shouldn't have much use for your French if you did," Chute agreed. "Ben is a dashed accomplished fellow, Miss Austen—and he keeps my nose to the grindstone far more than I should like. I had thought to sneak away on horseback this morning, and claim a day of liberty, but you see how Man and Nature conspire against me. I have only just got done with West, and Ben shall be wanting me about my correspondence soon."

I glanced up at Mr. L'Anglois's face. A little smile played at the corners of his expressive mouth, and his dark eyes glowed. He was an excessively handsome young man—yes, I could detect with regret that he was a decade younger than myself—and possessed redoubtable skills as well. Any Englishman retained by the Comte d'Artois—who was brother to the new-crowned King of France, Louis XVIII, and an exacting mountebank by every account—must be a man of efficiency, tact, and considerable learning. Easily capable of composing an acid charade on the fly—but any of the minds surrounding me should do equally well.

JANE AND THE TWELVE DAYS OF CHRISTMAS · 77

That Mr. L'Anglois had lost his situation at the Comte's departure from his Audley Street residence was as nothing; few Englishmen should consent to repair to France, or serve a foreign royal when English alternatives were at hand. That L'Anglois was a prize William Chute valued I could readily believe. I rather wondered at his having won him. William Chute has served the Crown as an MP these two decades at least—but without ascending to any Cabinet, or holding a respectable Portfolio. Compared to the Comte d'Artois, he is a cypher. But perhaps Mr. L'Anglois had tired of fame.

"If Mr. West is finished, sir," he said to Chute, "I should like your signature on a number of documents."

"Of course." Chute turned once more towards his book room. But L'Anglois's purpose was stayed by the entrance into the library of young James-Edward, who had been absent some hours in the billiard room with Mr. Gambier. He came charging through the door, his breath coming in great gasps.

"Sir!" he cried to William Chute.

My brother snorted and threw down his pen. "A little conduct, if you please. You are no longer among the harum-scarums of Winchester."

"What is it, lad?" Chute said.

"A messenger, sir—asking for you! He rode up out of the storm. We heard a pounding at the front door—and there being no servants to answer, as it is St. Stephen's Day—"

"Of course. Most inconvenient. I shall come at once. An Express from London, I suppose?"

James-Edward looked doubtful. "I do not think so. He is in Naval uniform."

And, indeed, a military figure—booted and spurred and enveloped in a riding cloak of dark blue—strode impatiently into the library at that moment. He brought a tide of cold air with him.

"Lieutenant Gage at your service," he said, sweeping off his hat and bowing to Chute. "Late of Ghent. I bring news from Admiral Gambier."

7

THE FEAST OF ST. STEPHEN

Monday, 26th December 1814
The Vyne, cont'd.

" The Admiral is well, I trust?" William Chute enquired.

"Perfectly well, sir, I thank you—and bade me offer Lady Gambier and her family his warmest blessings for the season," Lieutenant Gage replied. "I carry private correspondence for Lady Gambier, as well, that I am instructed to place into her hands. But first—" He glanced round the library, suddenly conscious of an array of silent faces, and coloured slightly—although that may have been merely the return of blood and life to a visage frozen by weather. "I beg your pardon. I incommode your guests."

"Nonsense," Chute replied. "Eliza, dear, you must take this gentleman's things and bring him a hot rum punch. We shall be in my book room. Langles, I shall want you as well."

The Lieutenant was relieved of his cape and hat; the three men exited in all the relief of those given a job of work in the midst of a tedious winter day; and we whom they abandoned, were left staring at one another.

"Only fancy, Jane," my mother observed, "that poor young man has been journeying through the storm! Breast-high, they say the drifts are, on the Basingstoke road—not even the mail coach has got through. It is to be wondered that he did not perish!"

"I suppose the spur was great—and his news urgent."

"Indeed," Eliza Chute agreed. Her arms were full of the messenger's wet things. "I must venture into the kitchens, now, and endeavour to concoct a hot rum punch. Does anyone have an idea of how it is made? Of all occasions to be without one's cook!"

Martha Lloyd had just such a receipt in her stillroom book; I thought perhaps I might recall it. "Possibly," I managed. "And if the Lieutenant is frozen enough, he shall not regard the taste."

"Clever woman. Follow me, Jane."

I did as she bade, treading briskly from the library to the landing and thence down the great staircase. Eliza laid Lieutenant Gage's sodden cloak on a bench near the blazing Yule log in the Staircase Hall. The great oak trunk appeared hardly diminished from last evening. I warmed my hands an instant, then followed Eliza's quick steps along the East Passage to the kitchens. The passage was dimly-lit by guttering wall sconces. In this, too, I saw the absence of servants—the tapers should never have been left so long untended. Daylight was retreating swiftly before the heavy fall of snow, and if we did not take care, we should find The Vyne plunged in darkness before long. I must remind Eliza to secure a supply of candles, and engage the gentlemen in the laying of fires throughout the bedchambers, well before we were forced to retire.

Eliza had barely pushed open the baize-covered door before the sound of laughter and singing greeted our ears.

> *A jolly wassel-bowl,*
> *A wassel of good ale,*
> *Well fare the butler's soul,*

That setteth this to sale;
Our jolly wassel.

"Providence, Jane," Eliza said briskly. "Mrs. Roark has already made rum punch—at my direction—for the enjoyment of the servants on their free day! I had entirely forgot. But they shall not miss a draught, if we beg one for the poor Lieutenant."

"Surely not," I agreed, with a spasm of relief. I have never been an apt pupil in the kitchen. "Perhaps we might beg some candles, as well?"

LATER, WHEN THE STEAMING glass had been presented and gratefully received at the door of William Chute's book room, Eliza fretted a little about her helpless state. "I am persuaded I should ask the Lieutenant to remain here tonight," she said as she peered out the darkling library window at the unabated snow, "no matter how urgent his dispatches prove. It is unthinkable that anyone should venture again into such weather—and with darkness falling!"

"Surely he may find a bed in the servants' hall," Mary sniffed. "Or be sent back to the Angel in Basingstoke. It is not as tho' you owe him any special consideration, Eliza—he is only a messenger, after all. I wonder that you admitted him to the house! I was reared to leave the Express fellows at the door."

"He is not an Express," Eliza said repressively, "but an officer of the Royal Navy. Having several such in your family, Mary, I should have thought—"

"Frank and Charles are Post Captains," she retorted witheringly. "They are not sailors, whatever you may think."

"Most assuredly they are," my mother said tranquilly. "And have been, since the age of fourteen—twelve, in Charles's case. Do not make yourself ridiculous, Mary. Our men of the Navy are the most distinguished in England."

"And we may offer him only a cold supper!" Eliza persisted. "Mrs. Roark will have laid it out in the dining parlour. It hardly seems fair to the poor man—and then there is his bed to be thought of. Fresh linen. With the maids free of work tonight, I shall have to see to changing it myself, if the Lieutenant is to be accommodated."

"Let him sling his hammock," Mary said with disdain.

Eliza might have retorted, but a clear, low voice from the library doorway enquired, "What Lieutenant?"

Miss Gambier had returned from tending her aunt.

"We have had a messenger from Ghent," Eliza said. "Do come in and sit down, Mary—I am on the point of going for Madeira and glasses. Should you like a little? I may be able to discover some macaroons, as well."

"Ghent?" Miss Gambier looked from Eliza to myself. Her countenance paled. "What of my uncle?"

"He is perfectly well. A matter of business, only, we are assured."

"The Treaty," she said faintly. "And the intelligence brought by . . . a lieutenant, you say. Who is the messenger?"

"A fellow by the name of Gage. My dear girl," Eliza said sharply as Miss Gambier sank to a chair and placed a hand to her lips, "are you ill?"

"Thank you, no," she replied breathlessly. "It is just the shock— that news of my uncle should come, through such a storm—"

She turned abruptly as the door to William Chute's book room swung open; and I thought, at that moment, that all her heart was in her face.

"Miss Gambier," Lieutenant Gage said, with a gaiety in his voice that had been absent before. He crossed the library and bowed smartly before her. "I bring letters for both you and her ladyship."

Did I imagine it—or did Miss Gambier's lips move in the single word *John*?

"May I wish you," he said, "a very merry Christmas?"

LADY GAMBIER'S HEALTH WAS so improved that she appeared in the Saloon before our cold supper, elegantly arrayed in a gown of dark grey with an overlay of black lace. Her composure was absolute, and if she sedulously ignored most of us, her benign smile fell often upon the interesting messenger from Ghent. Lieutenant Gage had pressed the Admiral's letter into his lady's hands immediately upon her entrance; but rather than excusing herself to enjoy its communication alone, Lady Gambier merely uttered her favorite phrase—so kind—and tucked the missive into her reticule.

There being nothing more to wait for, we proceeded two-by-two into the dining parlour. The Lieutenant's presence was thus an immediate advantage—for he evened our numbers. Miss Gambier, to nobody's particular surprise, was on his arm, and Mr. L'Anglois was forced to look lower—and carry in Cassandra.

"You are acquainted with the Lieutenant," I murmured to Edward Gambier as he gallantly steered me the dozen steps from the Saloon to my dinner.

"We saw a good deal of him in Brighton last summer," he agreed. "The Admiral was there, dancing attendance on the Regent, so naturally Gage was forced to trail after him and hold his hat and walking-stick. Should hate the office, m'self. These Navy chaps want to be chasing the French in a fast frigate, not doing the pretty to a lot of old court-cards."

"Fast frigates have been singularly unlucky of late," I observed.

The Americans had seized any number of them in battle. But Mr. Gambier appeared not to attend.

"And then Prinny sent my uncle off to Ghent at the end of September, to talk sense into Mr. Adams and the other colonials. I suppose the old fellow must have done it, if Gage is back in England again!"

"Did the Lieutenant inform you when you might expect Lord Gambier's return?"

"He did not. P'raps Aunt Louisa knows. Uncle will have written her the particulars."

The cold collation set out by the housekeeper in deference to St. Stephen's Day was a summary of past delights—platters of the various viands left over from Christmas dinner. I contented myself with cold beef, some excellent cheeses, and a slice of black pudding; a selection of pickles rounded out my repast. A quantity of fruits was also on offer—apples, pears, and oranges. The informality of the meal sat oddly with our careful toilettes—I had put on my beloved claret-coloured silk, a gift from my brother Henry. Cassandra wore a pale green gown of excellent cut she had obtained in Canterbury, whilst on a visit to Edward at Godmersham. What we should do on the morrow, when our fund of finery had all run out, I did not trouble to think.

The simplicity of the meal, however, encouraged a sort of intimacy that the closeness of the weather, and our nearer acquaintance of four-and-twenty hours, only deepened. With the exception of my brother James's wife, we were all disposed to laugh and be easy, to toss jokes at one another and engage in snippets of serious conversation. I was seated, this evening, between Mr. L'Anglois and the Lieutenant—who had Mary Gambier on his left hand. I suspected Eliza's work in this; the change in Miss Gambier's whole person since the arrival of John Gage suggested that a love-match was in the air, and it should have been cruel to separate them by the length of a table. I was inclined to leave them in peace, and let them talk the evening away; but I found that the Lieutenant's manners were too good. He would not permit the neglect of one dinner partner, for the prior claims of another.

"You are quite the hero, Lieutenant," I said lightly as he bent his gaze upon me. "To ride nearly fifty miles, in drifts and driving snow, from Portsmouth to Basingstoke! It is a feat worth publication in the papers—or a place in the betting-book at White's."

"It was my duty," he said seriously. "I ought, perhaps, to have changed my horse and stopped the night in Basingstoke—but Admiral Gambier had charged me with letters to his family, as well as the conveyance of official papers to London. Given the state of the roads, I thought it best to reach Lady Gambier while the daylight held, and break my journey here."

"We are far more engaging than any company you should have found at the Angel," I assured him, "and you have relieved the general tedium of a snowy day. We are all in your debt."

"Forgive me, Miss Austen—but are you, by chance, a relation of Captain Frank Austen?" he said.

"His sister!" I beamed at him; Frank is very dear to me, whether sailing the high seas or turned on shore. "He has served twice under Admiral Gambier, I know—was it then that you made his acquaintance?"

"Far earlier," he replied. "Around the Year Five—before the Trafalgar Action. I was fortunate enough to sail with the *Canopus* as a midshipman. It was Captain Austen who taught me to read a sextant, and command a gun crew, and board a French vessel with my sword drawn."

It had been nearly ten years since Frank had commanded the
Canopus; the Lieutenant must have been a lad of eighteen or twenty
at the time. I wondered why such a personable young man, and
enjoying an admiral's influence, had not achieved the next step in
rank of Master and Commander, or Post Captain. We were lately
done with a punishing war against the French—when any number
of zealous sailors had earned both fortune and advancement through
their actions. Much as Buonaparte was deplored, and his exile cause
for rejoicing, his existence these fifteen years has been a boon to the
ambitious in the Royal Navy—provided they survived their battles.
So many sailors were second sons, forced to seek their fortunes on
the high seas; few could marry without the taking of rich prizes.
No lieutenant, tied to an admiral on shore, could hope to share in
such wealth; and I thought I understood a little of Miss Gambier's
melancholy. Her brother had confessed their parent died in debt. It
was to be presumed she lacked a private fortune. If she had lost her
heart to Lieutenant Gage last summer in Brighton, hers was a sad case.

But it did not do to wander in thought at the dinner table. "How
fortunate you are," I said to my companion, "to observe the negotiations in Ghent! You will understand that with two brothers serving
the Admiralty, I am anxious about this American War."

"Two brothers?"

"I may also claim Captain Charles Austen, lately of the Atlantic
Station. He is presently gone into the Mediterranean—a sadly flat
business, now Buonaparte is cast upon his rock!"

"—Unless he chuses to leave it," the Lieutenant said facetiously.
"Only think what glory for your brother then! But the Atlantic Station
has indeed given cause for anxiety. Our ships have taken a drubbing at
American hands. I doubt any at the Admiralty expected it. Commerce,
not broadsides, has generally been the American object."

"They are not unintelligent," I protested. "Having shewn them how to rout British infantry in the last war, we have lately been teaching them the finer arts of gunnery in this one! The *Constitution*'s engagements with our *Guerrière* and *Java*—on separate occasions, in different parts of the world, and under different commanders—demonstrated that. Both ships were dismasted, I believe, and burnt as hulks? And this, from a forty-four-gun frigate!"

"I see you have closely followed the Naval dispatches," Lieutenant Gage said with a smile.

"News of the *Constitution* is everywhere, I assure you. The Americans have taken five British warships in her—and will take more, no doubt, if the war continues. Nothing of our methods has escaped their notice—neither improvements in the design of vessels, nor in maneuvers, nor communications. We cannot end hostilities soon enough, lest Britannia's rule of the waves be entirely overthrown."

In the heat of my feelings, my voice had increased in volume; and I saw that it had fallen into one of those odd silences that sometimes seize even the most animated of dinner tables. Most of my companions were staring at me—James with disapproval.

"Pray remember where you are, Jane, and do not run on in the wild way you are suffered to do at home. Lieutenant Gage can have not the slightest interest in a woman's idea of politics."

"He may, however, admire her knowledge of Naval tactics," the Lieutenant said.

"You are all condescension, sir." James was at his most pompous. "I fear the attention my sister has won, with her frivolous publications—she has lately taken up the amusement of novel-writing—has entirely gone to her head. She fancies herself an Authority, tho' she has not a syllable of Latin."

"Neither does the crew of the *Constitution*," Raphael West said quietly.

I met his curiously penetrating gaze and coloured. There was a spark of laughter in West's eyes. He did not suffer fools; James, therefore, must be a delight.

"Your father is an American, I believe, Mr. West?" Mary enquired.

"No, ma'am. He is a Philadelphian."

Among general laughter, she protested, "I do not understand!"

"To be a native of Philadelphia—the birthplace of freedom, unless one is talking to a Boston man—is to know a higher order of allegiance than mere country. What we British fail to understand," West continued, "is that America is first a collection of states, more singly dear to their inhabitants than any collective idea of a republic. My father should always admit to Philadelphia, before he should claim America."

We British.

Was West, indeed, an English subject? I wondered. Certainly he spoke as one; had been reared and educated as one. But his father was living an exile of sorts—celebrated by the Crown; a principal mover in the foundation of the Royal Academy; an object of esteem among a people who were not his own, and with whom his country had twice been at war.

"The late Benjamin Franklin was also a Philadelphian," William Chute observed, "and a damned friend to the French."

"As was my father," West returned coolly. "There was a time when his sympathy for the French experiment made him unwelcome in this country. From being Surveyor of the King's Pictures at Windsor, he was banished to Paris. But once the Monster showed his true stripes—once Buonaparte crowned himself Emperor—like every friend of Liberty, my father could not but be disgusted. He renounced the tyrant and returned to London. Sensible men understood and forgave him."

"Paris," breathed Mary. "You must take us to Paris, James, now that the Emperor is overthrown. I long to see France before I die."

All the Austens were so accustomed to Mary's intimacy with death that we did not flutter an eyelash at this statement, but Thomas-Vere Chute positively choked on his wine in surprise.

"My dear Mrs. James," he sputtered, and then looked with sympathy at my brother. Whether his fellow-feeling was born of grief at Mary's secret decline, or grief for James at being burdened with her, I could not say.

Mary sighed tragically, and struck an attitude I mentally appellated: Beauty Expires.

"And how do you regard this American War, West?" Mr. L'Anglois asked.

"As a fight we ought not to have chosen," he replied. "The object, I understand, was to secure our territories and Naval stations beyond the present American borders; but it would seem to arise in truth from more petty concerns. Quarrels over the impressment of American seamen. The desire to inhibit rival trade—"

"But surely," I said, "the American alliance with France—the intimacy between the two nations—must be regarded as pernicious?"

"With Napoleon dethroned, who can say? France is an unknown quantity. Having helped Louis to his throne, we might find the French better friends in future."

"Damned good thing Buonaparte has been routed," William Chute interjected. "With our best troops—Wellington's crack Peninsular units—cavorting in Baltimore and the swamps of Louisiana, we should never be able to answer a French threat if one came. Told Wellington as much myself, when last we met in London. Feel damned exposed with our veterans being months across the Atlantic. Thank God for the return of a sensible Bourbon in Paris, I say!"

"Hear, hear," Mr. L'Anglois intoned, and glasses were raised.

Once we had drunk the French King's health, Eliza turned the conversation, and I was not afforded an opportunity to expose my deplorable opinions again; but as we ladies rose to leave the gentlemen to their port, the Lieutenant stayed me with a word.

"I think I may assure you," he said in a lowered tone, "that the conflict is over. I cannot impart specifics—that should be a breach of duty, and my news must properly be saved for the Admiralty—but as I informed Mr. Chute, a treaty between ourselves and the Americans was signed two days ago in Ghent."

"Then the season is indeed one day of peace," I said. And left him.

No mention of charades was made in the drawing-room this evening. Eliza attempted to rally her guests with the setting out of card tables. My mother dearly loves games of chance—although gambling at Commerce is more to her taste than a hand of whist— and fell in with her hostess's plans immediately. Miss Gambier and Lieutenant Gage sat a little apart, engrossed in a tête-à-tête; Mary attempted to form an engaging picturesque, her head bent low over Caroline and her book. I assumed this was for Mr. Raphael West's benefit—he had appeared in the drawing-room tonight with a leather bound notebook in his hands. But immune to the appeal of the maternal bond, he crossed the room to where Cassandra and I sat over our coffee cups.

"Your interest in the American War persuaded me to unearth this book," he said, as we made room for him on our settee. "I was fortunate enough to visit the States some years ago, on a private errand of my father's, and made numerous sketches. I thought perhaps you both might wish to see a little of the place that has figured so largely in your brothers' fortunes."

I am no artist; that talent belongs to my sister, who employs her pencil as I employ words: to capture the likeness of home and landscape. Cassandra is so modest in her own valuation as never to produce a sketchbook whilst an artist of Raphael West's stature should be by; not for Cassandra, the vain posturing of a Mary Austen with her charcoal and paper. She had entirely escaped West's notice, being naturally of a retiring and self-doubting nature. But her intelligent comments as we reviewed the sketches—regarding light, and vantage-point, and scale of the subject—revealed her inclination to him; and without pressing her upon the point, he voiced an interest in seeing Cassandra's drawings one day. She coloured, doubted, and was silent.

"My sister has received no formal training," I said gently, "and must shrink accordingly from the censure of such a master as yourself."

"I am no master," he said abruptly. "I shall end my life as a student, Miss Austen—for Art is an exacting god, and accepts nothing but genius. But tell me: What do you think of America?"

"It seems strange and wild," I observed, "more violent in Nature than the pastoral beauties of England."

"Untamed," Cassandra amended. "It puts me in mind of Derbyshire, Jane—the monstrous formations of rock near Bakewell. Even the Pinny at Lyme—surely you recall?—has crevasses and rifts in the cliffs like these."

"You give us log cabins, but no cities." I glanced at West's profile as he studied his own work. "Surely there are some, however recent in their construction? Washington City was said to be burnt down by our forces."

"Washington was established, as its name suggests, quite recently," he replied, "and was thus built largely of wood. But the older cities—Philadelphia, Boston, New York—have many fine buildings of stone and brick. These sketches, however, were made in the Blue Mountains north of New York, along the Hudson River. Native tribes were once numerous there. I am not surprized, Miss Austen, that you see savagery and violence in their lines."

West's art was astonishing—his charcoal drawings surging and vivid with life, fantastical in their representations. Under his hand, a felled tree became a vanquished god, all twisting branches and gnarled trunk, as though the gargoyles of an ancient cathedral had bewitched the forest and taken it for their own. Grotesqueries animated his landscapes; Nature warred; no spot was left serene. The notebook was a glimpse into a turbulent soul entirely masked by the gentleman's well-bred façade. He had claimed passion, rather than the cool Platonics of his father's art; but I saw the Gothick and the Romantic struggling for a Classicist's soul.

Was the violence in the landscape—or in the man?

I might have voiced the question aloud, but for the sudden recurrence of Christmas in our midst.

Eliza had appeared in the doorway with a large, shallow bowl in her hands. Blue flames danced along its surface, casting eerie shadows on her neck and face. "Quickly!" she cried. "Snuff the candles, before the effect is run out!"

We hastened to do as we were bid, each of us dousing the nearest light.

Eliza swayed across the room like a Vestal, the flickering bowl in her hands. She set it on a table William Chute had swiftly cleared of its oil lamp.

"Snapdragon!" she cried, and stepped back. "Children—the three of you must snatch your raisins first!"

THE THIRD DAY

8

THE CHILDREN'S BALL

Tuesday, 27th December 1814
The Vyne

I do not know exactly what woke me in the middle of the night—an unaccustomed noise, perhaps, for certainly the vast pile of The Vyne is rife with them. I sat up. A shaft of moonlight cut through the draperies nearest me, which were imperfectly drawn. The snow had ceased. I pulled on my dressing gown, for the fire had burnt low and the bedchamber was chilly. My window gave out on the lake and The Vyne's north front, the rear of the house; an unbroken carpet of white glowed beneath me, fringed with black trunks. It was a bewitching sight.

The moon was low in the sky, opaque and agate, brushed with cloud. I judged that the hour was near dawn. Thoroughly awake, I glanced over my shoulder at the sleeping Cassandra. If I lit a candle to write in my journal, the light might disturb her. Better to use the early hour to deliver young Caroline's third gift.

This was a neat carriage dress for day-wear, made of chestnut-coloured French twill, with a brown velveteen spencer and a dashing tartan silk turban for Jemima's curls. A rabbit-fur muff and a gathered velveteen reticule completed the costume. I had even persuaded the cobbler in Alton to fashion a pair of diminutive brown leather boots. The perfect attire for a Fashionable lady's airing, in Hyde Park or around her country estate.

The prospect of a hunt being distant, until a general thaw should be achieved, James and Mary might wish to depart The Vyne so soon as this morning. Cassandra and I had therefore decided last night that a carriage dress would be perfect for Jemima's needs. I gathered up the doll's clothes and moved noiselessly to the door.

There I halted, every nerve in my being aquiver.

A low murmur of conversation—words indistinguishable, but tone unmistakable—filtered to my ears from the passage beyond.

A woman was speaking, her voice angry and defiant; a man answered, calm but vaguely threatening. Blast these heavy oaken doors! I could make no sense of the words. Never mind that I had no right to do so—that at such an hour, and in such a place, this must be a private conversation. I did not hesitate to overlisten it. The scene was one more clew, if any were needed after the ugly end to our charades, that all was not well at The Vyne.

I laid the doll's clothes on the washstand and pressed my ear to the door.

"Be damned to you," the woman said with the sudden clarity of a bell.

"Very well, madam. I will know how to act."

There was an instant's silence in the passage, as tho' all breath were suspended. Then the man—for he was still there—heaved a queer sort of sigh, part agony, part relief. I heard his steps turn and pace swiftly past my door.

I gathered up Caroline's gift and waited for the space of ten seconds. Then I turned the knob and peered down the hallway in the direction of the vanishing footsteps. I saw no one, but the distant glow of a candle flickering along the walls told me that the unknown gentleman was moving away from me.

I glanced to the right—and saw Mary Gambier.

"Good morning," I said. "I thought I heard voices."

"So did I," she said, and closed her door.

NOT JAMES'S VOICE. NOR William Chute's. I did not think it was Edward Gambier—nor could I find a reason why he should threaten his sister from the hall passage in the early hours of morning. That left four other gentlemen: Thomas-Vere Chute, Benedict L'Anglois, Lieutenant John Gage—and Raphael West.

I remembered the tortured tree limbs and dwarfed figures in his sketches, the undercurrent of menace in the unknown man's voice.

I would wait for Cassandra to wake, before delivering Caroline's present.

"YOU MUST PROMISE TO return to us once your duty to the Admiralty is done, Gage," William Chute said.

The Lieutenant stood on the south side of the Staircase Hall before the front door, his blue cloak caught at his neck and his hat once more upon his head. One of Chute's grooms had saddled the messenger's horse, rested and mettlesome after a night in the stables. The lad waited on the porch outside, ready to throw Gage into his stirrups.

"That is, if you're able to cut your way through these drifts!" Chute continued. "I wonder you bother to attempt it."

"Folly," Eliza chided. "Pray listen to sense, Lieutenant Gage, and remain with us another day or two. Your news will keep—and far better to arrive in London with it safely, than to falter in the attempt!"

The Naval messenger smiled awkwardly. "I fear I have already delayed too long, and will merit any penalty for tardiness the Admiralty chuses to impose." His eyes drifted to the staircase, where Mary Gambier stood with her hands clasped and her countenance as expressionless as marble. Her aunt had not appeared that morning; it was her habit to take her breakfast on a tray in bed. "Your liberality in welcoming a stranger, Mrs. Chute, shall not be soon forgotten."

"But you must return to us! Surely they cannot detain you so long in London. We shall expect you in a few days' time."

"I cannot promise," he said with difficulty, "tho' my heart wishes it. You are all kindness. But my time—indeed my life—is not my own. I must go where duty and the Admiralty bid."

He doffed his hat, bowed to us all, and turned towards his horse. Painful, to watch a publick leave-taking between two hearts that must yearn to bid each other *adieu* in private, and far more tenderly. I hoped the Lieutenant and Miss Gambier had snatched a moment to say their farewells.

The groom offered the stirrup; the Lieutenant mounted with grace, and took the reins. He raised his hand and with one earnest, parting look for the lady standing on the stairs, he laid his heels to the horse's flanks and was away.

"Nice lad," William Chute said, as his butler, Roark, swung closed the great front door. "We shall hope those fellows are satisfied with his intelligence, and give him leave, eh? There might be a hunt in the offing, by the time he is returned to us!"

WE SETTLED ONCE MORE at the breakfast-parlour—a room Eliza called the Strawberry Parlour, for Horace Walpole's having slept in it some fifty years since—in groups of two and three. Lieutenant Gage's departure had brought us all to our feet, and now we were treated to cooling tea and cold toast. The chafing dishes of eggs and pheasant and ham, however, were still warm. The servants had resumed their labours on Eliza's behalf, so no crisis was too great for her resolving.

"Take away all these cold plates," she ordered, "and bring us fresh tea and coffee. The snow may be done, but I declare the temperature is frigid! The poor Lieutenant, to be abroad so early on such a brisk morning!"

"I am sure he is accustomed to it," James's Mary said indifferently. "For he must often have walked an icy deck at sea. But I am so delicate, you know, that the least chill might carry me off. James was for returning to Steventon this morning, but I protested most violently. I cannot risk my health in venturing forth in such weather, no matter how sound your carriage and coachman might be, Mrs. Chute."

Particularly, I thought, when such interesting guests should be left behind at The Vyne.

"James, however," his wife persisted, "should rather see me in my grave than endure another hour of frivolity!"

"How Gothick your mind does turn, Mary," Eliza said equably, "when it has nothing better to do. Cassandra, I am thinking of getting up a Children's Ball for Twelfth Night. I wonder if I might consult you about the various courses for the dinner—and whether Jane would be willing to create some Character Cards for the masquerade?"

"I shall help you!" Thomas-Vere cried with a note of ecstasy in his voice. He was arrayed this morning in a shocking waistcoat of puce silk, figured with gold butterflies, and his wig was powdered silver. "I adore masquerades!"

"Popishness," James muttered into his newspaper.

"I beg your pardon, Mr. Austen?" Eliza enquired, startled.

"Popishness." He snapped his pages closed. "Paganism. Twelfth

Night revels devolve from the Roman Saturnalia, my dear Mrs. Chute, as I am sure you are aware."

"Nonsense," my mother said comfortably. "Do not be a spoilsport and a prig, James. Your father was very fond of presenting a sprig of mistletoe to every young lady of his acquaintance on Twelfth Night, as I recall."

"Then I confess I must regard his Christian doctrine—not to mention his taste—as questionable," James retorted. "The Roman Saturnalia is a feast of Inversion, when the natural order is turned topsy-turvy. Nobles go as servants, and servants as noblemen. All distinctions of birth are ignored. Anarchy is thus the order of the day, ma'am, and a defiance of God's Plan. It is an excuse for every kind of debauch in the name of liberty. Nothing less than the late revolution in France, to be exact."

"But what have guillotines to do with my masquerade?" Eliza demanded, bewildered.

James hunched a shoulder. "I daresay a Children's Ball may be innocent enough. But the rituals of Twelfth Night were bred in evil, and no good can come of perpetuating them. They ought to be consigned to the ash-heap of history, as Rome has been."

"I take it you abhor the Classical world, Mr. Austen?" Raphael West enquired. His eyes were half-shuttered by indolent lids, but I detected a satiric glint.

"I flatter myself I appreciate the beauties of Classical form and Classical thought," my brother said grudgingly. "No man who has been privileged to study at Oxford can fail to acknowledge our debt to vanished times. But I must plead the propriety of present improvements upon ancient ways. We in England have amended what Rome gave us, for the better."

"Exactly so," Mary agreed, "which is why there cannot be the slightest objection to Mrs. Chute's masquerade. I am sure it will be the most English party imaginable. But Cassandra cannot possibly be of use to you, Eliza, in planning your dishes," she continued, "for she is not a married woman, and has never studied domestic economy! I should be very happy to consult with you. It does not do to go to spinsters, you know, for the elegance of one's entertainments."

Unless, I thought, one was in the habit of lying on a sopha in a chilly winter room. Spinsters were infinitely useful for fetching firewood and ham, whilst one lay in contemplation of the Abyss.

"Mary," James said warningly. "You cannot mean to attend this Saturnalia. For one in the throes of spiritual battle, the temptations of frivolity—of giving oneself over entirely to pleasure—"

"It is a Children's Ball, James." She leaned close to him and said in an audible whisper, "I am sure it is meant to honour our Caroline and James-Edward. Miss Wiggett is only an adopted child, after all."

"Thank you," Eliza said crisply. "We shall gather our plans in the morning room—shall we?"

IT IS CUSTOMARY TO call the Twelfth Night fête a Children's Ball, because dressing-up and faerie tales are the order of the evening; but persons of all ages must enjoy the entertainment. Never mind that it is the children who play at King and Queen; we others form their Court, in cunning guises chosen at random from Character Cards. I should have expected Eliza to have purchased her set in London; I was pleased to discover that we should be set to devising them ourselves. There is such scope for wit in a set of Characters, as I have cause to know.

The morning room was a pretty little chamber off the Staircase Hall, given over entirely to Eliza's pursuits. Here she conducted her correspondence after breakfast, drew up her orders for the housekeeper, Mrs. Roark, and wrote lists of provisions to be ordered from London. The room was one of the few at The Vyne that felt fresh; instead of heavy oak panelling, its walls were painted a cheerful yellow. One wall had been decorated with scenes cut from prints and carefully pasted onto the plaster; it was a scheme Eliza had undertaken for Miss Wiggett's amusement, after the pair had glimpsed a similar Print Room in London.

"The winters are so dreary, you know," Eliza said wisely, "that it helps to pass the time. My Caroline is so industrious! She enjoys looking among the print collection—William's ancestors were forever collecting them—and chusing which complement others, and deciding the arrangement on the wall."

"She has a good deal of natural taste," I said.

"Yes. It is priceless in a young lady—and cannot be taught." She glanced at James's Mary as she said this, and pressed her lips firmly together. As a hostess, Eliza Chute was a saint—and far more forbearing than I should have been.

She set my mother at her own pretty little writing desk, to make out innumerable cards of invitation in her perfect copperplate hand; some sixty or seventy persons, I suppose, were to be invited—not counting their children! Cassandra and Mary were arranged on one settee, while Thomas-Vere and I secured another. We were supplied with paper and pen, and endeavoured to ignore such phrases as Twelfth Night cake and Claret Cup in the effort to form our own plans. Thomas-Vere was all that was enthusiastic and amiable in an assistant.

"We must prevail upon West to sketch a figure for each of our cards," he burbled, "for he is a master of caricature."

"And if only he may be prevailed upon to sign them," I observed, "we might frame the cards afterwards."

"Miss Jane!" Thomas-Vere tapped my hand with his quizzing-glass and attempted to look arch. "Profiting from the charity of genius?"

"But perhaps Mr. West does not mean to remain in the country so long," I added. "It is over a week until the ball, and I daresay he will wish to return to his family by and by."

"I do not think he possesses any," Thomas-Vere replied. "Other than his redoubtable father, of course. The brother is estranged, and West's wife has been dead these three years. His daughter is lately married."

Eliza's intelligence, therefore, was correct. Three years a widower! And no glowing young girl had captured West's heart? I might have pursued the interesting conversation, but Thomas-Vere jumped to his feet. "I do not know why I did not think of it before," he said. "West must assist us. With his hand and our wit, Miss Jane, the Characters shall be all that is fanciful and engaging. You do not object?"

I did not, and he exited the room with alacrity. In his absence I scribbled a few names on my paper—Lady Lavish, Miss Candour, Guy Gallant, Frederick Fop. The latter would be suited to Thomas-Vere. I had once played Miss Candour myself, at a vanished revel. The rôle consisted of telling every other guest exactly what one thought of him. I had enjoyed the masquerade enormously.

Mary, now . . . if I could contrive it, she should figure as Signora Topnote, the Italian soprano. That should delight her vanity; and discourage her from talking throughout the evening.

The door to the morning room burst open. Thomas-Vere stood with his hand on the knob, his breath coming in gasps. "Eliza, do you know where William is gone?"

"I thought to see about the dogs," she replied, a small frown between her eyes. "What is it, Tom?"

"Lieutenant Gage's horse has returned," he said. "Without its rider."

9

THE BROKEN TRAIL

Tuesday, 27th December 1814
The Vyne, cont'd.

We four ladies rose as one and followed Thomas-Vere to the Staircase Hall.

The butler, Roark, stood in the open front door. Beyond, beneath the portico, was the groom who had saddled John Gage's horse. His cap was in his hand. He looked discomfited and scared—less at the tidings he had brought, than at being kept waiting in the cold to repeat them.

"What is it, Tibbin?" Eliza asked.

"The messenger's gelding, ma'am. Made his way back to the stables. I thought maybe the gentleman was come back to the house, and the horse'd got away from him."

"Thank you, Tibbin. Have you seen your master?"

"He's at the kennels about the dogs," the groom said.

"Pray fetch him at once."

Tibbin pulled his forelock and turned without a word. As Roark swung closed the door, I observed the groom making for the stableyard at a run; the gardeners had swept the carriageway from yard to portico clear of snow. They were progressing further down the carriageway in the direction of the road, but had not yet swept above fifty yards beyond the front door. It seemed probable, however, that we should be able to return to Steventon on the morrow. Pale sunlight turned the white landscape to flashing brilliance; the persistent drip of melting snow sounded from each of The Vyne's many eaves. A thaw was setting in.

"The Gambiers ought to be told," I said. We ladies and Thomas-Vere still stood in the Staircase Hall, our backs to the cheerful Yule log. "If he has been thrown—and unable to make his way back . . ."

"A broken leg," Thomas-Vere said firmly.

"Or neck," Mary observed.

At that moment, William Chute's heavy boots could be heard tramping down the east passage; he had come up from the kennels through a rear door and the servants' wing.

"My love," Eliza said as the green baize door behind the staircase was thrust open. "You met Tibbin?"

"Aye," William replied, "and I have told him to collect a search party of stable lads. I returned only to inform our guests—some of the gentlemen may wish to join me. I shall find L'Anglois in my book room, but do you know, Tom, where are West and Gambier?"

"Gambier is in the billiard room. I searched for West earlier," Thomas-Vere replied, "and could not find him."

"Has anyone seen Miss Gambier this morning?" Eliza enquired.

"I did," Cassandra said. "When the rest of us returned to the break-fast-parlour after Lieutenant Gage's departure, she went another way."

"To her bedchamber?"

Cassandra shook her head. "I suspect that she is in prayer, Eliza. She was making for the Chapel."

THE CHAPEL AT THE VYNE is justly famous. Indeed, there can be few places so magnificent outside the royal Tudor palaces. It is very ancient, the foundations being lost in Norman times; tho' the present arrangement of antechapel, chapel, and Tomb-chamber date from Henry VIII's time. They were later embellished with the fanciful decorations of the Strawberry Hill aesthete, John Chute. I am told that two closet galleries once existed, overlooking the nave above the heads of simple worshipers, so that the Tudor Master and Mistress of The Vyne (a notable family by the name of de Vere, long since extinguished) might worship in private piety. There are choir stalls of dark wood lining the walls that equal nothing, I believe, except those in St. George's Chapel at Windsor. The vaulted ceiling is webbed with moulded plaster veins, picked out in gold. Paintings in the Italian stile are ranged above the north and south walls—they charm the eye into believing that a Gothick cloister lies just beyond one's reach. The Four Evangelists and angels soar in their architraves. Glorious stained glass, dating from the sixteenth century, winks like scattered jewels above the altar. The floor is partly of marble and—what is far more engaging—partly of glazed Flemish tiles, commissioned in Antwerp. Their faces are covered in a riot of pictures: animals and birds, fruit and leaves, heads in profile and full face; even a Harlequin fool. The tiles beguile one to look down, the windows to gaze up—and so one may practise both humility and ecstasy, in the pursuit of one's God.

Mary Gambier was on her knees before the altar, which stood on a raised wooden platform. It held no other decoration than a simple gilt cross. At the rustle of our approaching skirts, she lifted her head. But she did not move. Her hands remained clasped, her countenance expressionless.

"My dear," Eliza Chute said, coming to a halt before the raised dais.

"What is it?" Miss Gambier said. "What news have you come to tell?" Her voice was strained.

"No news. But we are uneasy. Your friend the Lieutenant—"

She rose from her knees. "What about him?"

"His horse has returned riderless. The men have organised a search party."

Miss Gambier closed her eyes an instant. A wealth of emotions passed over her face—fear, pain, resignation, anger.

"Then I must go with them," she said. Her eyes opened once more, dry of both emotion and tears. "Will any of you join me?"

Tho' I could not ride, I might search on foot. "I will," I said.

In the event, we had not even time to don our pelisses, much less our boots. We had achieved the upper landing and would have turned down the passage to our bedchambers when I happened to glance out the tall windows giving on to the lake. A sad little grouping of figures, dark against the snow, toiled through the unbroken drifts of the north front. They bore another among them.

I put a hand on Miss Gambier's shoulder.

She turned, her gaze following mine. "They have found him," she said. And in her voice there was something like relief.

We sped down the staircase and made for the east passage. As we achieved the green baize door to the kitchens, however, it swung open—and revealed Edward Gambier. He was undoubtedly come in search of his sister.

He stepped into the hall, the door closing behind him. His open countenance was white and drawn. "Mary," he said, and drew her into his arms.

"Tell me," she choked. "I cannot bear the suspense."

"He is gone, Mary. He is gone."

"How?" I demanded.

Gambier looked at me over Miss Gambier's head. "His neck is broken."

For once, it seemed, James's wife was correct.

ELIZA CHUTE, FOR ALL her Fashion and charm, is an excellent woman; and she proved her goodness in the care and sensibility bestowed upon Mary Gambier in the ensuing hours. She first broke the news of John Gage's death to Lady Gambier—who had been laid down on the couch in her bedchamber, recruiting her strength. Lady Gambier went at once to her niece, and I hope had words of comfort for her. Eliza then gave orders in the servants' hall—the Lieutenant's clothes were to be dried and pressed, and his corpse properly laid out, and a bier placed in the Chapel with candles burning all around. Impossible, of course, to make funeral arrangements, until someone could be sent to the Admiralty and Gage's people found. Even a poor lieutenant may have a widowed mother, or a spinster aunt, who must wish to know the circumstances of his death.

"I shall write to Gambier," the Admiral's lady said stoutly, with the first resolution I had yet seen in her. "He felt for Gage as tho' he were his own child. It is a sad waste. He ought to have died for King and Country!"

"What makes you think he did not?" I murmured.

But no one in all The Vyne appeared to regard the Lieutenant's death as anything but an accident. I waited for some expressions of unease to overcome at least one of my companions—and waited in vain.

Eliza set out a cold collation in the dining parlour, and those who retained an appetite sat down to eat their fill. I pled a headache. When my companions had left me, I hurriedly put on the pelisse and boots that had not been wanted an hour before, and slipped quietly through the door to the south porch.

The gardeners' clearance of the carriageway drifts had been abandoned due to the necessity of the search party, but the way was easy for some hundred yards. After that, I halted before a wall of white some four feet high. Where Lieutenant Gage's horse had broken through was obvious; the trail was further trampled and mauled by the search party that had followed it. I gathered my skirts—I was wearing a round gown of grey cambric beneath my pelisse—and began to trudge forward through the packed and tumbled drifts.

A quarter of an hour later, I had almost reached the end of the carriageway and gained the Sherborne St. John road. The distance, impressively long and winding when viewed from the comfort of a closed carriage, is tediously protracted when attempted on foot; and had the exercise not warmed me to the core, I am sure my teeth should have been chattering with cold. My hands were stiffening in their gloves and I could no longer feel my toes inside my boots. But my labour was about to end: beyond a turn in the carriageway I glimpsed the snow-covered roof of a small outbuilding—an ice house, by its design, snugged into a slope that descended gently to the road. A few bare trees framed the landscape. The horse's trail came to a sudden halt here, in a whirl of displaced white.

To my surprize, I was not alone.

Raphael West stood in the middle of the carriageway, his back turned to my approach and a sketching book raised in his right hand. After an instant's pause for surprize, I picked my way through the snow and gained his side.

"Miss Austen," he said calmly.

"Mr. West." I glanced at the sketchbook; his left hand was moving rapidly and carelessly over the paper, outlining the scene in charcoal. Where I saw only empty space and disturbed ground, however, he had supplied a tumbled horse and a prone figure. As a scene of violence, it was excessively probable.

"I expected to hear that the horse reared and threw the Lieutenant," I observed, "but you seem to think the horse fell. Was there ice beneath the drifts?"

"There is none there now." He glanced up at the weak sun, fading towards the western horizon. "Perhaps it has melted. I do not know. Nor can I tell how much you apprehend of horses—having been raised in a parsonage with little in the way of riding."

"Very well. May I ask you to explain your sketch?"

"From the appearance of the snow"—he gestured ahead of us and slightly to the left—"I should judge that the horse came to its knees there. It then panicked and thrashed about a bit to regain purchase under its hooves. Bucking up, it scrambled forward a few yards before turning back and nosing its fallen rider, who lay there." Again, the gesture with his charcoal, this time further to the left in the trampled drifts. "The imprint of Gage's left hand is quite plain if you chuse to walk up and look at it. He fell sprawling."

"Were you of the search party?"

"I came up with it a few moments after it departed the stable-yard. I had been working in the Oak Gallery when the hue and cry went up, and only learnt of the Lieutenant's mishap once the men had set out."

"But you saw the body?"

"I did."

"Was he lying where you suggest that he fell?"

Raphael West glanced at me sidelong. "He was not. His body was recovered over there"—he gestured to the right—"after his nag, no doubt, had bolted for the stables. But how the Devil did you guess?"

I shrugged lamely. "What man breaks his neck from falling into four feet of soft snow? Had a tree branch snapped and struck him—or his horse startled and thrown him—"

West smiled crookedly. "I should swear to it that the horse was brought down to its knees."

I stared ahead with narrowed eyes. "The trail goes no further?"

"It does not."

"And none joins it from the road?"

He shook his head.

Our eyes met soberly. "You are sketching a case for murder," I said.

"I thought it my duty," he replied. "The evidence, you see, is melting."

WHILE RAPHAEL WEST COMPLETED his second rough drawing—one that showed the final location of John Gage's body—I forced a path through the snow towards the ice house, and examined the trunks of the trees.

It was not long before I found what I expected—evidence of a kind that would not vanish in the sun.

10

ART IN THE DETAILS

Tuesday, 27th December 1814
The Vyne, cont'd.

I must suppose that the majority of ladies, gently reared, should have displayed a greater sensibility at the gallant Lieutenant's violent end. I ought perhaps to have wept over the scene, or suffered a passing faintness that must have excited Raphael West's anxiety. But I am no longer a green girl, and cannot be giving way to emotion when sober presence of mind is required. Moreover, I am a little acquainted with murder, and those who practise it; I have witnessed a number of mankind's depravities; and on occasion, I have had the good fortune to achieve Justice with nothing more than my wits to support me. The novelist's perception of motive and character is equally suited to the penetration of human deceit. I am determined never to apologise for my talents in either.

I spared a thought, then, for John Gage's earnest looks, and for the misery his passing must cause all those who held him dear—particularly poor Miss Gambier. Then I gathered my discoveries from the snowbank and presented them to Raphael West.

He studied my gloved palms an instant, then glanced at the sky. "It grows dark. Let us go back."

Half an hour later, we discovered William Chute in his book room. He was composing a letter to the Admiralty as he paced before his fire; Benedict L'Anglois was charged with transcribing it. Rather than disturb the MP and his secretary unduly, we had dragooned a footman into scratching at his master's door; a word only was required to admit us.

"I fear we must leave off our posing, West," Chute said as the painter ushered me before him into the book room, "until this sad business of young Gage is managed. Miss Austen! Your cheeks are flushed with cold, I declare! You have never been out-of-doors in this weather!"

"I have been walking, sir, to view the place where the Lieutenant died—and found Mr. West before me."

"Indeed." Chute frowned a little and looked from one to the other of us.

"If we might have a word in private, sir?"

"I shall just draw up this letter, Mr. Chute," L'Anglois said immediately, "and return with it for your signature."

"Very well. You will add everything that is appropriate, I hope?" Chute asked anxiously.

L'Anglois inclined his head and quitted the book room.

"I intend to send him immediately to London." Chute studied us intently. "How may I serve you?"

Raphael West set his open sketchbook on the writing table. "I have made several rough drawings of the site of Gage's mishap. Pray examine them, sir."

William Chute glanced over the drawings. West had added what he called "insets," smaller depictions of particular details, superimposed on each of the scenes. One such was a minute image of the snowy imprint of Lieutenant Gage's gloved left hand, where he had first sprawled in the drifts. The other was a similar picture of the impression of his right arm—upon which he had fallen, at some remove from his first position, in death.

Chute took infinite care in his study of the sketches. Then he looked up and met West's gaze. "How is it that a man with a broken neck may pick himself up, walk a few steps, and keel over again?"

"I can think of only one cause," West replied calmly. "His neck was not broken by falling from his horse."

"But—you would suggest that Gage died after he was tossed? I have never known a similar case; and I have witnessed a few untimely deaths on the hunting field, I may say. Indeed, I have never known a man to break his neck and walk, much less survive."

"Nor have I. That is not what I would suggest."

Chute's eyes strayed to my troubled countenance. "Miss Austen, ought you to be here? Surely you will like to take some refreshment with my wife. The fire is better in the library."

"Miss Austen wishes to show you what she discovered," Raphael West said, "at the base of two trunks, near the place where Gage died."

I opened my right hand. Some twisted lengths of wire winked in the firelight.

"What are these?" Chute exclaimed.

"All that could be retrieved of the trap that brought down Lieutenant Gage's horse," I said. "I would guess that we shall find the whole, once the snow is entirely melted."

Despite his preference for country life, Chute has benefited from his years of parliamentary service; he is sharper and more adept than I should have guessed, at weaving a whole cloth from a few strands of wool.

"You mean to say that this . . . foul contrivance . . . was stretched across my carriageway?"

"It must have been invisible with the heavy fall of snow, particularly if it was put there last night—and covered with drifts by the early hours of morning."

"We shall have to look to the horse's knees," Chute said grimly.

"Hot fomentations to the wounds," West suggested, "which, judging by the fineness and strength of this wire, will be clean and deep."

"Good God!" Chute exclaimed. "It is in every way infamous! To rig such a trap, with the intent of toppling any poor innocent making his way through the snow—"

"Not any innocent," West warned. "Lieutenant Gage. The Admiral's messenger."

Chute paused, and looked from one to the other of us. "You believe he was toppled, and while rising from the ground, was set upon by an unknown person, and . . ."

"Killed," I said succinctly.

"Depending upon the angle of the attack," West added, "it should not require inordinate strength to snap back a man's head; and the signs of struggle should be lost in the trampling of the horse—which was so much alarmed, it bolted for its stable."

Chute drew a gusty breath. "Some brigand, I suppose. A wastrel or vagabond cast up from the Sherborne road, and ready to prey upon any chance stranger."

There was a pregnant silence. "No, sir," West said regretfully. "The snow is unbroken from the direction of the Sherborne road, as you must see from my sketch of the ground. No brigand can have come from there."

Chute studied West's drawing once more, and his expression altered. "Do you mean to say—"

"That the Lieutenant was killed by someone belonging to The Vyne? Yes, sir."

"Damn your eyes!" Chute cried. "I will not have my people suspected! It is a farrago of nonsense from first to last! The man was thrown from his horse and died. He is not the only rider, I am sure, to suffer such a fate."

Neither West nor I spoke; we did not review the facts as we had shewn them; we merely waited for Chute's fury to die, as a flaring log might settle into embers.

He wheeled and paced a few steps, then paced a few more towards us. A formidable figure, when stiffly upon his dignity; but when I expected him to order us from the room, he halted and studied us both uncertainly. "It's a bad business."

"Yes," I said gently. "You will understand how bad when I tell you that the small outbuilding that stands near the carriageway—an ice house, is it not?—probably harboured the killer. There is a far smaller trail of prints from the road to the building; and the wire was set among the trees at just that point. Mr. West and I found the place empty, of course—but it was not so this morning."

"He waited there until Gage's horse went down," Chute said. "Despicable blackguard."

"Tell me, sir," West interjected. "Was the Lieutenant's dispatch bag found on his person?"

"It was not."

"Nor upon his horse?"

"The bag must be buried in drifts," Chute replied. "I shall order a search for it, when once I am done reporting the sad intelligence of the Lieutenant's death to the Admiralty." He groped his way towards his chair and sank heavily into it.

West stepped closer to the writing table. "Forgive me, sir, but I must ask you—were the papers the Lieutenant carried of such grave importance that another might kill to obtain them?"

Chute raised watery brown eyes, remarkably akin to one of his hounds. "He carried the Treaty signed in Ghent a few days ago, between Great Britain and the American delegation. As I have been closely concerned in the Government end of negotiations—being privy, on the House side, to Lord Castlereagh's dispositions in the matter— Admiral Gambier wished me informed. Gage shared the substance of his dispatch with me yesterday. I glanced over the Treaty, and bade him carry it to London with all possible speed."

Viscount Lord Castlereagh had been at the Congress of Vienna since September. In addition to being Leader of the House, he was Foreign Secretary—and as such, expected to negotiate for Britain.[3] In Vienna, it was said, the Four Powers would redraw the map of Europe—and when such an undertaking was at issue, the resolution of the American War must be secondary. Still, it was the Treaty signed in Ghent that had gone missing.

"For what does the document provide?" I asked.

"For an end to all hostilities between our two nations," Chute replied. "—And precious little else, I might add. We have prevailed in none of our chief points, while the Americans have realised most of theirs. Still—that is neither here nor there. I am sure the Admiral did his best. I do not know how Castlereagh will regard the terms."

"Surely Admiral Gambier will have sent a copy of the Treaty to Vienna?" West said. "He acts, I believe, for Castlereagh in the Ghent negotiations."

"Undoubtedly he will have sent the Viscount a copy. But the

---

[3] The Congress of Vienna ran from September 1814 through June 1815. Representatives of England, France, Austria, and Russia met to discuss European political futures in the aftermath of Napoleon's abdication and exile. New boundaries were established not only for France but for the Netherlands, the Duchy of Warsaw, and various German states and Italian territories.—Editor's note.

Treaty itself—with signatures—was in Gage's possession. He was charged with reaching the Admiralty; the Admiralty was to deliver the document to the Home Secretary, in Castlereagh's absence. After the Cabinet had reviewed and understood the terms, it was to be sent to Parliament. The Treaty must be read and debated in both the House and Lords, before it is ratified."

"With the Treaty lost—"

"Surely it will be found in the snow!" Chute said imploringly.

"Send out your search party again, sir," West suggested.

Chute rose and rang for a footman. "I shall, indeed. But we three know they will find nothing. Gage is dead—and there is no reason on earth to rob and kill a dispatch rider, unless you wish to prevent his intelligence from arriving."

THE FOURTH DAY

11

THE ODOUR OF DEATH

Wednesday, 28th December 1814
The Vyne

Cassandra undertook to present our gift to Caroline in the early hours of the morning. Jemima's latest gown was a simple white muslin dress for day-wear, with a triple flounce at the hem and flowers embroidered at the bodice; a pale blue spencer and a jockey bonnet completed the costume. I had managed the embroidery—sewing is one household task in which I excel—and Cassandra had fashioned pale blue slippers from a discarded bit of satin. I did not stir when she departed on her faerie mission; yesterday's exertions in the snow had thoroughly exhausted me.

I encountered Caroline a while later in the Staircase Hall; she was sitting on the bottom step, staring thoughtfully at the burning Yule log. She had tied a black ribbon around Jemima's arm. She knew nothing, to be sure, of murder—but sudden death will distress a child.

"James-Edward says we must leave The Vyne today," she told me mournfully.

I sank down on the step beside her. "Shall you not like to be at home?"

She shook her head. "Nothing ever happens there. No one visits us. It is terribly dreary in wintertime. Even you will be leaving soon, Aunt."

"Not until after Twelfth Night," I promised. Thank Heaven no word had come to poor Caroline of the promised Children's Ball! To be denied such a treat must cause anguish; and it seemed doubtful that Eliza should hold a revel, under the circumstances.

William Chute had proved himself a man of action in the hours after our meeting in his book room. Sparing no expence, he had despatched his letter to the Admiralty via an Express. A similar missive had been sent to Admiral Gambier in Ghent. A groom had ridden off through the drifts on one of Chute's own hunters to Hackwood Park, home of the second Lord Bolton, who is a Justice of the Peace in the locality; he was expected to wait upon Mr. Chute this morning. Chute holds a similar title but recused himself from acting in the present case of murder. The little awkwardness of having hosted both victim and killer made the matter a delicate one.

Finally, he had tramped out himself to the scene of the Lieutenant's death and overlooked the ground. There, with despairing hope, he set a party of gardeners to sweeping the drifts in an effort to secure the missing dispatch bag. After several hours, they succeeded in securing only the remainder of the cunning wire that had brought down the Lieutenant's horse.

Miss Gambier took her dinner on a tray in her bedchamber last night. There were any number of questions I longed to put to her. Who was the person that had uttered threats at her door in the early hours of the morning? Did she suspect the same person of having written the mysterious charade? And if so—had either event anything to do with the Lieutenant's murder?

What had driven Miss Gambier to her knees in the Chapel at the exact hour of Lieutenant Gage's death?

I could not, with propriety, interrogate the lady in the depths of her grief. Indeed, I had no right to interrogate her at all. I could not even voice my suspicions to William Chute—Miss Gambier was a guest in his household, and he was preoccupied with the fate of his American Treaty. It was probable that Miss Gambier's private affairs had nothing to do with an intrigue of State.

But the questions persisted, all the same.

Before the servants, Eliza was at pains to put a good face on events, and we brushed through dinner tolerably well—tho' the tone of conversation was both subdued and tedious. Edward Gambier, in particular, was singularly inattentive, and without Mr. L'Anglois—who was gone on horseback to the Admiralty—we lacked one disinterested voice in our midst. It was left to James to introduce a topic of conversation— never to be preferred. He pontificated on the increasing numbers of Evangelicals in the Church, and his belief that the increase in piety must be the saving of us all. Thomas-Vere declared, in shocked tones, that he believed Evangelicals to frown upon so harmless an amusement as dancing. Beyond this, ecclesiastic debate did not venture.

It was only when we had all assembled in the drawing-room over coffee that Chute made a sort of speech, brief and to the purpose, which must astonish those who knew him as a garrulous sportsman. I began to apprehend the talents that recommended him to such an exacting Cabinet member as Castlereagh.

My brother James had just announced his intention of removing the Austen party to Steventon in the morning, "provided the carriageway and surrounding lanes are tolerably clear; for we cannot allow ourselves to add to your burdens at present. I shall, of course, be most happy to return and preside over funeral rites in the Chapel for the unfortunate Deceased—always supposing that his family do not wish the disposition otherwise."

"So kind," Lady Gambier murmured.

"I must ask you to remain here until I have spoken with Lord Bolton," Chute replied. "I expect him to pay us a morning call."

"Bolton?" James's countenance brightened visibly. "I should be happy to meet his lordship at any moment. I did not know he intended to spend the holidays in Hampshire."

"In the usual way, he should have gone into Leicestershire, for the hunting," Chute agreed, "but Lady Bolton is in daily expectation of her confinement. Indeed, I should like all of you—including Mr. West," he added with a particular bow, "to remain at The Vyne until the inquest should be over. I do not think we can properly avoid one, now."

James frowned; Thomas-Vere was startled, and Gambier confused.

"Inquest?" he repeated. "Over poor John? Why the Devil should a Coroner be called, because a fellow is thrown from his horse?"

"It is customary when the Deceased is in the employ of the Crown," Chute replied.

I did not think this was true; but it satisfied a number of those present. William Chute meant to play a deep hand. He might have informed his house party that a trap had been laid—foul play suspected—that the Ghent papers were missing—but how should it avail him? He did not wish to alarm the innocent, or put the murderer on guard. And even did Chute order a thorough search of The Vyne and its outbuildings, he should discover nothing of the stolen Treaty in that vast and ancient pile. Whoever had killed for the spoils, would be certain to hide them well.

It remained to decipher which among the Christmas guests the murderer might be. I did not for a moment believe the servants to be implicated; they had been enjoying their freedom on St. Stephen's Day, and could hardly have known even of Lieutenant

Gage's arrival. The idea that one of them would lay a trap for his horse—or steal the Treaty—was absurd.

"Lord Bolton!" Mary murmured with satisfaction as we mounted the stairs to bed an hour later. "He is excessively handsome, Jane, and very good *ton*. James and I are forever meeting him and his lady—a sweet creature!—when we are gone into Basingstoke. Such a gentleman will not have come in your way before this. You will wish to be loitering in the Staircase Hall when he is announced, I am sure, to see what a Great Man looks like. I wonder the Chutes did not invite Lord and Lady Bolton to dine whilst we were here. It might have been just that select and intimate party one could expect from a Member of Parliament. But we find only the Gambiers and Mr. West."

It appeared that Raphael West's *éclat* had worn thin in Mary's eyes. I suspected his indifference to her sketchbook—and her poses—was largely to blame.

"Lady Gambier, you know, is not truly genteel," she persisted in an undertone, "for her husband's title was only got through the Navy."

And worse still, I thought, she is cousin to poor dead Anne.

"James says a clergyman's wife ranks higher than a duchess," Mary concluded, "in being closer to God."

"I wonder you can bear to live with the man," I replied, and bid her goodnight.

I LAY AWAKE FOR some hours, my mind a welter of ideas. A treaty was naturally of importance to the parties involved—in this case, Britain and the United States. But why should an individual resort to murder to steal it? When the principal negotiators must be cognizant of the details, and preparing to present them to their respective governments for vote and ratification, surely the paper—even signed—was a matter of form. If one wished to alter the outcome of events, better to kill the negotiators themselves!

And why should anyone beyond the two Governments involved, wish to know the Treaty's terms?

I exerted my wits to puzzle it out.

The negotiations at Ghent were to end the present war. That should alter relations between the United States and Britain in numerous ways. Trade, for example, should resume unfettered by both parties. American territorial rights should proceed unhindered by British claims. And the British Army—His Grace the Duke of Wellington's crack Peninsular troops—should be returning home . . .

What had William Chute said, over Christmas dinner? —that with the troops elsewhere engaged, England was vulnerable?

Who might value such intelligence?

A foreign government, of course.

Foreign agents, who could wish to delay the news of an end to the American War. Or the issuance of new orders, for those same crack troops.

Russia's Czar, I recalled, had wished for British military support during his late conflict with Napoleon—who had foolishly penetrated so far as Moscow, only to see it burnt by its inhabitants. French losses in the retreat had been terrible; the Russian winter accomplished what British troops could not. We had been deaf to Russian pleas in 1812—because our armies were two continents distant. Now that Napoleon was exiled to Elba, and the Czar was rebuilding his city—the disposition of Wellington's men could no longer be of interest to him. Unless the Czar's future designs affected England's interests.

Surely no one at The Vyne might figure as a Russian agent?

Thomas-Vere?

The idea was laughable. Which argued for its consideration.

Edward Gambier?

He was in a position to know something of politics, through his uncle, but seemed to have little aptitude for the subject; and he was not yet even of age. At merely twenty, he thought more of the shine on his Hessians than of England's vulnerabilities. Or was this merely a pose, intended to bamboozle the credulous?

Mr. L'Anglois? His name was French enough.

Raphael West?

Here my thoughts slowed in their whirl. One had been secretary to the Comte d'Artois, with connexions to the new Bourbon King. The other was an American—tho' to all outwards appearances, as English as myself. West's celebrated father had been a friend to French radicalism. Did any of this argue for the murder of Lieutenant Gage? France was now England's ally—was she not?

And then there were the women. I could not undertake to think about them now.

I tossed and turned on Eliza Chute's comfortable pillows. For aught I could apprehend, the Treaty's theft had but one effect: it slowed the end of the war with America. Until a fresh copy of the signed document could be obtained, no treaty should be ratified in Parliament—or in the American Congress. Hostilities, therefore, would continue. Word passed slowly, in any case, across the Atlantic. It might be a full six months before Wellington's crack troops came home.

Who, at The Vyne, wished England vulnerable?

LORD BOLTON ARRIVED IN a chaise-and-four at half-past eleven o'clock. Cassandra and I observed his appearance from the upstairs landing, as he exited his coach in a curly-brimmed beaver and redingote; he was a gentleman of medium height and spare appearance, not much above thirty years old. His father had been simple Tom Orde, of a numerous Hampshire family. Mr. Orde married the illegitimate daughter of a duke; upon her inheritance, remarkably, of the duke's estates, Orde was created Baron Bolton of Hackwood Park. His son, in turn, married the eldest daughter of Lord Dorchester—the Hero of Canada and the Victor of Quebec. The vicissitudes of Fortune are indeed marvellous.

James's Mary had been loitering about the Staircase Hall since breakfast, and hurried forward almost in step with the butler, Roark, who must have been astonished to find his office of taking the great man's coat and hat usurped; but Mary remembered herself just in time, and contrived to put a question to the butler as he was on the point of pulling open the massive front door.

"Oh, Roark!" she cried. "Does Mrs. Chute require any assistance in the hothouses? For it must be proper to bestow a few flowers about the Chapel. The odour of Death might otherwise prove offensive with time. A clergyman's wife may be a fund of knowledge in such cases, you know."

"I shall inform my mistress," Roark replied with dignity. He stood with his hand upon the door, waiting for Mary's withdrawal. She did not move. Lord Bolton lingered in the cold on the doorstep. Mary's determination and Roark's concern for his lordship's health won out; he opened the door.

"Why, Lord Bolton!" Mary said, with infinite condescension. "Do hurry within doors—the cold this morning is dreadful!"

Cassandra and I leaned carefully over the balustrade to glimpse the top of the curly-brimmed beaver.

It was removed and handed to Roark, who possessed himself of the redingote as well. His lordship's mild brown curls inclined towards Mary.

"Indeed it is . . . ma'am," he said doubtfully.

Mary simpered. "Mrs. James Austen," she supplied.

"Delighted to . . ."

"—Of Steventon Parsonage. I daresay you must have hunted with my husband on countless occasions. We were introduced, once, in Basingstoke! At Ring Brothers, I believe it was. Your lady was so kind as to admire my cloak. How does she get on? Is she in good health?"

"Excellent health, I thank you," Lord Bolton replied in tones of bewilderment. So Mary had scraped an acquaintance with that sweet creature in the middle of a Basingstoke shop!

Cassandra's hand was pressed to her lips and her eyes brimmed with mirth. I could not look at her.

"If your lordship will allow me," Roark said. "Mr. Chute is expecting you."

"Thank you, Roark," Lord Bolton said, and followed the butler with what we could only imagine was relief.

Cassandra and I scurried off to our bedchamber, and buried our heads in our pillows. Absurdity is a blessing that is best shared.

1 2

A CATALOGUE OF MOVEMENTS

Wednesday, 28th December 1814
The Vyne, cont'd.

I could not presume upon my brother's patience with the Law—he should no doubt declare himself to follow a higher authority than Mr. Chute's, in any case—but I might expect him to remain at The Vyne so long as Lord Bolton did. He should hover with scarcely more aplomb than his wife about the threshold of the book room, in the hope of a chance encounter with the Baron; for there is no doubt that Lord Bolton has many valuable livings within his gift, and for all his Evangelical phrases, James should never miss an opportunity to secure his livelihood. But perhaps I wrong him there; he once refused two hundred pounds per annum for holding a curacy, merely because he could not travel the necessary distance to the parish of a Sunday. Perhaps James is not so much a mercenary as an admirer of the Great. He will want to be returned to Steventon in good time to prepare his sermons for New Year's Eve and New Year's Day; on the morrow, therefore, we must certainly depart.

That afforded me little time to learn, as best I might, where each of The Vyne's people was during the period—so brief as half or three-quarters of an hour—between Lieutenant Gage's departure yesterday and the return of his horse to the stables. Most of the guests had no inkling, as yet, that Lieutenant Gage was murdered. All but the guilty party should own their whereabouts frankly, if properly approached.

Three of the Austens—Mary, Cassandra, and I—were entirely excluded from suspicion. We had been seated together in the morning room, debating the merits of *puits d'amour* and sack cream with Eliza Chute. To this list of irreproachable females I must add my mother, for I refuse to credit that a lady of five-and-seventy, who is subject to occasional gout, should be capable of breaking a strong young Naval officer's neck. Thomas-Vere Chute might also be absolved—except that he had quitted our conference in the morning room for an interval, to search for Raphael West. Admittedly, he had not been gone very long—and at his return his clothing showed no signs of his having been out in the snow—but a good coat and pair of boots might have disguised the signs of violence; and he was decidedly out of breath when he burst upon us once more.

If Thomas-Vere had turned traitor, it must be for want of funds. He had not the passion for a political polemicist. He was likely an expensive creature, however—Taste being a fierce master in the realm of Dress, Art, and the pleasures of the Theatre—and a clergyman's means are slim. For all I knew, he might frequent gaming hells; the Dandy Set often did. As William Chute's brother, with unquestioned intimacy in the Member's household, he should be a ready tool for any foreign power willing to pay his fees; and he was silly enough to find the rôle of spy amusing.

I decided to go in search of the gentleman.

The house party had arranged itself in groups this morning. My mother and Lady Gambier were in the Saloon, a comfortable and brightly-lit space with an entire wall of windows giving out onto the lake. The Chutes' pianoforte was here, a lovely rosewood instrument with bronze caryatid mounts on the legs; I longed to practise my polonaises—Mr. L'Anglois had been as good as his word, and left his sheet music in my keeping—but I profited from circumstance, and directed my attention to Louisa Gambier. At the hour the Lieutenant had been killed, she was taking breakfast on a tray in her room; once the body was recovered and Miss Gambier overcome, Eliza had sent a servant to her ladyship, to advise her to attend to her niece. I must ask Eliza if Lady Gambier had indeed been discovered in her room. She might, however, have been anywhere during the interval between Lieutenant Gage's departure and his sad return. For none of us had seen her. Implausible as Lady Gambier's guilt must seem, it behooved me to talk to her.

"I am glad to find you at ease here, ma'am, and recovered enough from your indisposition to join the rest of the party," I said.

"So kind," she murmured, and adjusted her spectacles to peer more closely at her embroidery. Lady Gambier's frequent resort to her bedchamber and her smelling salts would lead one to believe her a fragile creature, but she is stout enough in appearance, with a heavy knot of grey hair and a thick body expensively clothed. I studied her profile and could find nothing of James's late Anne in its lineaments. And yet they were cousins.

"I have been telling her ladyship about Anna's wedding," my mother confided. "She remembers our dear Anne from General Mathew's day, but never chanced to meet with her daughter. My first grandchild, married! I cannot count how many I must own, now—nearly thirty, but for the loss of Charles's poor mite only a few months ago." She lowered her voice in a confiding way and leaned towards Lady Gambier. "My son's wife died a week after being brought to bed at Sheerness, and the child survived only a fortnight."

"Very sad," her ladyship murmured.

I could not think this a happy choice of subject. Lady Gambier, as my mother should have considered, had never borne a child. But she surprised me by offering a confidence in her turn.

"I could never bear to live aboard," she declared, "and to his credit, the Admiral has never asked it of me. Such filth and sickness! Such a coarse mode of life, among low sailors! The situation is not fit for a lady."

"With such opinions of the Service, you must have been very attached to the Admiral to marry him," I observed.

Her ladyship glanced at me contemptuously. "I had been on the shelf for any number of years, Miss Austen, when James Gambier paid his addresses. It was unlikely another offer would ever be made to me. Mary feels a similar urgency—but the Navy would not have answered. So I told her. But so it ever is. The Young do not wish to profit from the experiences of their elders."

"Was there . . . an attachment between Miss Gambier and Lieutenant Gage?" I suggested diffidently.

"If there was," Lady Gambier said, "it is all at an end, is it not? Miss Gambier is in no danger of throwing herself away, now."

She set down her embroidery and looked me full in the face. Her dark eyes were pitiless.

"You are to be congratulated, ma'am, on having preserved her from a folly worse than death," I said.

My mother, I am sure, detected my bitterness.

I found Thomas-Vere Chute in the billiards room, at the far end of the house—a place I had never had occasion to enter before, as it lay beyond the drawing-room and a small anteroom between, which Eliza liked to call her China Room. Having failed to find the elegant clergyman in the library—where my brother was loitering in some agitation and the hope of a chance meeting with Lord Bolton— I abandoned the upper floor. The sound of clicking ivory balls led me through the drawing-room and porcelain displays beyond, and there, to my satisfaction, was not only Thomas-Vere, but Edward Gambier and my nephew, James-Edward.

Thomas-Vere was dressed all in black, as became a man of the cloth; but this was so unusual—he was an addict of sartorial splendour—that I must assume it was in respect of the Dead. His wig this morning was steel grey, a sombre hue, tied with black satin ribbon.

"Miss Austen!" he cried. "How delightful! We had hoped to make West stand as our fourth, but he is nowhere to be found. Pray, take up a cue and we shall set the balls afresh."

"Aunt does not play," James-Edward broke in. "There is no table at Chawton Cottage."

"But happily," I replied as I took down an idle cue from the rack, "there is a handsome one at your Uncle Edward's house in Kent. I have long been in the practise of playing there, James-Edward, so be careful what you are about. I shall claim Mr. Chute as my partner, and we shall give you two young exquisites a drubbing. Win? Lose? Or Carombole?"[4]

"All three," James-Edward said, his chin lifting dangerously. "It would be devilish flat, otherwise."

"Very well," I replied, purposely ignoring the cant language that

---

[4] From Jane's language, she is describing English billiards, which employed two white cue balls and a single red object ball. A winning game employed the two cue balls; the player scored two points by pocketing the opponent's ball. In a losing game, the player scored by caroming off the opponent's ball and pocketing his own. Carombole play combined both techniques with a third—the object ball. To score, players must carom off both the opponent's cue ball and the object ball. By 1800, the three forms of play were generally combined to form English billiards.—Editor's note.

should have won a stinging rebuke from his father. "Sixteen points, sirs, a penny per point. Mr. Chute and I shall give you and Mr. Gambier two points to start, as a handicap."

This was a notable bit of bravado on my part, but no matter; if James-Edward and his partner beat us soundly in a matter of moments, I should have more time to interrogate Thomas-Vere. But in the event, we were smartly matched. Mr. Gambier was a proficient, as befit a languorous gentleman who spent his hours in the clubs of Pall Mall and the country houses of the Great. His fingers were steady, his shots deft. James-Edward betrayed all the excitement inevitable in a Winchester schoolboy, and was prone to slashing his cue across the green surface like a swordsman. His ball was rather more apt to leap in the air and land on his opponent's toe, than find a pocket. Happily, I had chosen to wear my half-boots of jean that morning, and was thus impervious.

I was a careful and deliberate player. What I lacked in dash, I more than made up for in accuracy. Thomas-Vere, however, was a flamboyant soul. He pirouetted about the table like an opera dancer, deploying his cue behind his back. If the essence of a man is revealed in his play, then Thomas-Vere was a gambler: he never hesitated on the brink of risk. Sometimes his shots went wide; but more often than not they went home. This naturally underlined his native complaisance.

"Our luck is in, Miss Austen," he confided as we approached our turn, four points in advance of our opponents. "Observe, callow fellows, as I carom both cue ball and object!"

He contorted himself into a human knot, the better to achieve the necessary attitude, and thrust his cue home. Our ball struck the red one, then skittered towards the table's bank, missing our enemy's cue ball by a hair.

I eyed the result resignedly. "I believe, Mr. Chute," I said, "that

I prefer skill to luck. Winning, sirs!" And I shot our ball off theirs, into the pocket.

"Ho-hey!" Thomas-Vere cried, and applauded with his long, white hands.

Edward Gambier bowed. "Honoured, ma'am, to lose to so pretty a player."

"I have not got any pennies at present, Aunt," James-Edward stammered, "but perhaps I may meet my obligations in a few days' time." It was customary to give the children their Christmas Boxes—small gifts of loose coins—on Twelfth Night. I might have told my nephew to think no more of his pennies—but that should have shamed him before Mr. Gambier, who was obviously a favourite.

I curtseyed to James-Edward, therefore. "I shall accept your vowels, sir—and request the honour of a second match, when you may win your own back again."[5]

James-Edward flushed. "With pleasure. We shall have to play tonight, Aunt, for Papa says we are to leave tomorrow."

"Impossible!" Thomas-Vere cried. "How is The Vyne to endure the remainder of the season, without the Austens to give it spice?"

"You must secure Mr. West as your billiards partner," I replied. "Tho' he seems a most elusive gentleman. You could not find him yesterday, as I recall—when you quit the morning room."

"Aye," Thomas-Vere said, and his gaiety fled at the memory. "I soon gave up the search, however, once the groom knocked upon the door. Poor Gage!"

"You chanced to be crossing the Staircase Hall, I suppose, when the groom appeared?"

---

[5] "Vowels" were I.O.Us—in the form of the debtor's initials, signed to an acknowledgment of the debt.—Editor's note.

"Not directly," Thomas-Vere replied. "I had looked into this room, thinking West might be with you, Gambier—"

"And I told you I thought he was about his sketching of your brother, in the book room," Gambier replied.

"Of course. The poses, for the Parliamentary picture." I felt a curious sense of relief. Naturally Raphael West had been occupied yesterday morning after Lieutenant Gage's departure—he would wish to conclude his job of work and be away from The Vyne.

"But it was all a hum," Thomas-Vere said petulantly, "for when I hurried up to the library, neither he nor William was there. William was down at the kennels, as the groom told us but a few moments later. It was when I descended once more that I found Roark standing agape at the front door, all the cold blowing in, and the groom with his hand on the gelding's reins."

He was correct, of course. Chute had walked up from the direction of the kennels; I had forgot. I had forgot Raphael West's own words, as well, as we stood together in the snow.

"He mentioned something to me about having been in the Oak Gallery. That is just beyond the book room, is it not? Perhaps he intended to sketch—found Mr. Chute absent—and wandered into the Gallery itself," I suggested.

The Oak Gallery is a long, many-windowed passage lined with portraits and pictures. It runs the full width of the house along the west side, and is accessible only from the book room and the Chutes' bedchambers, which are at the rear of the house. These are the former Royal bedchambers, and the Oak Gallery similarly dates from Henry VIII's time. I had not looked into it during this visit to The Vyne, because Chute and his secretary were forever closeted in the book room, discouraging my entry—but I may attest that the Gallery is one of the most remarkable remnants of early-sixteenth-century architecture extant in England. It is lined from floor to ceiling with linenfold panelling, carved with various noble arms. Seven mahogany benches march down the centre, covered in leather, so that the interested aesthete might pause and rest while surveying the paintings. I could easily comprehend Raphael West lingering in such a room, his sketchbook in hand.

"I do not think West was entirely honest, then," Mr. Gambier volunteered in his bluff way, "tho' I cannot think what it matters, where he was. But when I saw him, just after breakfast, he was in the Chapel—speaking to my sister."

13

SUSPECTS

Wednesday, 28th December 1814
The Vyne, cont'd.

Lord Bolton disappointed his more ardent admirers by declining Eliza Chute's offer of refreshment. He asked to view Lieutenant Gage's body—which was by now decently laid out on a bier in the Chapel, awaiting its coffin from Sherborne St. John—and then departed in the direction of the stables. There, I presume, he examined the gelding's knees, which had suffered from the cutting impact of the wire. As a gentleman long accustomed to horses, he profited, I am sure, by the latter inspection far more than the former. Broken necks cannot often have come in his way.

Lord Bolton then called for his carriage and made his *adieux*. He went away looking anxious and harassed, perhaps as a result of Mary's begging him to "remember me to your sweet lady, and pray accept my sincerest wishes for her health and happiness." As her ladyship was hourly in expectation of her fifth child, Lord Bolton undoubtedly felt his place was at home rather than in Eliza's Saloon, where a nuncheon had been laid out—but James's earnest entreaty that he "honour us with your excellent horsemanship when next we ride to hounds" must have sped him on his road. The Great dislike above all things to be toad-eaten.

"You have put the fat into the fire, and no mistake, Miss Jane," was all William Chute would say as he helped himself to stewed pig's feet and—joy beyond imagining for Mrs. Austen!—cold brawn. "I should have liked to have avoided an inquest, with the Treaty gone missing, but Bolton feels it would not do. One must consider the wire you found. To call Gage's death Misadventure is hardly honest, whatever concerns of State might argue; and so Bolton believes we must empanel a jury, and present the evidence."

"When is it to be, sir?"

"In two days' time," he replied. "But stay a little, and I shall explain."

It was evident from the disposition of our party about the Saloon that his lordship's visit, and the close conversation in the book room, were of general interest. All but Benedict L'Anglois and Miss Gambier were present; and presumably her formidable aunt would relate the particulars to her. We sat in groups of twos and threes. I settled by Cassandra, and we were soon joined by Thomas-Vere, who seemed to regard us as in some wise his property while at The Vyne. All of us had plates laden with good things: cheese biscuits and stewed plums; slices of ham and radishes; cold tongue and suet pudding. William Chute appeared in our corner with a decanter of Madeira. I thanked him, my face upturned to his, and felt a sudden prickle of consciousness along the back of my neck. Raphael West was regarding me with his usual penetrating gaze. He stood on the opposite side of the Saloon, next to Eliza and James. With a word of apology, he left them, and crossed to our corner.

"Mr. Chute," he said with a bow.

"Mr. West." Our host inclined his head. "I suppose you are

wanting some stronger stuff than Madeira, eh? A glass of claret, perhaps?"

"Thank you, no. I merely wished to learn what determination you reached with Lord Bolton, as to the inquest."

"We are all on tenterhooks, Will," Thomas-Vere said archly. "The vulgar whiff of a publick enquiry must excite the interest of each of us. Do not be keeping your business close to your vest, I beg."

William Chute glanced about the Saloon. As if aware of his roving eye, everyone but Lady Gambier turned to him expectantly. She maintained an aloof self-sufficiency; I now knew that for a pose.

"There is the figure for your sketchbook," I murmured to Raphael West. "That appearance of indifference is an art won only by decades of study. You would do well to capture it."

"I prefer the engaged mind to the retiring one," he replied. He let his notebook fall open at his knee; to my astonishment I observed a sketch of myself—crouched over the knot of wire I had discovered in the snow. I looked up at him swiftly and would have spoken, but William Chute forestalled me.

"You all must know that I have been speaking to Lord Bolton this morning regarding an inquest on Lieutenant Gage's death," he said to the room. "We are agreed that it is more than probable the Lieutenant did not die by accident, as was assumed."

There was the briefest of silences. Then, "Good God, man!" my brother James cried. "You cannot mean he killed himself?"

"No," Chute agreed. "I should think that most unlikely."

"You mean," said a clear, low voice from the doorway, "that Jack was murdered."

All our heads turned as one. Miss Gambier stood there, her face white as paper.

"Nonsense," Lady Gambier said crisply. She rose from her retired position and stared coldly at her niece. "Do not be making a cake of yourself, Mary. If you cannot master your worse nature and appear in publick with the composure required of a lady, you would do well to remain in your room."

I saw Eliza shift uneasily and raise one hand, as if to stop the unfeeling words. Edward Gambier took one step towards his aunt, his brows knit in anger. But anything he might have said was forestalled by the Master of The Vyne.

"That is exactly what I meant, my dear," William Chute assured Miss Gambier, as tho' her ladyship had never spoken. "Will you not join us? A glass of Madeira would do you good."

"Thank you, sir." Without the slightest notice of her ladyship, Miss Gambier glided towards a chair Raphael West held out for her. "I should like a glass of wine."

While her host fetched one, James began to bluster. "But this must be nonsense, Chute! Or at the very least—a grievous mistake. It is impossible for Lieutenant Gage to have been murdered. Why, the tracks of his horse never reached the road!"

So James, too, had noticed that fact.

William Chute pressed the glass of Madeira into Mary Gambier's hand. "You are correct, Austen. Gage's horse did not leave The Vyne park. Which makes the matter much more personal—and dictates clearly that I may take no hand in the investigation myself. That is why I have sought advice of Lord Bolton. He has elected to notify the Coroner in Basingstoke. He hopes to have a jury empanelled the day after tomorrow—Friday. Your sister will have to give evidence."

"My sister?" James looked about the Saloon wildly. "I take it you would refer to Jane. I cannot allow it, Chute. To be appearing in a vulgar proceeding such as this—"

"Vulgar?" I said mildly. "When Lord Bolton is the mover?"

"Do you expect him to attend?" Mary asked. "With perhaps Lady Bolton?"

"Do not be ridiculous, my dear," James said sternly. "Her ladyship is about to be confined. Do not be giving countenance to Jane's deplorable thirst for publicity. You know full well how she contrives to involve herself in other people's murders, with no greater object than the achievement of Justice—which had far better be left to Divine Providence!"

Raphael West leaned close to my ear. "Do you, indeed? How very intriguing."

"Mr. West will also appear," Chute said, "as I must, myself. Miss Austen will be in excellent hands, James; I shall take prodigious care of her, and carry her to Basingstoke Friday morning."

"But, sir," Edward Gambier broke in, "what is it all about? From your remarks, I understand you to mean that someone belonging to The Vyne killed poor Jack. I must suppose you to suspect one of the servants. But why should any of them commit murder? They cannot have known Gage from Adam."

"I do not suspect my servants." Chute's countenance was bleak. "They have all been with me for years—generations, in some cases. Besides, they were at liberty on the day of Gage's arrival—St. Stephen's Day—and were probably too foxed on rum punch to have roused themselves early the following morning. No, I do not suspect the servants."

There was a sharp and deadly silence.

"He suspects his family and friends," Thomas-Vere drawled.

Mary uttered a shrill shriek.

"How very charitable of you, Will!" the clergyman continued, with false mirth. "So refreshingly apt in this Christmas season, when peace and goodwill walk among men. If one of us is to be gaoled and hanged, may we at least know why? As our good Gambier enquired—why should any of us kill Gage, whom we barely knew from Adam?"

"The document he brought from Ghent has been stolen," Chute said abruptly. "It was a delicate paper; he was to have delivered it to the Admiralty, and from thence to Parliament. You see why I must take the Lieutenant's death as a matter of the most serious moment. He died in the execution of his duty, on business for the Crown."

Lady Gambier thrust aside her embroidery and walked in her stateliest fashion to the Saloon door. "Tricks and stratagems," she said coldly. "I do not believe a word of it. The man fell from his horse and died; you will discover this paper of yours in the spring, when the snow melts. In the meantime, the Gambiers shall not remain to be insulted at The Vyne. We shall quit this unhappy house tomorrow."

"I cannot allow it, my lady," Chute said quietly.

She stopped dead in the doorway. "What did you say?"

"I cannot allow you, or your niece or nephew, to leave. None of your whereabouts at the time of the murder may be corroborated." William Chute, I gathered, had also been asking questions—probably of his servants. "Indeed, I must insist that you remain under our roof at present, until the inquest, at least, shall be over."

"How dare you, sir!" Lady Gambier blazed. "What is this impertinence? Shall I find my things searched, for a murder weapon?"

"Not for the weapon—Miss Austen has already discovered that." He inclined his head in my direction; Miss Gambier glanced at me swiftly. "But all my guests' rooms are even now being searched. Only the gravest necessity should prompt such an outrage, and I am deeply conscious of the injury I do to all of you—but I have ordered the housemaids and footmen to go through the belongings of every person at The Vyne. The stolen paper must be hidden somewhere, and if it may be secured, a great deal of future unpleasantness may be avoided."

"I suggest you search the hearths, then, as well," Raphael West interjected. "We cannot exclude the possibility that the paper in question has been burnt; and if so, some evidence might remain."

"But why destroy what one would kill to obtain?" Mary Gambier cried. "It does not make sense!"

"Which is certainly why none of us will put up with such impertinence," Lady Gambier hissed.

"I cannot agree with you, Aunt," Mr. Gambier unexpectedly said. "If all within The Vyne's walls are to be guilty until proved innocent, it is not for us to be excepted. I shall remain, Mr. Chute, and willingly, until you have put a name to Jack's murderer."

"Then you are a fool," his aunt declared. She had turned, at last, in her place in the doorway. "Do you not know what may come of this, Edward? —The injuries that may be visited upon all your family—for the sake of a common sailor?"

"Now it is you who are speaking nonsense," he returned stoutly.

She stared at him an instant in fury, then swept out of the room.

A LITTLE FLURRY OF wonder and hasty conversation ensued among the remainder of the guests. Thomas-Vere secured his brother's attention by the simple expedient of grasping the collar of his jacket, and talking at him in a modulated form of his usual high-pitched cackle. My mother said prosaically, "It must be impossible, I suppose, for Jane to go in publick without exciting the attention of the violent. I am very sorry for it," and my brother James's wife chose that moment to fall from her seat in a dramatic and entirely fictitious swoon.

James so far forgot himself in the excitement of the moment as to dash the contents of his Madeira glass in his wife's face, which succeeded in rousing both her consciousness and her wrath. She had donned a white muslin gown this morning—far too youthful for her years, and too paltry for the winter's chill—and it was now thoroughly stained with the caramel-coloured wine. Her sputtering only increased the confusion. Eliza called for hartshorn; her husband muttered, "Well, well. Mrs. James. You must always be enacting a Cheltenham tragedy." Miss Gambier looked on with scorn.

Eventually, Mary was compelled to rise from the floor, and in a fainting condition—leaning upon James and effecting to stagger—she was conveyed upstairs. More than one person heaved a sigh of relief when my brother's wife had disappeared from view.

I rose and gathered my reticule, conscious of a person hovering near.

"I wonder, Miss Austen, if you would accompany me to the Chapel," Mary Gambier said.

I turned and gazed at her. It was an application from an unexpected quarter.

"I should like to see . . . Lieutenant Gage, but cannot bear to go alone. I confess I have not the courage."

I suspected that she prevaricated a little, but being anxious myself for a tête-a-tête with Miss Gambier, I acquiesced.

"I was excessively surprized to learn that you discovered the means by which Jack—Lieutenant Gage—was killed," she began as we made our way across the Saloon and into the dining parlour. The Ante-Chapel connected to it, and passing through the rooms was the quickest path to the Chapel itself. I made a mental note of that fact—which I had not consciously considered before. One might reach the Chapel—or leave it—by two different routes through the house. I could not at the moment see any significance in the fact, but stored it away regardless. Mary Gambier was still speaking. "I had been told he was thrown from his horse."

"He was," I replied. We passed the dining table with the sugar sculpture at its centre, the greens and ribbons fading a little. No fire was yet kindled in the hearth in this room, and the air was chill. The gaieties of Christmas night seemed memories of a distant age. "His neck was broken, as no doubt you were informed. But his horse was not brought down by accident."

We had reached the Ante-Chapel. It is a small room that owes its existence entirely to John Chute, Walpole's friend, and is meant to serve as a sort of vestibule to the more ancient Tudor chapel beyond. There are sacred pictures on the walls and a few wooden chairs bearing the Chute crest. I sat down upon one of these. "Stay a moment, and I will tell you what I found."

"Very well." She sank into a chair beside me.

"Lieutenant Gage's horse struck a wire strung between two trees at exactly the height of its knees. The wire was buried in the snow, and thus invisible. I found the ends, tied to the trunks—and later, when the snow had melted, Mr. Chute found the entire length."

She frowned slightly. "You walked out to the scene of his death? When?"

"A few hours after it occurred. I found Mr. West before me. He was sketching the ground, lest evidence of violence melt away in the sunshine. It is his conclusion, from his interpretation of the marks, that the Lieutenant's neck was broken after he picked himself up from his injured horse—by an attacker who came upon him from behind. I assume that it is to explain his sketch—and its implications—that he is wanted at the inquest."

She rose abruptly and paced back and forth across the stone pavings, her hands working at the ends of her shawl. "Why did either of you feel an interest? What can have spurred your concern?"

It seemed an odd question. I should have expected her to

exclaim at the fact of the wire, and wonder whose malice had set such a trap.

"I suppose," I said slowly, "that I have felt some mystery surrounded you from the moment we arrived at The Vyne, Miss Gambier. You were embarrassed on Christmas Night by a rude charade you were the first to solve—and appeared to take very much to heart. On another occasion, I heard you arguing with a gentleman outside your bedchamber door—and heard that man threaten you. Lieutenant Gage was the object of your affection. Lieutenant Gage died barely four-and-twenty hours after appearing at The Vyne. I rejected the idea of an accident from the first. Even without the later intelligence that the poor man had been robbed of his dispatches, his death was bound to interest me."

She stared at me fixedly, and drew a deep breath. "You blame me. For his death. You think me responsible."

"I blame his murderer," I said calmly. "Can you put a name to that person?"

Her lips parted, and for an instant I thought she might tell me all her tortured thoughts. But she said only, "I wish to see Jack."

14

GROPING IN THE DARK

Wednesday, 28th December 1814
The Vyne, cont'd.

He looked as the Dead often do: as tho' he had discarded his body like an old suit of clothes, and had escaped for parts unknown. Those clothes were the same—his Naval uniform—and the soft brown hair waving over the forehead looked real enough to touch. But Lieutenant Gage might have been a wax effigy, for all that remained of his spirit and understanding; it was the utter lack of animation in that still form that must have convinced Mary Gambier of what she already knew. She fell to her knees before the bier—Eliza had thoughtfully provided a *prie-dieu* for those wishing to pay their respects—and commenced a silent and relentless weeping.

It was a quiet and restful place, there beneath the vaulted ceiling. Eliza had somehow found a few blooms in her hothouse, and had placed them near the bier—forced lilies, whose scent masked the underlying one of decay. She had placed candles in the Chapel's iron holders, and these must have been constantly replenished by the maids. They shed a gentle golden light on the Lieutenant's countenance.

I stood in sympathy a few feet behind Mary Gambier for some minutes. Then, as her weeping did not ease, I placed my hand gently on her shoulder. She flinched.

"You may leave me now, Miss Austen," she whispered. "I am quite all right. This place holds no terrors for me, anymore."

I EXITED THE ANTE-CHAPEL by the East Corridor, which took me swiftly back to the south side of the Staircase Hall. The great Yule log lay on the hearth, its heart still intact but its outer layers scorched and glowing; a quantity of ash had begun to collect at its edges. The hearth, naturally, could not be swept each day. I stared into the flames and allowed my pity for Mary Gambier to touch my heart. I might have pressed her on several points—might have urged her to answer my questions, divulge her suspicions, confide the truth of her connexion with John Gage—but her grief had persuaded me to silence. There would be time enough, after the first flush of sorrow, to learn her secrets. For now, I knew that she had cared for Lieutenant Gage—that he had been brutally taken from her—and that she held herself to blame. She had all but declared as much. The picture of misery was complete.

My eyes began to blur from the heat and light of the fire. I blinked, and as my vision cleared, saw what my preoccupation with the flames had missed: a scrap of paper, partly-burnt and lying in the collected ash. The oddity of such a thing caused me to bend and pluck the scrap from the hearth.

It was a sketch—violently done, in angry strokes of charcoal—of a woman, stretched naked upon a cross. I might have called it obscene, had not the bravura of the technique elevated the image beyond such words. There was something of Mary Gambier in the head, turned in profile to the right shoulder.

"Ah. The lady with the deplorable taste for publicity. And the desire for Justice that is not God-given."

Raphael West.

He was standing in the north vestibule, looking at me. I held out the drawing.

"Is this yours?"

He approached me without haste, took the thing from my hand, and studied it impassively. "It is not. These strokes were made by a right-handed person, and I use my left. Where did you find it?"

"In the ash." I glanced down at the hearth. "Someone tried to burn it."

"Miss Gambier? Or the artist?" He crouched down and poked with his finger through the grey powder. It was a relief to be in the company of a man whose wits moved so quickly that he required few explanations. I had not met with a similar mind in years, and the sudden realisation of my lack brought unexpected tears to my eyes.

"Nothing else," he murmured. "Should you like to take a walk, Miss Austen?"

I glanced out at the South Porch, the white winter light dazzling my eyes. Explanation enough for tears, if he required one. "Yes," I said.

I ran up the stairs and fetched my pelisse. Cassandra was reading a book by the bedchamber fire. She looked up, startled. "Jane! What is this Mr. Chute has been saying about a murder weapon? How can you possibly have encountered one? Mary would have it that you invented the whole, from a desire for notice, but Mamma gave her a decided set-down. I should have done as much myself, only that Mamma was before me."

"Thank you, my dear." I kissed her cheek. "Keep the fire well built-up, and we shall have a comfortable coze when I return from my walk. I shall then tell you all."

"Your walk?" she repeated; but I could not stay. I dashed from the room, my sister's protests following me.

"Tell me what your brother meant, when he claimed you involved yourself too often in murder," West began, as we passed through the great door and out onto the South Porch. The carriageway lay before us like a mud-brown riverbed, its cover of snow melted.

"It is true that I have had an inordinate amount of experience of the evil men may do," I returned thoughtfully.

"Are all murderers male?"

"Not all." I glanced at him sidelong. "I have known several women, of various ages, who determined to play God. Murder requires no especial strength or talent, Mr. West, unless it be for deception. It is the most democratic of arts—and it hides in plain view. We are so accustomed to the sudden accident or illness that may snatch away an innocent; we do not think to question Providence, particularly in the deaths of children. That is the vilest form of murder—the one I cannot forgive."

He frowned at me. "You have witnessed such a thing?"

"Discovered it, more properly. An entire family of children poisoned, in order to secure the father and his fortune.[6] I have known those who kill from madness; those from the spur of desire; those who kill in cold-blooded anger and calculation; those who kill for fortune; and those, remarkably, who kill for love. I have come to believe that the murderous heart is in some wise the most human."

He looked all his astonishment. "But your books! They celebrate

---

[6] Jane refers here to the account of her experiences published as *Jane and the Stillroom Maid.*—Editor's note.

so much that is admirable in human nature—gratitude, and generosity, and . . . the dignity of one who acts always from the best principles."

"True." I lifted my shoulders. "But I write also of human folly. We should not detect the noble qualities in others, were we not smothered with self-interest and arrogance, blindness and vanity, insincere words and ambitious hopes. Say rather that I understand the human heart, Mr. West—both in its evils and its blessings—and you shall be nearer the mark. One has only to find the motive, to find the murderer."

"That kind of penetration—I can readily apprehend how it might aid you in exposing a murderer—but how has the opportunity to do so come in your way? Living as you do in the country, retired and— Forgive me," he said abruptly. "I presume upon our acquaintance."

I laughed. "There is sometimes a value in advancing years and all lack of social distinction, Mr. West. We spinsters, sitting in our corners while the handsome and the wealthy dance away their dissipations, are afforded remarkable openings for detection."

He flushed, and turned his acute gaze upon me. "That is not what I would mean to suggest—that you have no measurable worth, because you are a woman and unmarried. I should not offend you in such a way for the world. It has been long and long since I have met with such a remarkable intelligence, and I am happy in the chance that brought us together. I merely found it incomprehensible that so much violence could surround a parsonage in a simple Hampshire village like . . . Steventon, I believe you called it?"

I could not laugh at him again; he was too serious for mockery. I pressed his sleeve, therefore, and hastened to assure him of my pardon. "You are correct, sir. I have travelled more, perhaps, than my simple life betrays. And for a period, I was honoured with the friendship of an excellent man—somewhat highly placed in Society and Government, whose acquaintance exposed me to a most varied experience. My brother James could not like that acquaintance; and so he chuses to deplore the activities associated with it."

"That pursuit of Justice, better left in God's hands."

"Exactly."

"Does your friend have a name?"

"He did. Lord Harold Trowbridge."

"Good God!" West cried, then recovered himself. "He has been gone some years, I think. You have my sympathy."

"You knew him?"

"I knew of him; I must believe the whole world did—or at least, that World that centres itself in Pall Mall."

I inclined my head.

"But come." He glanced at the sky and the westering sun. "It grows cold, and we shall not have light enough, soon, for this walk of ours."

"Stay," I said impulsively. There was something I could not avoid asking him; the intimacy of being alone in his company demanded it. "Where were you, when John Gage was killed?"

His eyebrows rose. "As to the exact moment, I cannot say precisely. But if you will accept a general period— That is what I wished to show you. Come."

He turned to the left and walked the length of the South Front, deviating sharply around the out-thrust end of the kitchens and service wing. Beyond lay the exterior entrance of the Chapel, hard by the Tomb-chamber.

This was a Gothick addition of the Strawberry Hill Chute, and contained a monument in marble to Chaloner Chute, who was Speaker of the House of Parliament during Cromwell's time. The cenotaph was erected a hundred years or more after his death; the Speaker's body lies elsewhere, and so "Tomb-chamber" is at best a misnomer. It all seemed like a bit of stage-craft to me, or a garden folly brought indoors; although impressive enough, there was little but boasting behind it.

"You wished to show me a marble statue of a man, reclining with his head under his arm?" I asked tartly as we stood by the exterior door.

"Not really," West replied. His voice had lowered. "Miss Gambier is in the Chapel, I think?"

She was; and at his words, I remembered Edward Gambier's statement that West himself had been there yesterday when Gage was murdered. I opened my mouth to speak, but West's upraised hand forestalled me.

"We shall enter only the vestibule, and must not speak or make overmuch noise. She will not be disturbed, and shall assume we are merely servants moving beyond the range of her sight."

I nodded to show that I understood, and he pushed open the door.

The vestibule to the Chapel and the Tomb-Chamber is quite small, offering barely room for two persons. One cannot enter the Tomb-Chamber itself without first walking through the Chapel. West, however, had no intention of doing either. He eased the door closed behind us. If we turned to our left, we should immediately enter the East Corridor, with the kitchens leading off it. As West had observed, Miss Gambier would assume any scuffling from that quarter to be the work of the servants.

He held his finger to his lips, glanced down the East Corridor— which was empty—and leaned forward. His sensitive artist's fingers pressed a carved shield in the centre of a section of linenfold panelling immediately opposite. The panelled section swung inwards.

I stared at the gaping hole in the wall and then at West. He ducked into the opening and motioned for me to follow. I gathered up my skirts and did so with little grace and an unfortunate bit of thumping, pulling the panel nearly closed behind me. "Can we get out at the other end?" I hissed.

He was standing several feet below me, on a riser of a descending stair. He nodded.

I closed the door and swayed a little in the sudden fall of darkness.

"Give your sight a moment to clear," he whispered. "Then follow me. Careful of your tread on these steps; they are centuries old."

I closed my eyes for the space of several heartbeats; and when I opened them, the darkness was lighter. I could perceive shapes in it. West, for example, was a bobbing movement below me, already descending the hidden stair. I reached forward with my toes in trepidation and found the first step. Then another. The descending passage was narrow and low, so that I stooped a little, my shoulder grazing one wall. It was lined with wood, which had decayed to dust in places. I concentrated on the careful footsteps of my companion in front of me, and refused to consider the possibility of vermin.

"Where does this come out?" I whispered.

"To tell you would spoil it."

I hurried a little—his voice suggested he had moved away from me more than I could like. I did not glance behind me; there were terrors in the dark, in the close air of the sealed passage. Terrors, too, in what might lie ahead. I was seized of a sudden with the conviction that I had been lured to my death by a madman—by the very one who had engineered John Gage's end, and meant now to silence me for having discovered his wire! What a fool I was! I stopped in my tracks, my heart pounding, and strained to see before me in the darkness. If I turned and ran for the passage door like a heroine of Mrs. Radcliffe's, should I find it immovable, and die screaming as my fingers clawed at the impassive panels? Should I be cut down with a wire round my neck, my fleshless skeleton to be revealed only years hence?

"Take my hand," West said, his voice soothing. "There is nothing to be afraid of."

He had turned on noiseless feet and come back to me. I reached out my fingers and felt his, rough but warm.

Later, I understood that we walked perhaps eight minutes more in that lightless tunnel. But at the time, it might have been an hour or ten. I could not have said. I only knew that I felt immense relief when the blackness turned to grey, and I could perceive Raphael West's sleek dark head before me. He was ascending a stair. My foot tested a step, and then another. A few seconds more and he raised the latch on a common wood door.

He pushed it open and drew me into the small space beyond it: low-roofed, its batten walls lined with shelves, sawdust beneath our feet. The room was windowless. Directly opposite was a second door. This had a square pane of glass at its top, and I could glimpse daylight. Oblongs of black and white. Patches of snow against bare tree trunks.

"What is this place?" I asked.

"The ice house," he said.

15

DIVIDED ALLEGIANCES

Wednesday, 28th December 1814
The Vyne, cont'd.

"The ice on the lake is not yet thick enough to cut and stack in blocks in this room," Raphael West observed, "or we should not have found space to enter."

"You were here when John Gage met his death?" I said stupidly. "Then you must have seen his murderer! Or—"

"—Or killed him myself." His gaze was satiric. "Pray believe, Miss Austen, that I did not."

"Then—"

"I was not standing inside this building when Gage's horse went down." He unlatched the far door and stepped out into the snow. "I suspect, however, that his murderer was. As he—or she—waited for the horse to spring its trap, I was searching diligently for the passage we just traversed. I did not find it yesterday morning; I had been convinced the entrance was hidden in the linenfold panelling of the Oak Gallery, when, with a very little thought, I should have perceived that it was far more likely to be near the Chapel. Those escaping their enemies will either bolt from a house or claim sanctuary; and our tunnel is ideally situated for either."

"I had heard that you were seen in the Chapel," I observed, "in conversation with Miss Gambier."

"—Who, if interrogated, may be able to recall my appearance there." He gave me a wry look, well aware of my motive in discovering his whereabouts. "Her presence inhibited my search; I withdrew by the East Corridor, probably at the very moment Mrs. Chute led your party in search of Miss Gambier. I heard a cavalcade of ladies' feet, but did not stay to learn what the bustle was about. That intelligence came later—from Chute himself."

I followed West from the ice house. The shadows were long on what little of the snow remained; where Lieutenant Gage's body was found, a bare and muddy patch marred the landscape. The tree where I had discovered one end of the entrapping wire was not five yards from where I stood, by the edge of the carriageway. "Sanctuary," I repeated. "To what can you possibly refer?"

"To William, Third Baron Sandys," he said. "The Sandys family owned this place in Elizabeth's time, long before the Chutes were thought of. The Third Baron committed the grievous error of joining the Earl of Essex in his rebellion against Elizabeth, and when Essex failed, Sandys was imprisoned in the Tower. He lost his fortune and his life as a result; Elizabeth seized The Vyne, and used it as a sort of royal lodging-house when the Duc de Biron came from France to call. The Vyne has long been rumoured to hide a bolt-hole. Colonel Henry Sandys, who fought for the Crown against Cromwell, certainly employed it to come and go unnoticed, during the Siege of Basingstoke."

I looked from the muddy ground to the tree trunk, to the ice house, and back again. "In any event, it is an admirable means of fetching ice to the kitchens in summer. Only think how conveniently situated!"

"Did you not wonder," West said chidingly, "how Gage's murderer came and went in such a depth of snow, without appearing inside The Vyne with his breeches wet and his boots rimed with ice? The murder was well-planned; he probably adopted his coat in the tunnel, and changed his boots on the return journey. Both coat and boots might be restored to their rightful wardrobe during the night, for he expected no one to follow his footsteps underground."

"But you were looking for the passage before you even knew the Lieutenant was dead," I protested. "It will not do!"

"That is true." That calmness again, almost a weariness. "I had been told to look for it."

"Mr. West," I said carefully, "my toes are exceedingly cold. You will escort me back to the house now, if you please. And along the way, you will explain exactly who you are."

"I WAS REARED BY my father—I am his firstborn son—to cultivate what talent I had for drawing," he said, as we strode briskly along the muddy carriageway in the fading light, "but I must acknowledge that I spend only a part of my hours in the pursuit of Art. My father chides me continually for this; he regards me as wasting a God-given talent equal to his own. But I assure you, Miss Austen, that I do not possess the gifts of Benjamin West. They are unique to his genius.

"For years, I chafed under the perceived necessity of being worthy of him; of equaling or surpassing his achievements; of proving myself my father's heir. I will add that it is a burden my younger brother felt even more acutely, bearing as he does my father's name. He parted from our parent in an unfortunate fit of temper, with rebukes and harsh words on both sides, and in ten years has seen my father only once—at my mother's funeral rites, ten days ago."

"I am sorry to hear it," I said.

West hesitated. "I should perhaps explain a little of my father's circumstances, which will in turn help you to apprehend my own. Benjamin West was born in the colony of Pennsylvania, the tenth child of an innkeeper. He received no formal education; he learnt to mix paints from the Indians, who showed him as a child how to blend clay and bear grease to form a crude pigment. Even now, he stands as an autodidact—his genius lies entirely in his ability to represent the world on canvas and paper, for he can barely spell when asked to put down his thoughts in print. In 1763, he came to this country already a success in his own. My mother joined him a year later, and they were married at St. Martin-in-the-Fields. My parents reared their children in an odour of success created chiefly by the patronage of His Majesty, George III—who so admired my father's Death of Wolfe that he appointed him Court Painter."

"I have seen it," I observed. "It is a remarkable picture—tho' not equal, in my opinion, to his Death of Nelson. But my preference for the Navy may influence me there."

West smiled. "I was raised, as a result, in a luxury the innkeeper's son cannot have dreamt of. I have lived as an English gentleman, and have never been expected to own a profession or earn my keep, other than as my natural talents incline me. Being freed of the necessity to make my way in the world as Benjamin West did, I never achieved his degree of ambition or dedication to art."

"But this burden—your belief that you ought to follow your father's path—"

"—was one I cast off when my brother broke with our family," he replied. "I determined that it were better to be deemed a failure in my father's eyes, than to sunder myself from him forever."

"I see." The bulk of The Vyne's east wing—the kitchens and the Chapel—loomed before us as the carriageway curved towards the house, and I was conscious of a desire to slow our walk, despite my chilled body, so that I might hear the whole of West's confidence.

"My father never returned to Pennsylvania, as I believe you know. He endured the political stings of residing in this country during the war between his colonies and the Crown; his success became all the greater, and His Majesty's patronage only increased; he was named President of the Academy, succeeding Joshua Reynolds. And yet . . . something of the colonist remained."

I glanced at him sidelong. His footsteps slowed; he came to a halt and faced me in the gathering dusk. "The rise of Buonaparte, and what my father regarded as a noble experiment in enlightened government in France, won all his interest. When his ardour was met with suspicion and contempt in Government circles, he broke with His Majesty's court and removed us all to Paris. I was then married, and a father myself. From 1801 until 1804, during the Peace of Amiens, I lived with my young family in France. Because of my father's fame, I came to know many of the principal figures in Buonaparte's circle. My father was celebrated by the French as an American, a friend of Democracy and the Citizen, rather than an Englishman—which is what I have always considered myself to be. He painted any number of portraits of the newly-Great in Paris, while I grew more and more disillusioned with the abyss between their professed beliefs and their actions. When Buonaparte crowned himself Emperor in 1804—thereby embracing the corrupt tradition he had pledged to overthrow—my disgust was complete. The Treaty of Amiens was broken; England undertook to blockade the Continent, as Buonaparte commenced the building of a vast invasion fleet intended for Kent."

"I was in Kent during the Great Terror of 1805," I broke in soberly. "I shall never forget the oppressive expectation of French troops. And to know, daily, that my brothers were sailing on the blockade!"[7] I could not continue; my fear for Frank's and Charles's lives has always coloured my perception of Buonaparte.

"I went to my father and told him I had no choice but to remove with my family to England," West continued. "He begged to join me."

My feet were entirely numb; but I would not have quitted the carriageway for a King's ransom. "His disgust, then, was equal to your own?"

"It was. My father experienced a complete reversion of feeling against Buonaparte, and upon his return to England, threw his support entirely behind the British cause. He was an old man, and his sins were forgiven him. He became once more President of the Royal Academy. He painted his Nelson. But I found that I, Miss Austen— as a younger man, an American by blood if not by education, and a person of some note in Society—remained suspect in the eyes of Government. I had moved too easily among our enemies whilst in Paris; I was known to be intimate with those whose chief object was our annihilation. I appeared, like every other indolent gentleman of easy circumstances, to have very little employment and far too much time on my hands. I was tasked, therefore, by men of power, to provide evidence of my loyalty."

"You were required to give information," I said slowly.

He nodded. "I see you are familiar with the game."

"I was schooled by one of its proficients."

"Lord Harold?"

"He stiled himself the consummate man-about-town, and was everywhere received as a gentleman and a Rogue—but it is understood

---

[7] Jane refers to events previously disclosed in *Jane and the Genius of the Place.*—Editor's Note.

by very few that he was one of the Crown's most trusted spies," I said. "He reported to the Admiralty—which directs such intrigues against the Enemy, through the employment of the Secret Funds."

"I know," West returned drily. "They have supported me for a considerable period. I am certain there are those who would regard the tactics employed against me as nothing short of blackmail. I did not wish my family—young or old—to be shunned as traitors. I did not wish to move through the streets of a country I loved, under the constant eye of suspicion. And so I acquired, over a period of time, a second avocation."

"You became a spy. Against the French? Or the Americans?"

"Does it matter?"

I studied his face. "Of course! An important treaty with the Americans has gone missing; its emissary is murdered. Did you know John Gage intended to break his journey at The Vyne, Mr. West? Is that why you chose Christmas to complete your sketches of the Honourable Member, William Chute?"

"I did not anticipate it," he said bleakly. "Neither Gage's arrival, nor his violent death. Indeed, the events of the past few days have been so unexpected that I cannot account for them."

I frowned in perplexity. "From the frank disclosures of your narrative, I am convinced you were sent here—not solely by your father, but by the Admiralty. You were told to search The Vyne for a bolt-hole. What, then, is the object of your intrigues?"

"To find and expose a dangerous French spy," he replied. "If I am not mistaken—the very person who killed John Gage."

THE FIFTH DAY

16

GHOSTS

Thursday, 29th December 1814
The Vyne

Early this morning when I crept into the nursery wing to lay Jemima's latest offering at her feet, I nearly stumbled over the figure of young Caroline, wrapt in a blanket, and slumped in a sleepy huddle near the bedroom door.

"My dear girl!" I whispered, as I attempted to gather up the formless mass and carry it to the empty bed. "You will catch your death! How long have you been lying there—and why, in Heaven's name?"

The fire had long since gone out; there was ice in the washstand basin; and Caroline's fingers, where they emerged from the blanket, were deadly cold. But she was wide awake in an instant. I do not think she had slept soundly all night.

"Aunt," she croaked.

I held my finger to my lips and glanced round sharply, to know whether she had awakened Miss Wiggett in the other bed. That young lady was far too old to be sleeping in the nursery wing, but I suspected she had been displaced from her usual room to make way for her mother's guests.

"Is it morning?" Caroline demanded.

174 · STEPHANIE BARRON

"Yes. Although still dark outside, at this hour. Why were you not in your bed?"

I sank down onto the cot beside her. She had pulled the clothes up to her chin and was attempting, without success, to disguise her shivering. "Because I meant to be brave," Caroline said. "James-Edward says there is a murderer about, and that he cuts off a person's head with a length of wire. If the murderer were to come here, Aunt, I should not like to be in my bed. I should prefer to be hit by the door when it swings open, so that I might awaken the household with my screaming."

"What a heroine you are," I returned, admiringly. "You should do very well in one of Maria Edgeworth's novels. Her ladies are always possessed of stout lungs. But I do not think you need fear a murderer, poppet. James-Edward is merely trying to frighten you. It is what brothers do, when they are home from school and bored."

"Truly? But Lieutenant Gage—"

"—did not have his head cut off with wire. Beheadings are only for Royals, as you well know."

She shivered in earnest. "I wish we were not sleeping so near the Chapel," she said forlornly.

I understood, then. The nursery wing is two flights above the Chapel itself, and does not extend over it—but it is true that of all the inhabitants slumbering in The Vyne, young Caroline should be nearest to a ghost, if Lieutenant Gage's unquiet spirit chose to walk abroad. I had an idea James-Edward might be responsible for this unfortunate notion as well, and resolved to speak to the odious boy about it.

"Miss Gambier has been holding vigil at the Lieutenant's bier for hours, Caroline," I said reprovingly. "If she may endure it without fear—she who truly knew and valued him—certainly you may do so."

Her expression cleared. "Then that is why there were so many footsteps."

"Footsteps?"

"Outside my door last night. In general it is very quiet, for nobody comes up here, you know—it is only us children and Crokie. Miss Crokehart—she is Miss Wiggett's governess. But now you mention Miss Gambier, perhaps it was she who came and went so often. I felt sure it was a ghost."

"Miss Gambier retired rather early last night."

"But perhaps she could not sleep—and did not like to go through the Staircase Hall, lest anyone saw her. There is a stair at the Chapel end of this corridor, you know, for the servants—they come from the kitchens that way."

I wondered very much whether Mary Gambier had spent the night on her knees in the Chapel. Such penitence must augur an unquiet mind. As if divining my thoughts, Caroline added, "Miss Gambier may have been afraid that the poor Lieutenant was lonely. Or cold. Or perhaps she had a secret to tell him."

A secret to tell.

"Try to stay warm in bed until the fire is laid," I told my niece briskly, "and only when it has been lit and has warmed the room, may you get up. I shall say nothing to Mamma about how I found you—but pray promise to sleep in your bed tonight."

"I promise."

I rose to leave her. One chilled hand grasped my arm.

"Did you not bring me a present?"

The child had a refreshingly human failing—one moment going in fear of her life, the next considering of material gain.

"I did." I reached into the pocket of my dressing gown and withdrew Jemima's costume. This was a frilly bit of nonsense intended for a night rail and a dressing gown. Cassandra had been its chief author; she had chosen a fine gauge of cream-coloured lawn and trimmed it lavishly with lace. I had merely embroidered rosebuds at the neck and hem of both pieces. But Caroline was in transports.

"The very thing!" she said, holding the night rail up to her doll. "For you know, Aunt, I did not like her sleeping in her fine clothes, and it would not do to remove them. We cannot have Jemima take an inflammation of the lungs."

MY BROTHER JAMES'S WIFE had sent word that she was far too ill to appear before us last evening, and took her dinner in bed on a tray. Mary Gambier, on the other hand, had not hid herself away, but joined us in the dining parlour, where she sat wan and silent throughout the meal. Her brother chose to sit by her, and spoke to her once and again in a lowered tone. I was glad to see that she ate a little of Eliza's excellent dinner.

Later, when we repaired to the Saloon, she avoided the slightest chance of a tête-à-tête with any of our party by seating herself beside her aunt. As my mother was the only creature capable of enduring Lady Gambier's society for more than five minutes, Miss Gambier was safe from scrutiny or questioning by the impertinent.

I sat at the pianoforte. I had been assured that no one expected a brilliant performance; we were all overshadowed by the knowledge of the inquest on Friday, and most of The Vyne's guests were disposed this evening to read or converse quietly. For my part, I welcomed the chance to lose myself in music. I managed a little respectable Mozart, the new polonaises Mr. L'Anglois had shewn me being too boisterous in a house of mourning. Music provided a mental screen for more important activity—I had much to consider, of all Raphael West had disclosed. I wished to trust him, for the simple reason that he recalled the intelligence and spirit of a gentleman now several years gone; but the awareness of my little fever of admiration for Raphael West rose in my mind as a kind of warning. I could not know what he was. I was too susceptible to flattery. He had singled me out as confidante—and such discernment on the part of a gentleman was rare enough that I must be susceptible! I could not, therefore, trust the power of my reason. I had too few sources of objective information about the painter. Was West, as he claimed, in search of a French spy—or was he an agent of the Americans, intent upon destroying the fragile peace lately achieved in Ghent, before news of it should ever reach Washington City?

West had seated himself beside Cassandra, and was perusing her sketchbook. How unfortunate for Mary, that she had chosen to exclude herself from our company this evening—she who was so eager for the instruction of a Master!

As tho' she had read my thoughts, my brother's wife appeared that moment in the doorway of the Saloon, arrayed in her dressing gown (sadly limp from too-frequent wearing) and a lace cap, supported heavily by the arm of her son.

"Mary!" James said chidingly. "You should not have attempted such exertion. Are you sure, my dear, that it is wise?"

In a failing voice she begged him only to secure her a chair by the fire, and settled herself languishingly in it. James placed a cushion behind her back, and set about determining where the fire screen ought to be placed, to do her the most good.

"Should you like a cup of tea, Mary?" Eliza asked.

"It would maudle my insides at this time of night," she mourned. "But perhaps a little ratafia can do no harm."

The drink was procured, and the attention of the room searched for a new object of interest.

Cassandra, I observed, had wisely closed her sketching book.

"Well, Chute," my brother exclaimed as he stood near his wife, absorbing the lion's share of the warmth, "what did your search of the house disclose this afternoon? Have you secured the Lieutenant's pilfered document—and determined that the notion of murder was only a hum?"

"I have not," Chute said abruptly. He had returned to his preferred Christmas employment over the punch bowl, and was grating nutmeg into a quantity of rich cream beaten with eggs and brandy. "Eliza was good enough to look through the ladies' effects, while I surveyed the gentlemen's. A maid and a footman accompanied us both. The Roarks undertook to search the servants' rooms, and several of our men went through the principal cupboards. We found nothing."

"Surely, sir, you expected no more," West observed quietly. "Whoever killed to secure the document, will have secured it in truth."

My brother James snorted and looked pugnacious. He thrust his hands into the rear waist of his breeches, his coattails fanning behind him. "Poppycock! You found nothing because there is nothing to find! May we Austens be allowed to depart for Steventon on the morrow? You must own, Chute, that the sad tragedy has worked dangerously upon my wife. She should not be forced to remain. It is too injurious to her health."

"Why should it have worked upon her?" Miss Gambier demanded, rising from her position by Lady Gambier's side. "Of what personal interest can it be to Mrs. Austen, if John Gage is dead?"

"Sit down," Lady Gambier hissed. She seized a fold of her niece's gown as tho' to force her submission. Miss Gambier twitched it impatiently from her aunt's grasp and stepped towards Mary.

"Would you borrow the grief of those who loved him, with a view to making yourself interesting? You are nothing but a ghoul! I shall view your departure gladly, and bid you farewell with alacrity."

"Miss Gambier!" James said forcefully. "You forget yourself. My wife has done nothing to merit such reproaches. She is a sensitive creature, a martyr to her nerves, and must feel the presence of the Deceased acutely. Had it been possible to bury him decently— but the necessity of retaining the corpse for the inquest—and all the embarrassment of a publick proceeding—the knowledge that she is, herself, tarred by this unfortunate brush—the idea of murder—"

He came to an uncertain halt. Miss Gambier stared at him with what I may only call contempt. Mary held a handkerchief to her face, as tho' suppressing sobs. There was an uneasy silence.

"Forgive me," Miss Gambier said. "I should not have spoken. I hardly know what I have said, indeed. Pray excuse me—I must retire."

She quitted the room with dignity.

In the silence that followed her exit, I closed the pianoforte and rose from my bench. Music seemed the grossest offence in the face of such grief; and I found I longed for my bed. I began to make my *adieux*.

"But, Aunt," James-Edward implored. "You cannot go upstairs so soon. You promised to give me a match at billiards!"

"So I did." I raised my brows meaningfully at the boy; in his enthusiasm he might refer to "penny points," and James was never one to look kindly upon gambling. "Let us go immediately, my dear, or I shall fall over from weariness."

Thomas-Vere and Mr. Gambier joined us; and by the time we were done—and I had allowed James-Edward to beat me soundly—the Saloon was emptied of life. I urgently wished to consult with Raphael West, but I should have to wait for morning to do so.

CASSANDRA WAS STIRRING WHEN I returned this morning from the nursery wing.

"Did you succeed in your errand, Jane?"

"I did. Caroline said it was just what was wanted. She is a delightful child; but I begin to think that James's anxiety is warranted. Not for Mary, mind—but for Caroline. She is afraid of murderers and ghosts. We would do well to remove to Steventon as soon as possible."

"I cannot be easy myself," Cassandra said, pushing herself upright against her pillows. The maid had already visited our room, and the fire was crackling merrily. She had left a tray of tea on a side table; I poured out a cup and handed it to my sister.

"Have you met the Lieutenant's ghost, traversing The Vyne's corridors?"

"Do not joke of such a thing, Jane. The poor young man was brutally cut down, in the prime of life, and with all his prospects—" She broke off, her eyes misting, and hurriedly sipped her tea. Cassandra lost her Tom Fowle at just such a young age, in what must be regarded as a sort of murder—for he was constrained to accompany his patron's regiment to the West Indies, as clergyman, and died there of yellow fever. Two persons' lives were blighted in Tom's loss; and I had an idea of Mary Gambier's future pain, in studying my sister's face.

"I am sorry," I said contritely. "I ought not to have said it. But you looked so strange!"

"Mr. West showed me the drawing you found yesterday," she said quietly.

"While you were sitting together, last night?"

She nodded. "I suspect his interest in my work was in part a process of detection. He first ascertained, by scanning my sketches, that it was not my hand that had effected that crude depiction of

Miss Gambier. Then he offered the drawing. He asked whether I knew who might have produced it. But I could not say. I confess, Jane, I found it a frightening thing. There is a suggestion, in its lines, of one not quite sane."

"I thought as much myself." I curled up beside her on the bed with my cup of tea. "I was reminded, at first, of the strong and violent lines of Mr. West's own work—his gnarled trees and crude vagrants. But he denied it was his hand. He claimed to know the sketch had been done by a right-handed person—and that he favours the left."

"I agree with him there."

"Cassandra—we know that Mary is an adept with charcoal. But who else in this house may claim such a talent?"

"Thomas-Vere draws a little," she said reluctantly. "But he has never allowed me to glance at his pictures. I suppose there are many who have been schooled in sketching—and yet are loathe to admit as much in publick."

"That complicates matters."

"But, Jane." She set down her cup on the boulle dresser and regarded me earnestly. "You and Mr. West believe this thing has some significance—tho' it was discarded in the fire, to be burnt. Does that not suggest that its maker repented of the garish scrawl, and wished it destroyed?"

"True. Why was it drawn in the first place, however? The image of a naked woman—a lady of our acquaintance—hanged on a cross? It is the third mystery I may place at Mary Gambier's door. And that is at least two mysteries too many."

"You refer to the charade," Cassandra said. "And the sketch makes two. What is the third?"

I told her of the threatening conversation I had overlistened, the very dawn of Lieutenant Gage's death.

Cassandra merely shook her head. "What can the concerns of Mary Gambier—in life, or on paper—have to do with that poor man's murder? William Chute is convinced he was killed for what he carried. Not because of the woman he may have loved."

"Must it be one or the other?" I mused. "May not the two motives be confused—or even intended to confuse?"

Cassandra straightened. "You mean—that Lieutenant Gage was killed for Mary's sake, and the document stolen as a sort of diversion?"

I stared at her. "It is possible, I suppose." Cassandra, naturally, knew nothing of French spies; but perhaps West's preconceived notions had clouded his judgement. "In that case, Miss Gambier must know the killer. It ought to be the very same person who spoke so harshly to her, mere hours before the deed was done."

What had the man offered as his parting shot?

Very well, madam. I will know how to act.

Was this the source of Mary Gambier's guilt—that she had known it in her power to prevent John Gage's death, and had withheld whatever his killer demanded?

A feeling of dread rose within me, from the pit of my stomach to the centre of my throat.

"Good God," I whispered, and bolted to my feet. "The danger—"

"What is it, Jane?"

I stared at my sister wildly. "Mary Gambier has been living with the very person she believes murdered her lover. Dining, conversing, even sleeping under the same roof . . . when she owns the knowledge to have him hanged! Do you not see, Cassandra? Both of them know that she knows . . ."

17

THE WAGES OF SIN

Thursday, 29th December 1814
The Vyne, cont'd.

Idressed quickly, pinned up my hair—which reaches now past my knees—and pulled on a serviceable, if spinsterish, lace cap, to hide the haste with which I had completed my toilette. Cassandra was not far behind me, although she persisted in believing I exaggerated Miss Gambier's risk. I tapped on that lady's door immediately upon quitting my own, but received no answer.

And there I hesitated.

It was as yet only eight o'clock, and I supposed it possible Miss Gambier still slumbered—if indeed she had been restless in the night and upon her knees in the Chapel, as young Caroline thought.

"Does she answer?" Cassandra enquired.

I shook my head.

"Then leave her, Jane. Rest is what the grieving require."

We descended to the breakfast-parlour. It was empty save for Mr. L'Anglois.

"You are returned from your errand to London, sir!" I cried.

"But a half-hour. I beg your pardon—I am only just come from the stables to the table, in all my dirt. I stopped only to apprise Mr.

Chute of my return." He rose and bowed to us both—and very cordially remained standing until we should be seated.

"How did you find the roads?" Cassandra ventured.

"Indifferent so far as Woking, ma'am, but when I reached Hounslow, I perceived a marked improvement. And my return was as nothing at all—the turnpike entirely clear!"

"James will be happy to know it." Cassandra unfurled her napkin. "He is determined to depart The Vyne today."

"We shall be sorry to lose you," L'Anglois said with an earnest look. "And before you have had a chance to essay my sheet music, Miss Jane!"

"I played a little, last evening," I admitted, "but not your polonaises. I did attempt to find you the morning of Lieutenant Gage's death," I added, with hasty improvisation, "but when I went in search of you after breakfast that day, I could not discover you."

This was a gross untruth, naturally, but let us see what the gentleman produced by way of answer.

"You should not have troubled to do so," L'Anglois said. "I assured you the music was yours for the asking—It ought to be played."

"I made a noble attempt to find you. I glanced into the billiards room and the library. Seeing the door to Mr. Chute's book room standing open, I even glanced in there—tho' with what trepidation!"

This last was a second falsehood; I had spent the whole of the interval after breakfast on Tuesday in Eliza's morning room; but I knew that L'Anglois's employer, William Chute, had been in the stables—and so might risk the suggestion that the book room was empty. I was determined to drop any number of handkerchiefs merely to observe whether L'Anglois picked them up.

"I am sorry to know that you were put to so much trouble," he said earnestly. "I shall secure the sheet music directly you are finished with breakfast, Miss Austen, so that you may practise when you chuse, in peace."

A clever fellow, Benedict L'Anglois—and not to be readily drawn. Vexing, that he refused to confess where he had spent the morning of Lieutenant Gage's death—but was it instructive? Did it confirm my suspicions—that a man lately employed by a Royal French household had deliberately buried himself in Hampshire, for an object far more important than the advancement of William Chute's career?

Or did I refine upon a trifle?

The maid appeared, and poured out my tea. I ordered toast; my spirits were so unsettled I could not consider the steaming silver dishes arrayed on the sideboard. The question of Mary Gambier returned to worry me. To be asking after her when half the household were yet abed, was to look too particular; but I attempted a little subterfuge. When the maid had departed, I rose suddenly as tho' I had forgot something I required, and went after her.

"Has anyone been into Miss Gambier's room," I asked her, "to lay the morning fire?"

"I cannot say, ma'am. Would you like me to ask?"

"Indeed. I must leave The Vyne today, and should like to say my farewells to Miss Gambier, but do not wish to disturb her if she is still sleeping."

The maid dropped a curtsey and went into the serving wing without another word. I dawdled in the passage, aware of the sound of new voices in the parlour behind me; Edward Gambier and Raphael West had come down. Cassandra uttered a soft laugh at something that was said. One of the three men with whom she sat might be a murderer. I felt my heart accelerate.

The maid reappeared. "Lucy made up the fires this morning,

ma'am, at half after six o'clock. She says that your sister was asleep, but you were not in your bed—and neither was Miss Gambier."

I had been in the nursery wing. Where had Miss Gambier been? The Chapel? If so, she had descended by the Staircase Hall. I could swear that no footsteps had passed the nursery door whilst I sat with Caroline.

I returned to the breakfast-parlour. We should probably discover that Miss Gambier was still at prayer. Surely I refined too much!

"Nothing is to be done at the Congress without Castlereagh," Mr. L'Anglois was saying. He turned with an air of condescension to my sister. "You will apprehend how vexatious we find this, Miss Austen, when I explain that Castlereagh is not only Foreign Secretary, but Leader of the House. In his absence, our poor Mr. Chute is buried in duties—which I fear he is not attending to as he ought. This affair of the Lieutenant has distracted him from his work."

Cassandra had long been aware that Lord Castlereagh combined most of the vital services of Government in one brilliant frame; she was not to be deceived into believing William Chute his proxy; but she merely smiled at Benedict L'Anglois. To be continually underestimated is a woman's lot.

"You are abroad early, Miss Austen," Edward Gambier observed as he lifted the silver lids on the various dishes. The odour of kidneys assailed my nostrils. "Eager to be away, I expect—as we all are. Devilish flat in the country at the moment, tho' Chute thinks it possible we may take a gun and a dog out, this morning. Will you hunt with us, West?"

"Gladly," he said. His eyes drifted to mine. "Is it certain you are to depart, Miss Austen?"

"My brother James rules our party," I replied, "and James is anxious to be gone. But, Mr. Gambier—surely your sister and Lady

Gambier cannot be wishing to be away! Surely Miss Gambier is fixed at The Vyne until the Lieutenant's funeral rites are held."

"I have not discussed the matter with Mary," he said. "But Aunt would leave on the instant, if she could. I begin to think it would be a kindness to the rest of the party if I should get her la'ship away—she don't always behave as she ought. Deuced high in the instep. Sets people's backs up. Regular Tartar, Aunt Louisa!"

"Have you seen your sister this morning?" I asked. "I should like to take my leave of her. But when I knocked upon her door, there was no answer. Perhaps she is yet asleep."

He shook his head. "I looked into her bedchamber before I came down—the room is empty. I expected to find her here, in fact—but if she's already taken her breakfast, no doubt she's gone to the Chapel."

L'Anglois raised his head from his newspaper frowningly. "In the little time that I have been returned to The Vyne—perhaps three-quarters of an hour—I may say that Miss Gambier took no breakfast."

Cassandra and I looked at each other.

"Should you like me to walk to the Chapel with you, Jane? I have quite finished."

The maid had not yet appeared with my toast. "Why not?"

"I shall come with you," L'Anglois said.

IN THE END, ANXIETY proved infectious. The entire breakfast party rose from their seats and hurried with me across the Staircase Hall and along the East Corridor. There is a native stillness to sacred places that dictates one step softly; I pushed open the door to the Ante-Chapel and crept inside.

She lay facedown in a silk dressing gown at the foot of Lieutenant Gage's bier. Her guinea-gold hair was undone and one arm outstretched, its fingers curled in supplication. I could see no obvious wound, and for an instant hoped she slept.

"Mary!"

Edward Gambier hurried past me to his sister's side. He lifted her still form and turned it. And at that moment I knew, beyond all shadow of doubt. Her eyes were staring at the vaulted ceiling, her neck rigid. She had clearly been dead some hours. As Mr. Gambier raised her in his arms, supporting the wretched figure, a small glass bottle rolled across the Flemish tiles.

I stooped to pick it up.

Laudanum.

I handed the thing to Raphael West, who studied it with knitted brows.

"She is so cold," Mr. Gambier cried. His looks were wild; he was attempting to chafe his sister's wrists. "Will no one help me?"

"We must carry her from this place." Benedict L'Anglois sprang to Edward Gambier's aid, and would have helped him lift the dead Mary from the floor, but West's voice suddenly rang out.

"No," he said. "Leave everything as we found it. Miss Jane, would you summon William Chute, and bring him here?"

I hastened without a word from the Chapel, through the dining parlour and the Saloon. At the far end of the latter I encountered Roark.

"Mr. Chute," I said breathlessly, one hand against my stays. "Pray summon him. There has been . . .another tragedy."

The butler turned on his heel and mounted the stairs. I went to stand by the Yule log—its cheerful persistence a mute reproach—and recovered my breath. My fingers were deadly cold, as tho' Mary Gambier's chill were somehow catching.

Booted feet, heavy upon the steps beside me; I glanced up.

"Miss Jane," William Chute said. His countenance was flushed and his hazel eyes anxious. "What is it?"

"Juliet," I said, "dead beside her Romeo."

THAT IS HOW THE scene was intended to be read, of course—that the grieving young woman had taken her own life in the middle of the night, chusing to die rather than exist without her beloved John Gage. The guttered candles, as yet unchanged by Eliza's careful staff; the scent of the lilies; the bier raised before the altar and the girl sprawled in sorrow beside it—all spoke eloquently of a mortal bargain with despair. That was William Chute's assumption once he viewed poor Mary Gambier's body; and when West shewed him the empty laudanum bottle, his conviction was entire.

"Did your sister quack herself with these drops?" he demanded of Mr. Gambier.

"I do not know," the gentleman replied in a bewildered tone. "The contents of Mary's dressing case were entirely her own affair."

"You do not recognise the bottle?"

Gambier took it with shaking fingers. "It is the usual chemist's bottle," he said. "There is nothing to distinguish it as Mary's. Aunt may tell you more."

"Poor child," Chute said gruffly. "She could not endure her grief, we must suppose. Indeed, she was so sick with it she cannot have known what she was about. Self-murder is a dreadful thing."

Gambier closed his eyes tightly.

"Is it possible she took too much by accident, sir?" Benedict L'Anglois suggested in broken accents. His pallor was dreadful and his fingers shook. He must indeed have felt an attachment to Miss Gambier—and was now reeling from her loss.

"Naturally that is what occurred, Ben!" Chute snapped, as tho' his secretary were an imbecile. "You do not think Miss Gambier should have knowingly cut off her own thread? A Christian lady, reared in the strictest principles! We shall inform Lord Bolton just how it was. Distraught—unable to sleep—and perhaps dosing herself overmuch. Now, gentlemen—let us carry her to her bedchamber."

Impossible that it should be left this way—a probable case of murder, dismissed as accidental suicide! It was imperative that the two deaths be seen for what they were—destruction in tandem, stemming from the stolen Treaty, Mary Gambier's past, or both. I opened my mouth to speak, but as he moved past me to help lift the body, Raphael West shook his head ever so slightly in the negative. The gesture proclaimed, for one who was watching, that I should keep my opinions to myself. I stepped back, and allowed the solemn procession to pass.

"Miss Austen," Mr. Chute said hurriedly, "pray carry this dreadful news to my wife. Eliza will see that everything proper is done. And Miss Jane—pray summon your brother. It is only right that a blessing be said over the corpse."

SOME HOURS LATER, I observed from the upper staircase window the arrival of a tradesman's cart, presumably from Sherborne St. John. It bore the unmistakable draped form of a coffin—the one ordered for Lieutenant Gage. He would be placed in it and borne away for the Angel in Basingstoke—the principal coaching inn being the usual place for the empanelling of an inquest.[8]

As I watched, William Chute emerged onto the carriageway below

---

[8] It was usual during inquests of this period for the jury to view the corpse, which was generally held in a room adjoining the proceeding.—Editor's note.

and remonstrated with the carter, who turned his horses towards the Chapel entrance.

"Ordering another coffin," Raphael West said drily. He had crossed the landing so quietly I had not been conscious of his presence. "How exceedingly strange it must appear to the folk of Sherborne St. John!"

"Are you still convinced these deaths have to do with your French spy?" I asked softly.

"Are you not?"

"I find it incomprehensible that France should care whether we make peace with the Americans or not. Why should a French agent concern himself with the Ghent Treaty, when the new Bourbon King owes his throne to Great Britain? France is now our friend."

"Think, Jane," West said. "Not all French are Bourbons."

I started a little at his use of my proper name, and the tone that suggested I was the merest child. I glanced at him indignantly.

"Think how many men of power have been destroyed by Napoleon's fall," he continued. "Think how desperately they wish to see Louis XVIII fail. Consider how adept such men are at plotting—and how high the stakes of their success! Louis XVIII does not yet command the hearts or loyalty of the French Army. That remains entirely Napoleon's. If he chuses to lift his finger to them, from exile . . . All that stands between the Bourbon throne and humiliation is ourselves. Now. Tell me whether it is important to know if and when Wellington's crack troops will be returning from across the Atlantic?"

"You mean that if Napoleon leaves Elba—it behooves him to do so when our forces are still across the Atlantic," I said slowly. "Therefore, his supporters would delay news of the war's end—delay our troops' withdrawal—even by so simple an expedient as killing the messenger."

"Exactly. It will take weeks, in any case, for the Treaty to be ratified, and months for the news to travel to America. Add to that the present confusion as to the Treaty's whereabouts—the loss of the only signed copy—and one might well buy a year."

"But what can such surmises have to do with Mary Gambier?"

"I do not know. It is possible, you know, that she took her own life. She was distraught over Lieutenant Gage's death."

"Because she felt herself responsible for it. She refused to bargain for Gage's life."

West's eyes narrowed. "What the Devil do you mean?"

Ought I to share my secret knowledge—the conversation I had overlistened at Mary Gambier's door?

But what if it had been Raphael West who threatened and harried her affections?

I had not ascertained his whereabouts, that last dawn of Lieutenant Gage's life.

Nor did I know his movements in Mary Gambier's final hours.

He was perfectly capable of drawing that vile sketch, of the lady crucified. Indeed, no one at The Vyne was as capable.

And he had dissuaded me, only moments earlier, from voicing my suspicions of murder.

He stepped towards me, his hands raised as though to grasp my shoulders. "Tell me, Jane."

And die for my sins?

I stepped back, quite deliberately. "There is nothing to tell, Mr. West."

18

THE BLACKMAILER'S ART

Thursday, 29th December 1814
The Vyne, cont'd.

This time it was I, and not James or Mary, who hovered about the library in anticipation of Lord Bolton. As he advanced with William Chute upon the adjoining book room this afternoon, an expression of concern and dismay upon his countenance, I placed myself indelicately in his path. I could trust none of The Vyne's intimates—not even those I yearned to trust—with my dangerous knowledge. Speak too hastily, and I might end a corpse on the bedroom floor. In such a case, a Justice of the Peace—however young, rich, and indolent—is as a fresh umbrella offered in a Bath spring: a flimsy but publick witness to the deluge.

"May I present Miss Austen?" Chute said distractedly.

"Another of them," Lord Bolton murmured under his breath. He bowed, however, and said falsely, "It is a pleasure to meet you."

"I hardly think so," I returned. "You are come about the murder of Miss Gambier, are you not?"

Behind me, Thomas-Vere Chute gave a small shriek of dismay; he was turning over the plates of a *Gentleman's Magazine* by the library fire. Cassandra and Raphael West were in evidence—Eliza and my mother were with Lady Gambier, in Mary Gambier's room. James had blessed the corpse under strong protest; in his opinion, Mary Gambier ought to be forgiven from our hearts, but never offered Christian burial. His wife was immediately set to supervise the packing.

"Murder?" Lord Bolton repeated, and looked uncertainly at William Chute. Poor man, he was hardly older than Benedict L'Anglois, and ought better to serve as Chute's secretary than his Justice of the Peace.

"Certainly," I replied before Chute had a chance to answer. "Should you like me to explain?"

"Miss Jane—" Chute glanced warily at his lordship. "Pray come into the book room and sit down. We cannot be conducting our business before all the world."

Informing all the world had been my object. Once half The Vyne's guests had seen me importune Lord Bolton, the idea of murder—and my evidence—could no longer prove a danger to me. Raphael West had wished me to keep silent this morning; I was therefore compelled to speak. I bowed my head, the picture of meekness, and preceded William Chute into his tapestry-lined room.

What heaven to closet oneself in here, with a good fire burning! I seated myself on the edge of a chair and gazed at the gentlemen expectantly.

Lord Bolton took the settee.

"Now." Chute settled himself behind his desk and folded his hands beneath his several chins. "I have informed Lord Bolton of the sad accident that occurred last evening. He is agreed that an error of the kind Miss Gambier committed is all too common, alas, with the unguarded nature of laudanum drops, and the bewildering effect of grief."

"That is all very well," I said, "but it is nonsense to think that she did away with herself. Mary Gambier was a resolute creature—not to be thwarted by threats, and adamant when she believed herself in the right. When you speak of grief, Mr. Chute, I have an idea you refer to an attachment between Miss Gambier and the late John Gage. I am sure the Lieutenant's death was bitter indeed for Miss Gambier; but bitterness should not have persuaded her to self-murder. Rather, it must have spurred her to seek Justice."

"What can you possibly be talking of, Miss Jane?"

I gazed candidly upon William Chute. "I believe Mary Gambier was being blackmailed, sir, in an effort to wrest from her the Treaty of Ghent, or intelligence of its contents. As Admiral Gambier's niece and John Gage's beloved, she was likely to receive news of the Ghent negotiations well before the Government. It remained only to persuade her to disclose what she might know—by twisting the screws of publick disgrace. During the first evening I spent in this household I became convinced that the lady held a secret—one she did not wish disclosed—and that another at The Vyne meant to use that secret against her. Two subsequent occurrences persuaded me that I was right."

"But you also believe, ma'am, that blackmail turned to murder?" Lord Bolton enquired. "Why should that be so—if the Treaty, as we suspect, was already stolen when Miss Gambier died? Why should Gage's killer despatch her, if she served no further purpose?"

"Because she must suspect him in Lieutenant Gage's death," I said reasonably. "Had the Lieutenant's end been accepted as an accident—had the clever trap that brought down his horse never been discovered, nor the theft of the document he carried—Mary Gambier might still be alive. I bear some guilt in this; it was I who discovered the wire and excited her suspicions. Although I cannot blame myself entirely," I added. "Murder will out—and for all her composure, Miss Gambier was too inclined to defy Fate."

"Pray explain yourself, Miss Austen," Lord Bolton said.

William Chute sighed. It is a hard thing, for a simple man who looks forward to hunting his grounds when he should be freed from Parliament, to be forced to contend with a complex matter of murder and state.

"You will recall, Mr. Chute, our game of charades Christmas Night."

"Certainly. Most enjoyable. Miss Austen is a dab hand at composing clever rhymes, Bolton," he supplied.

"But I did not compose the riddle that destroyed the cordiality of our evening," I said.

Chute shifted in his chair. "I confess I cannot quite recollect—"

"No one, Lord Bolton, would own to having introduced the charade whose solution was: natural son. The implication of bastardy was evident, and Miss Gambier—who solved the riddle—took it severely to heart. She quitted the drawing-room immediately, and her aunt, Lady Gambier, nearly fainted. She had to be escorted from the room."

"Bad *ton*," Bolton observed. "Very bad *ton*—eh, Chute? Even if there is a by-blow somewhere in the Gambier line, it don't do to be raising the subject before the ladies."

"Hear, hear," Chute said.

"Nothing further occurred until St. Stephen's Day, when Lieutenant Gage most unexpectedly arrived. Here was the murderer's Christmas gift, indeed! With the Ghent messenger under the same roof, Mary Gambier and her secret became even more important— for she was to be persuaded to do the killer's work for him. I suspect she was urged to wheedle the provisions of the Ghent Treaty from the Lieutenant—for it was obvious from the moment of John Gage's appearance that he was attached to Miss Gambier, and could deny her nothing. But she was made of sterner stuff than her tormentor understood. She refused to betray her uncle or her Kingdom—and so was forced to fail the man she loved."

Chute's eyes started a little from his head. "Are you suggesting that Mary Gambier was responsible for Gage's death? Impossible! We know her to have been in the Chapel at the moment of his death."

"We know her to have arrived there, at least, by the time Lieutenant Gage's horse returned to The Vyne. We found her upon her knees, praying—a curious activity for a bright Tuesday morning, do not you think?"

"But—" Lord Bolton shifted slightly in his chair and regarded me. "If indeed Miss Gambier felt herself somehow responsible—is not guilt reason enough for suicide?"

"Her murderer would like us to think so."

"This murderer . . ." Lord Bolten lifted his hands in a helpless gesture. "It strains credulity, I confess, that you posit his existence from a rude charade. Forgive me for being blunt—but you overcomplicate what appears to be a simple death from grief."

"I referred at the outset of our conversation to three incidents, Lord Bolton, between Mary Gambier and another. I have only told you of one," I said reprovingly.

"Very well." Chute eased one gouty leg with a grimace. "Go on."

"In the early hours of the morning following Lieutenant Gage's arrival," I continued, "I awoke to hear an argument conducted in the passage outside my bedchamber door. Miss Gambier's room is next to mine. Alarmed, I approached the door and made as if to open it, but halted due to the private nature of the tête-à-tête. A man was abjuring Miss Gambier to some action she did not like—I do not know the particulars. I heard her say clearly: 'Be damned to you.' And her interlocutor replied, 'Very well, madam. I will know how to act.' Should you call that a threat, Lord Bolton?"

"You have no idea who the man was?"

I hesitated, then shook my head. "I overlistened the conversation through a heavy wooden door. A voice is much distorted by such a thing. I can say only that the tone and accent were those of a gentleman."

Chute said heavily, "Let us be perfectly plain. You heard this speech on the very morning of Gage's death, Miss Jane?"

"Yes, sir."

"Why did you say nothing before?"

"Because Mary Gambier was silent."

"Ah." He sighed. "That is a point. One cannot in conscience reveal what another chuses should be private."

"Particularly when one was never meant to hear it."

There was a slight pause.

"And the third incident?" Lord Bolton demanded.

"I found a drawing," I said slowly, reluctant to introduce the subject of the obscene image; it and the hand that drew it touched me on the quick. "It had been thrown in the fire in the Staircase Hall."

"A drawing?—One of West's?" Chute demanded.

"I do not think so. Indeed, I gave it into his keeping—in the hope he might be able to discover its author."

"May we see it?" Lord Bolton asked.

One cannot in conscience reveal what another chuses should be private. But such was my unhappy lot. I went to the book room door and opened it. Raphael West looked up from his position by my sister; I thought it very likely he had been waiting for such a summons. I beckoned him silently, then stepped back to allow him to enter.

"Mr. West is an artist," Chute explained to his lordship, "and is staying at The Vyne on a matter of business. You will have heard of his father—Mr. Benjamin West."

"But this is the greatest of pleasures!" Lord Bolton cried, rising to bow at Raphael West. "I consider that there is nothing to equal your father's work in all of England—nay, on all the Continent! Did I not hear he is to be offered a knighthood?"

"My father would prefer a peerage," West said coolly. "How may I serve you, Lord Bolton?"

"Miss Austen spoke of a drawing she discovered."

"I have the fragment here," West said, and offered it to the two men. "Pray treat it with care; it is weakened from the flames."

Now the silence was palpable, and most uneasy. Chute whistled slowly under his breath, and Lord Bolton said, "I take it this is the deceased young lady?"

"That is a representation of Mary Gambier," West said bitingly, "but it lacks the grace and dignity of the original entirely."

Chute took it from Lord Bolton and set it gingerly on his writing table. "And you think this garish thing—tossed into the flames to be burnt—was done by Gage's murderer?"

"It is an image of torture and suffering; nay, of sacrifice. I can only believe," I said, "that once Lieutenant Gage was known to have been murdered—once the idea of an accident was dismissed—Mary Gambier's life was forfeit. She could name her blackmailer. She knew that he had schemed for the Treaty. And he knew that she knew. It was merely a matter of time before he struck."

Chute stared at me, his heavy brows knitted. "Who is this fiend?"

"One of your guests, sir," I said quite calmly. "Or perhaps your brother. It might even be yourself—although I cannot think why you should kill for information the Lieutenant came to The Vyne expressly to show you."

"Unless I were very clever," Chute said slowly, "and meant to use that presumption of innocence to cast the blame on another in my household." He pounded his fists on his writing table in sudden exasperation. "But it will not do, Miss Jane! Why should the fellow steal the Treaty at all? Of what possible use may it be to any but the principals involved?"

"I will answer that question," Raphael West interjected—and in as concise terms as possible, related the Admiralty's fear of a French spy.

"Do you mean to say, man," Chute exploded when he had done, "that you entered my house under a pretext? That there is not to be a grand picture in Parliament, and that I have spent a tedious deal of time in posing, to no purpose at all?"

"I should never presume upon your kindness in such a way, sir," West replied. "Nor should I misrepresent my father's work so grossly. There is indeed to be a picture—and your poses shall form a part in it."

Chute wiped his forehead with a handkerchief and studied West gloweringly. "Am I and my household suspected of treason?"

It was a bald question enough. A lesser man than West might have shied from it.

"Private communications between Lord Castlereagh and yourself, regarding provisions under negotiation at the Congress of Vienna, have, for some time now, been unaccountably known in Paris and Moscow," he said. "The contents of your correspondence, which you believe known only to yourself, are read and debated throughout the Continent."

"Then look to Castlereagh's staff for your traitor!" Chute exploded. "You do not need to come to Hampshire in search of him."

"I am afraid, sir," West persisted quietly, "that we do. A man was lately taken up for stabbing another in a sailors' tavern in Portsmouth;

and when his pockets were turned out, he was found to have a letter written in French in one of them. When the Navy fellows examined it, they discovered it to be written in cypher—and sent it immediately to the Admiralty. There it was recognised as one of your communications to Castlereagh. And the alarm went up at the highest levels of Government."

"Damn me," Chute muttered. He passed his hands over his eyes. "I have been suspected. My honour and fitness for service questioned. Does Castlereagh himself believe me a traitor?"

"I cannot think so. But the disappearance of the Ghent Treaty, while at The Vyne—"

Chute groaned aloud. "How am I to prove my innocence?"

"That is for me to do," West returned. "I may say that my first action upon learning of the Lieutenant's death—before any idea of murder arose—was to question your kennel-master, Jobe. He confirmed for me, in complete innocence of my true purpose, that you had spent the interval of Gage's death among your dogs—under not only Jobe's eye, but two of his underlings'."

This was news to me.

"Thank God for that." Chute grimaced. "You will be suspecting L'Anglois next, as my secretary."

"And as a man who professes a thorough knowledge of French," I pointed out.

"His long years of service to the Comte d'Artois, however, make him an unlikely suspect," West countered. "He is known among Government circles as an ardent Bourbon adherent."

And he was in London when Mary Gambier died, I thought. I could not believe the two murders unconnected.

"I am relieved to hear you acknowledge it," Chute said warmly. "I know no harm of Ben. It is true that he draws up my correspondence;

202 · STEPHANIE BARRON

but it is always I who seal and despatch it—and then, only by Express. Can it be possible that our system of publick messengers has been overturned by the Enemy?"

"You forget, sir, that the person who stole your intelligence also stole two lives," I observed, "and we are agreed that the party must be an intimate of The Vyne."

"Aye," Chute retorted bitterly. "Explain that, Mr. West! The Admiralty sends you here, with grave suspicions they did not chuse to share with your host, and two of my guests are murdered! You have neither exposed nor thwarted your French spy—you have only brought violence to my household!"

"And none regrets that more than I," he replied with a bow. "The traitor is at liberty to kill again. Which urges me to suggest that Miss Austen be conveyed from The Vyne as soon as possible."

I started, and glared at him.

"Hey?" William Chute said.

"Having been foolish enough to find the wire that brought down Gage's horse," West supplied, "having insisted in publick that Miss Gambier's death was murder—and having supplied evidence of blackmail to Lord Bolton—her fame will have spread all over the house. It will certainly have come to the ears of our murderer. Should she remain at The Vyne, Miss Austen's life cannot be worth more than a few hours' purchase."

THE SIXTH DAY

19

THE GAMBIER WEAKNESS FOR GAMBLING

Friday, 30th December 1814
Steventon Parsonage

In vain did I protest that the very publicity attendant upon my actions must serve as the greatest safeguard. In vain did I suggest that by sharing my intelligence, I had inoculated both myself and others against the epidemic of violence. It does not do to be reasonable and sanguine—to trust in the weight of the Law—when the instincts of gentlemen have been roused.

Therefore I did not demur when James announced, upon Lord Bolton's departure from The Vyne, that all the Austen party must quit the place for Steventon, if he was to have a hope of preparing his sermons for Sunday. To James's surprize and discomfiture, William Chute did not attempt to dissuade him, but instantly offered the use of his coachman and carriage for the journey home. It had been agreed among the conspirators in the book room that Miss Gambier's death was to be treated as an accident, and tho' I had referred to murder in the hearing of Thomas-Vere and others sitting in the library, no further mention of the word was to be made. There was to be no inquest in Miss Gambier's death, lest the murderer take fright and bolt.

Lady Gambier did not descend to bid us goodbye. Her nephew informed us that they awaited only Lord Bolton's permission to depart The Vyne, so that they might carry his sister's sad remains to Bath, where his widowed mother now resided. Jane Gambier— for such was her name—would be wild with grief at the loss of her daughter; she could not yet have received the news, which might arrive only with the body.

Edward Gambier looked decidedly ill this morning, and older than his twenty years. The gay clubman was fled. He pressed my hand most narrowly, and thanked me in broken accents for my kindness to his "poor sister." He shook James-Edward's hand with better energy, however, and said he should be happy to meet him again, if he was ever in Town—which must be the apogee of any sixteen-year-old schoolboy's ambition. Thus our departure was not entirely without its notes of fondness and regret.

"You have been very sly, Jane," Eliza Chute whispered as she kissed my cheek in the Staircase Hall. "I shall be much surprised if Raphael West is not paying his addresses to you before the week is out."

She was mistaken, of course—I suspected that if Raphael West had a *tendre* for any among the intimates of The Vyne, it must have been Miss Gambier—there was a harshness in his voice when he spoke of her, that augured pain—but I merely shook my head at Eliza and climbed into our borrowed conveyance. Dusk had barely fallen before we were pulling up before the parsonage door, and Mary was exclaiming how very small everything looked to her, now she had been staying at The Vyne!

Owing to Eliza's kindness, we had provisions enough in a hamper for a cold collation before the fire last evening, and after desultory conversation, carried ourselves off to bed. The spirits of the Austen party were a little lacking. Cassandra and I shivered our way out of our gowns—we had not bothered to change for dinner, in such a subdued environment—in a bedchamber quite barren of a fire. Mary, it seemed, had dismissed the servants for the duration of our stay with the Chute family, and they could not be got back again until morning. James had laid a fire in the parlour and banked another in the kitchen—but we should have to make do with our quilts for warmth until morning.

"It is a valuable lesson," Cassandra observed through chattering teeth, "in the vanities of life—and the complaisance one may feel, on account of very little more than creature comforts—to have glimpsed the ease of a Great House like The Vyne, where so many labour for the indulgence of so few."

"It is a lesson in parsimony," I snapped, "and nothing more. You know we were never allowed to sleep cold as children, in this house!"

We determined that Jemima's next gift, therefore, should be a fur tippet and muff I had fashioned from rabbit fur. Cassandra undertook to deliver them to Caroline's garret room at dawn, as I had "the inquest to be thinking of." The mere notion of setting one toe out of bed in the freezing hours of morning was so distasteful that I accepted her kindness without protest, and buried myself in quilts.

I slept fitfully, my limbs cramped, and awoke when Cassandra rose. I lay still in the heavy darkness, listening to the wind moan and cry at the bedchamber shutters, and endeavoured not to think of The Vyne. I ought to be thankful I was safely away from a household that had harboured a murderer. I ought to profit from distance, to consider my fellow-guests with ruthless clarity. But I thought of Raphael West instead.

I knew nothing of his true character. I could judge only that he possessed a keen mind and a penchant for guarding secrets that must make me chary with my trust. The regard I had begun to feel for him—the pleasure in his conversation and company—was rather a tribute to the friend I had lost some years ago. I valued independence of mind and engagement with the world—Lord Harold had taught me both. Of late, I had been too little doing things, too little abroad. I had allowed myself to retreat into the quiet of the countryside and the world of my novels, and had been content. A few days in the company of Raphael West had reminded me of that other life I had given up: one of conflict and risk, knowledge and power. Comrades and mortal enemies. West had reawakened emotions, in sum, that could only make me restless—and cloud my judgement. If I wished to expose the murderer of John Gage and Mary Gambier, I must push emotion aside—I must deny self. It was as well I was obliged to sleep in a miserably cold room, with the prospect of a similarly cold breakfast.

Feeling thoroughly blue-deviled, I reached for the clothes I had left upon a chair and donned them under the protection of the bedclothes. It was so frigid in the small bedchamber that I could see my breath, and ice coated the panes of the solitary window. Bracing myself for the Arctic currents swirling up my skirts and under my drawers, I got out of bed and broke the ice in the wash-stand. My cheeks ached where I splashed water on them.

Cassandra came down the passage. "Up already!" she exclaimed, "and dressed! I do not think I can bear it." She hurled herself back under the bedclothes without removing her dressing gown.

I left her huddled there and descended to the kitchen. I was not too proud to take my breakfast with Cook—if she had returned—before the spit and fire.

I WAS IN MUCH better case two hours later, when William Chute's carriage called for me on the way to Basingstoke. He had brought Raphael West with him. We would both be summoned to provide evidence at the inquest—"although you are not required to appear, Jane," Chute said kindly, "if you have not the nerves for it. You may remain secluded in one of the Angel's bedchambers, and give your evidence to the Coroner in private."

I thanked the good man, but spared him the knowledge that an inquest was very small beer for a lady of my experience. I did not like William Chute to think me a vulgar jade. He had recovered from his shocks of the previous day, and our conversation with Lord Bolton, to affect an easy good humour during our lengthy journey—Basingstoke being all of nine miles northeast of Steventon. Indeed, The Vyne party had come well out of their way to escort me to the inquest, for Basingstoke is but three miles south of Sherborne St. John. I was acutely conscious of the kindness shewn me, and the inexpressible consideration in refusing to consign me to one of James's carters or nags—and was fulsome in my thanks. Chute flushed red, and looked conscious, and turned the conversation swiftly to Miss Gambier.

"Now we are able to have a comfortable coze—mind that hot brick near your skirts, Miss Jane—I would be talking over the matter of this sad murder. What is your suspicion of Miss Gambier's secret, and who in my household should be killing her for it?"

This was blunt speech indeed.

I turned my gaze to Mr. West.

He regarded me steadily and sombrely. "You are persuaded the crux of the matter is an illegitimate child?"

"It seems possible, does it not? Why else should that charade have been read out for all our consideration? It was intended to embarrass one of the company. Only Miss Gambier, after hastening to solve the riddle, refused to exhibit a sense of shame. She offered contempt instead. For that, I must applaud her."

"But we cannot know that this putative child was hers," Chute protested.

"No. And now that she is dead, we will have difficulty learning anything at all," I agreed.

"Miss Austen and I know very little about the Gambiers," West observed. "Perhaps you, sir, who are better acquainted with the family—"

Chute sighed. "I am barely acquainted with Edward and Mary. It is true I have known Louisa—Lady Gambier—and her sister, Jane, from the time they were born. Their father, Daniel Mathew, was brother to old General Sir Edward Mathew—he who was Governor of Bermuda, or some such."

"Grenada," I supplied. The island had been much spoken of in our household, when brother James was married to the General's daughter, Anne.

"Exactly so. The General carried off the Duke of Ancaster's daughter, and did very well for himself. His brother Daniel also set up as a gentleman—living, I presume, on his wife's fortune. Daniel's daughters, Louisa and Jane, were both plain as pikestaffs, but paraded as heiresses. Long in the tooth, I will add, when the Gambier brothers decided to offer for them. Louisa went off first, to James Gambier—the Admiral—and Jane second, to Samuel. He was Commissioner of the Navy Board when he died last year—and ought to have left a tidy fortune to his children. But he had the Gambier weakness for gambling."

"So his son told me," I said. "Edward Gambier makes out that his prospects—and presumably, those of his late sister—are tied up completely in his uncle and aunt, who as you know are childless."

"They are not the first couple to look for an heir among cousins," Chute observed. He had done so himself.

Fortune, inheritance, debt—all may be grounds for murder, I

reflected. "Edward Gambier declared quite frankly over Christmas dinner that he hoped his uncle had not got a by-blow somewhere, to cut him out of his hopes."

Raphael West gave a whistle. "Did he, by God? I suspect young Gambier may have been living on his expectations this past year—and that he, too, inherited the Gambier weakness for gambling. He is too often seen at Watier's."[9]

"I suppose that is why he chuses to rusticate in the country now, and drink my port instead of his club's," Chute said thoughtfully. "Living on tick never answers. Despise the habit. It has been the ruin of better men than young Edward."

"Lady Gambier must exert an awful power," West mused. "For it is in her hands, is it not, if her nephew is to be saved from his creditors—or broken?"

"I believe she exerted that power freely over Mary Gambier," I added. "Her ladyship made it very clear that she suspected an attachment between her niece and Lieutenant Gage—and could not approve the match."

"Tho' he is aide to her husband?" Chute enquired in disbelief.

"That would appear rather a detriment in Lady Gambier's eyes," I managed. "She does not admire the Navy."

"Extraordinary." Chute turned to West. "You believe Louisa hated poor Gage enough to set a trap for him with that wire? I should not have said she had so much spite in her."

"I do not mean to say her ladyship murdered Lieutenant Gage," I amended hastily. "But she certainly negatived his suit. Of course, if there was a child in the case—"

---

[9] Gambling at Watier's was for high stakes and ruinously expensive, among the gentlemen's clubs of Pall Mall.—Editor's note.

"I do not suspect her of being in the pay of Buonaparte's confederates," West added quietly. "She can have had no need to kill for the Treaty, when her husband was its chief negotiator."

"What about young Edward, then?" Chute slapped his thighs and winced as the pain of gout took him. "Needs a bit of the ready—is willing to sell his uncle's state secrets to meet his obligations—falls into the clutches of the French—?"

"And when his sister refused to help him, killed John Gage," West concluded. "There would be an added incentive, in that Mary Gambier's expectations of inheritance should become her brother's, upon her death."

I shook my head. "Even if we accept Edward Gambier was capable of murdering his sister, how was it effected? Would Mary Gambier take a mortal dose of laudanum from her brother's hands, if she suspected him of killing Lieutenant Gage?"

"That is true. She was no fool," Chute muttered. "And she gave no sign of mistrusting Gambier. In the hours after Gage's death, Edward had been her chief support."

I recalled them seated together at dinner, Edward leaning attentively towards his sister. "What if the dose was introduced into her food?" I suggested, "and the bottle left by the body in the Chapel, to suggest self-murder?"

"That would be clever, indeed," said Raphael West. "The fatal drug might have been placed in her coffee, while in the Saloon—and the addition of sugar would mask any difference in taste."

"By Jove," Chute exclaimed. "That is the way to go about it, sir. You might almost have killed her yourself!"

West glanced at me—a sober, earnest look—and failed to turn the jest.

He knows, I thought, that I cannot trust him.

"Lady Gambier poured out," I said colourlessly. "Miss Gambier sat by her aunt and retired early to bed that evening." I did not remind the gentlemen of the scene between my brother's wife and the dead lady; scorn and rage were the last that any of us had known of Mary Gambier.

"If the laudanum was in her coffee, she may have begun to feel a drugged weariness," West observed.

"And yet she was most active," I countered. "My young niece, Caroline, sat up much of the night of Mary Gambier's death—alarmed by footsteps in the nursery wing corridor. The child was afraid Lieutenant Gage's ghost was abroad."

"That corridor leads to a back stair," William Chute said. "It descends to the Chapel."

"And given that Caroline was disturbed by footsteps," I mused, "and Miss Gambier perhaps already insensible—is it not possible that her killer chose the nursery passage to convey her body to the Chapel floor? In the middle of the night, he should not like to carry her through the Staircase Hall. He might meet any one of us."

"Villain," Chute said bitterly. "It does not bear thinking of. That helpless girl, dragged limp from her bed—and none of us able to save her. When I consider what I shelter in my house—that even now a killer breaks bread with my wife and child—"

"If only we could divine the mystery of the charade," I said in frustration. "I am sure it is the clew to everything, and Lady Gambier will never reveal it. The secret will go with Mary to her grave."

But our conversation was at an end. The horses were pulling up, and the footman jumping down from the rear of the carriage. We had arrived at the Angel Inn, Basingstoke.

I WILL NOT TROUBLE to relate the particulars of the inquest—how the publick room of the inn had been given over to a considerable

214 · STEPHANIE BARRON

crowd of curious onlookers; how the jury was empanelled, or by
whom; how the Coroner appeared, in all the dignity of a wig newly-
purchased for the Christmas season and ennobled by his judicial
dignities, when in the common way he was merely Mr. Stout, the
Basingstoke surgeon. We have all been treated to similar scenes
before. When the six men of the jury had been sent into a side parlour to view Lieutenant Gage's body, and had returned affirming
that they understood he had been dead some days, and had lost his
life to a broken neck, Mr. Chute was called to give an account of
St. Stephen's Day. Lieutenant Gage's arrival was considered; his
farewells the following morn; the return of his riderless horse, and
the discovery of his body.

"You did not summon a doctor, sir, when Deceased was found?"
the Coroner enquired.

"It was impossible, due to the condition of the roads. They had
not then been cleared of snow, and the thaw was only just setting in."

"You found the corpse at half-past eleven o'clock in the morning,
or thereabouts, by your best estimation—and Deceased had quitted
The Vyne some forty minutes or so before. Was the body still warm
when you discovered it?"

"Barely. It had been lying some minutes in a drift of snow."

The Coroner allowed Chute to step down, so that the true drama
of the proceeding might occur—which, to my mind, was the testi-
mony of Raphael West and myself. It was our evidence which must
turn the inquest from a common enquiry into a fall from a horse, to
an exploration of murder.

West was required to take his oath first. He did so with his
usual self-containment and faint air of boredom. I was well-enough
acquainted with the man now to know that his countenance looked
most weary when his attention was most acute. He produced his

notebook and explained the sketches he had made. The Coroner summed up his conclusions.

"And so you would insist that the horse fell—and the rider landed—in places other than where the body was found?"

"Yes, sir."

A faint murmur of speculation fanned through the crowd.

The Coroner knit his brows. "Are you suggesting the injury to Deceased's neck was so trifling that he was able to raise himself and change his position—tho' serious enough that he then expired? For if so, Mr. West, I must say that all my long years of bone-setting are against you. Deceased's neck was broken right through."

"I do not suggest it." Impossible for West to say outright what his evidence shewed; that was for the Coroner to conclude.

"Then I take it, sir, you would imply that Deceased's neck was broken after he fell from the horse—and not by the fall itself."

"From the disturbance in the snow, I can think nothing else."

"We cannot know, other than from this sketch, that you did see such a disturbance," the Coroner retorted. "The snow has since melted. This may be all artist's invention."

"Another guest at The Vyne was witness to my sketching. You will find her signature appended on the obverse of that paper."

The Coroner looked for my name; found it; and Raphael West was invited to stand down. It was then my turn to speak.

I told the jury of my walk to the scene of Lieutenant Gage's death, and of finding Raphael West at work there. I affirmed that the snow was unbroken from the place where the horse was brought down, to the Sherborne St. John road.

"Brought down," the Coroner repeated. "Surely you mean fell?"

"I do not," I said firmly, and told him of my discovery of the entrapping wire. "I then observed footprints in the snow, leading from the trees to the door of the ice house."

"Suggesting that whoever laid the wire, retreated there for shelter?"

"That is possible."

"Or waited there, with the object of breaking Lieutenant Gage's neck, when once his horse was brought down?"

"That is also possible."

"Did you look within the ice house?"

"I did, with Mr. Raphael West. We found it empty."

Mr. Chute was then recalled, and told how he had been informed of our discoveries, and had subsequently notified Lord Bolton.

"Do you know of any reason why Lieutenant Gage should be killed, Mr. Chute, on your grounds?" the Coroner enquired in his silkiest manner.

"He carried an important Government dispatch," Chute said, "which is now missing."

Another ripple of interest from the crowd.

The Coroner brought down his gavel, and adjourned the proceeding for an interval, so that the jury might partake of the Angel's ale, and Mr. Stout might organise his thoughts.

"I have secured a private parlour upstairs, Miss Austen, so that we might enjoy a nuncheon in peace."

"You are very good, sir." My shivering breakfast with Cook had been of so unsatisfying a nature that I was quite ready to admire the rabbit and leek pie, Cheshire cheese, and baked apples the landlord, Mr. Fitch, had sent up for us. Mr. Chute invited Lord Bolton to join us, and that mild young man informed us he was now the father of a son. Lady Bolton was doing admirably.

We listened to him talk of his wife's superb temperament—her treating a lying-in as tho' it were no more than having the headache;

her undiminished beauty; and what young Harry had said when told that he had another brother. Nothing—not even the matter of a double-murder in his preserve—could divert his lordship from his stream of relief and self-congratulation. William Chute was just refilling Lord Bolton's glass with claret, and raising his own to the health of the infant, when there came a knock on the parlour door.

It was Fitch, the Angel's innkeeper.

"Begging your pardon," he said with a nod to all of us as he stooped deprecatingly in the doorway, a second figure behind him, "but this lady is wishful of having speech with you, sirs, and when she told me her name, I thought it best to come straight to Lord Bolton."

"Her name?" his lordship repeated. "What is it, man?"

Fitch glanced almost slyly over his shoulder, big with news; but the woman he guarded pushed abruptly past him, and strode into the room. She had a child of two or three on her hip.

"I am Amy Gage," she said defiantly. "John Gage's widow."

20

THE WOMAN IN THE CASE

Friday, 30th December 1814
Steventon Parsonage, cont'd.

If this interval of confusion and violence during the Christmas season has taught me anything, it is to value the essential goodness of William Chute—a man I had been much disposed to regard as little more than a rough country squire, of scant education and commonplace gifts. I had been wont, in the past, to deplore the throwing away of such a woman as Eliza Chute upon a man who preferred an hour with his pack of hounds in the stables, to one of studied discourse in his ancestral Saloon. But I was moved to admiration and warmth by the alacrity with which he dismissed the interested innkeeper and ushered Mrs. Gage to a chair by the fire, chucked her boy beneath the chin, and offered both a share of our nuncheon. He succeeded in turning an awkward and uncertain moment to one of easiness; and I perceived that this was a habit acquired as much from his long years of service in Parliament as his standing in Sherborne St. John.

Having seen Mrs. Gage settled in her chair and her child supplied with baked apple, however, Chute's shrewd brain turned to more critical matters.

"I forget my manners," he said handsomely. "You will allow me to make you acquainted with Miss Austen—she has lately been a guest at The Vyne—with Mr. West, and with Lord Bolton, our Justice of the Peace."

She inclined her head to all of us, but said only, "You're the lady as was called to evidence. And the gentleman as made the drawings." Her speech, like her dress, was not refined; her skin was coarse and her teeth indifferent. A plain face and an ageing one; but I could trace in it the remnants of prettiness, and her figure was buxom. As a young girl, Amy Gage had probably been a coquette. Knowing something of the Navy, I suspected the Lieutenant had wooed his landlady's daughter, while posted in Sheerness or Deal.

"You will not be offended, I hope," Chute continued, "when I tell you that we had no notion of your existence, and thus could not inform you of your husband's death. How did you come to learn of it, Mrs. Gage?"

"The news is all over Portsmouth," she said. "How the Admiral's messenger was killed in performing his dooty. I went to the Port Commander and asked him straight. He told me there was to be a 'quest—he'd had it from the Admiralty Signals. He gave me coach fare to Basingstoke."

"Have you accommodation?" Chute enquired.

Amy Gage shrugged. "I'll shift somewhere for the night. But what's to become of me then, I'd like to know, and the boy? I've hardly enough blunt to give Jack a decent burial! How we'll live now he's gone, there's no telling."

"He will have a Naval pension, surely?" I suggested.

"On a lieutenant's pay? No better than a beggar's portion," she retorted contemptuously. "If he'd made Master or Post—but he couldn't get a ship, now Boney's gone to ground. No, it won't do. I'll put the child on the parish, I will, and go into Service."

It was plain from the trend of the woman's words that John Gage's death in itself was barely a source of grief. Shocked as I was at the fact of his having possessed a wife—when his attachment to Mary Gambier, and hers to him, had been quite clear—I felt a twinge of sympathy for the dead man. It seemed a reproach to his memory that his loss was measured only in pounds and pence.

"Provided you may prove the truth of your marriage to Lieutenant Gage," William Chute said smoothly, "you may discover there is a sum in keeping for you—having died as he did in the service of the Crown."

This was nonsense, as I very well knew. Every Naval officer dies in service to the Crown, whether he be on shore or at the Antipodes, for he holds the King's commission. But I perceived that Chute was angling for intelligence, and hoped the promise of coin might win it.

"I wear his ring, don't I?" Mrs. Gage said defiantly. "It's a fine thing when a respectable widow is made to feel no better than a strumpet. Ask Gambier if I'm John Gage's wife!"

"My dear lady," Chute said swiftly, "I offered no insult. It is customary, before bounties such as I mentioned are paid out, to ensure that the recipients are legally entitled to them. The claims, for instance of your husband's other relatives—an aged mother, per-haps?—must be weighed against your own."

With a sharp movement, Amy Gage turned to Lord Bolton. "Listen on him! Jack was alone in the world, until he found me. But you fine folk with your words and your laws will cheat me out of my due. It's the old story, as is seen all over Portsmouth—good men die, and their kin are turned out like slops from the bilge."

"Mrs. Gage—" Lord Bolton began, in consternation, but Raphael West forestalled him.

"When did you last see your husband, ma'am?" he asked quietly.

"Christmas Eve. He didn't ought to have come, being meant for London and the Admiralty—ought to have taken the packet out of Ostend, into Kent. But Gambier was wishful Jack should see her la'ship. Give her his letters. So Jack took a Navy cruiser to Portsmouth instead."

"Had he been absent from you long?"

"He's never home more than one night together," she said simply. "Spends all his time in Gambier's service. The child don't hardly know him. But that's all right. Jack made sure we had enough to live on. I don't know how we'll make do, now he's gone."

West ignored this reversion to a burning subject. "He left you Christmas morning?"

"Still dark, it was. And no word since. I didn't think nothing of that—until Sally at the Bosun's Whistle told me about the 'quest, and I went to the Port Commander."

The Bosun's Whistle was a Portsmouth publick house.

"This Sally," I broke in. "She knew to come to you? Tho' your husband was so lately returned, and so briefly? She was aware, I collect, that he was bound for the north on Admiralty business?"

Of a sudden, Mrs. Gage looked less sure of herself. Her gaze shifted from mine; her hands worked at her little boy's jacket. "No harm in raising a pint of bitter on a cold winter's night. Or passing the time o' day with a friend."

I glanced at Raphael West. A French cypher of Chute's correspondence had been found on a man seized in a Portsmouth tavern. Was it the Bosun's Whistle?

He gave no sign. "Did your husband tell you where he was bound, on the Admiral's private business?"

"I know now," she said darkly. "Bound for his death, he was. What

I want to know is, was his purse on him? Or did the fellow who did for him, take his coin too?"

There was an instant of appalled silence. Then William Chute said drily, "I shall instruct the Coroner, Mr. Stout, to deliver over your husband's effects, ma'am, once the inquest is done. If you wish to bury him, you may even have his body."

"Not I," she returned indifferently. "That's the Navy's affair. He did ought to be tossed over the rail in his hammock. Jack'd like to meet Davy Jones, and no expence about it."

I thought of Mary Gambier on her knees before the Lieutenant's bier, and felt a wretched chill in my heart.

Mrs. Gage rose from her chair and snatched the child back onto her hip. The little boy's face was liberally smeared with baked apple; he buried it stickily in his mother's shoulder. She strode up to William Chute.

"You write to the Admiral and tell 'im how we're left. Tell him I mean to put Jack's boy on the parish. If he wants me, he'll find me in Portsmouth—until I can bear the charge of lodgings no longer!"

THE REMAINDER OF THE inquest held no surprises for me. The Coroner's panel was summoned from its enjoyment of Mr. Fitch's barrels, and required to listen to Mr. Stout's guidance. Lord Bolton was respectfully asked if he had anything further to add—as Justice of the Peace for the Basingstoke locality—and he gave it as his opinion that further facts might yet come to light in the Lieutenant's death. With such clear direction from the established authorities, the six worthies of the jury retired to ruminate among themselves; and within very few minutes, pronounced a verdict of murder, by person or persons unknown.

The day being already far advanced, Mr. Chute was anxious to summon his coachman and have the carriage brought round from the Angel's yard. As Mr. West and I hurried from the publick room where the inquest had been held, I observed Lord Bolton approach Amy Gage. He reached into his coat and produced a notecase. No doubt the sight of that little boy brought to mind his own wife and child—delivered into far different circumstances this Christmas.

"Unaccountable," I said as we rattled over the icy cobblestones towards Steventon once more. "Lieutenant Gage married—it is in every way unaccountable!"

"Only if you assume that Mary Gambier understood the case," Raphael West returned. "It is probable that she was as ignorant of his circumstances as we were. Despite her clear attachment, she cannot have known him long or well. Gage was too often absent on his duties, and absent from England."

"Her brother told me that the Lieutenant was perpetually in service to Lord Gambier—following him about the Continent as a sort of aide-de-camp." I glanced at William Chute. "That is unusual in the Navy, to be sure, but the Admiral has been turned on shore these several years, and his duties have lain in administration rather than command. I suppose Lieutenant Gage served him as secretary, rather in the way you employ Benedict L'Anglois; and no mention of his personal life ever arose."

"To be sure," Chute replied. "I believe Miss Gambier made Gage's acquaintance only last summer, in Brighton. But to think he chose to marry such a woman! She is not at all like Mary Gambier—and we must hope Mrs. Gage knows nothing of that lady's existence, or sad end. Thank God Bolton did not wish to hold an inquest on Miss Gambier's death—only consider of the embarrassment for all concerned!"

We were silent a moment, while the early winter dark slowly took possession of the carriage interior. The flickering lights of the side lanterns became more pronounced against the dusky backdrop; I reached my toes to the hot brick, refreshed at the Angel, and wished I might already be at Steventon, in the privacy of my bedchamber, to consider of all I had learnt. I felt oppressed by the sordidness of The Vyne affair, beyond anything I had yet known; a weariness of deceit and betrayal overcame me.

"I could not help remarking that Mrs. Gage lives in Portsmouth," Raphael West said quietly. He opened his sketchbook and held one page to the side-lantern's light. I could just make out the image of a woman and child; he had been drawing Amy Gage while Chute questioned her. In the shape of the boy's head and the almond eyes, I recognised the technique of Benjamin West—who conjured from every such pair a Raphaelite Madonna.

"Half the Navy resides in Hampshire," Chute returned indifferently, "when they do not live in Kent."

"But our spy," West concluded, "was discovered in Portsmouth—at the very Bosun's Whistle Mrs. Gage is known to frequent."

THE SEVENTH DAY

21

LET OUT THE OLD YEAR

Saturday, 31st December 1814
Steventon Parsonage

New Year's Eve saw an end to the thaw. We awoke to a sky lowering and ominous, and a temperature sunk into its boots. Clouds built up all morning as Cassandra and I strolled briskly down Steventon's solitary street, to fetch chickens from one villager, cheese from another, and fresh bread from a third. We had invited Caroline to accompany us on our brief shopping expedition, and she was everywhere greeted with deference and affection as "Rector's Young Lady." We encountered a spinster Miss Sutter, a lady of uncertain years in genteel decline, who was happy to renew her acquaintance with "dear Mr. Austen's daughters," and appeared anxious to trace the outline of our younger selves in Cassandra's countenance and mine. But it is nearly fourteen years since we quitted the parsonage for Bath with our parents, leaving it to James's care—and that is a period. Every pore of one's thought and existence is changed. Miss Sutter turned next to Caroline, who was shifting from one cold foot to another.

"And you have lately been staying at The Vyne, I hear! What a Christmas treat, to be sure! Such grand gentlemen and ladies!"

No word of murder had penetrated through the snows, it seemed, to Steventon. Yet.

"And how is your Mamma? Lying down upon her sopha—or improved in health, with all the charm and distraction of her guests?"

Caroline justified the faith I have lately been placing in her quickness and understanding, by refusing to answer such leading questions, and merely displayed Jemima to Miss Sutter's dazzled eyes. The faeries had come up to scratch this morning, delivering a redingote of Prussian-blue wool; just the thing for a freezing walk along muddy lanes. Once Miss Sutter had declared herself amazed at Jemima's stile and beauty, we pled the cold and hurried back to the house.

Mary, having been torn from all the richness and stimulation of The Vyne, had declared herself most unwell this morning, and descended into what her son, James-Edward, called "a fit of the dismals."

"Is that a sample of Edward Gambier's cant?" I enquired interestedly.

"Thomas-Vere's," he acknowledged with shy pride. "I had no notion, Aunt, that he was such a great gun—for he is a clergyman, after all, and generally speaks in that high-pitched manner. But from Gambier's chaffing when we played at billiards, I came to know that Thomas-Vere is quite the man-about-town. Up to every rig, as they say! Although apparently he keeps exotic fowl in his lodgings, which he did not care to bring to The Vyne. I confess I did not quite understand. But perhaps I did not attend fully."

"Exotic fowl?" I repeated, my brows raised.

"Gambier was joking Thomas-Vere—all in fun, of course!—about his pockets being all to let, and Thomas-Vere unable to meet his losses at billiards, on account of his Bird of Paradise," James-Edward explained. "I gather Gambier has seen the bird when he was up in Town. But perhaps it is an exotic flower, and not a bird, after all? It must be very dear, particularly in the cold of winter months."

And from what I knew of Birds of Paradise—a euphemism for a brilliant Light-skirt, a Comfortable Armful, or a Bit of Muslin, Thomas-Vere's Bird would be just as expensive in the heat of summer, when she took to parading in Hyde Park in next to nothing at all. He might wish to keep his mistress secret from his intimate family; but then again, he might be required to approach them for a loan. Thomas-Vere was an admirer of opera—and opera dancers were not happy long on a clergyman's pittance. If the lady was a true High-Flyer, she would soon demand jewels and a pair of match-greys for her cunning phaeton. Had Thomas-Vere found another source of income?

Selling his brother's political secrets to the highest bidder, perhaps?

Entanglement with Birds and their inevitable expence laid even the most discreet gentlemen open to blackmail; and Thomas-Vere was never discreet. If Edward Gambier had chosen to broach the subject before a Winchester schoolboy, he must assume the Bird of Paradise was common knowledge.

Or that Thomas-Vere, suitably warned, might pay well for silence.

I mounted the stairs to my room and sat down with this journal and pen. There is nothing like a bit of ink to bring reason to the most disordered mind.

SUSPECTS

	Murder of Gage	Murder of Miss Gambier
William Chute	with his kennel master	in his bed?
Eliza Chute	planning Children's Ball	in her bed?
Thomas-Vere Chute	absent some moments	in his bed?
Edward Gambier	playing alone at billiards	in his bed?
Benedict L'Anglois	unaccounted for	absent in London

I looked up from the page. The movements of our party were variable at the time of John Gage's death. But anyone might have administered laudanum to Mary Gambier's food or drink. The only person entirely cleared of her murder was Benedict L'Anglois. He had returned to The Vyne less than an hour before her lifeless body was discovered, and no doubt the stable lads could attest to his horse's arrival. That interval was insufficient to effect murder; when found, Miss Gambier had been dead some hours. *She is so cold*, Edward Gambier had cried. *Will no one help me?*

Did innocence in one death clear L'Anglois of the other? Quite probably. There could not be two guests at The Vyne determined upon violence.

Mary, Cassandra, and I had been fixed with Eliza in the morning room at the moment Lieutenant Gage's neck was broken, our movements known. Of the remaining ladies, only Lousia Gambier—unattended in her bedchamber—and Mamma, at her needlework in the library, had gone unobserved. The breaking of a strong young man's neck, however, suggested the killer to be male. Edward Gambier or Thomas-Vere might have done it. So might my brother James.

Or Raphael West.

I knew where the first two gentlemen claimed to have been at the moment of the Lieutenant's death. I should probably discover that my brother was lost in slumber upon a settee in the Saloon at the time. Gambier claimed to have glimpsed Raphael West in the Chapel that morning—but at what hour, exactly? Mary Gambier could have told me—could have supported or denied Mr. West's search for a secret passage. To the ice house. Where Lieutenant Gage's murderer had lain in wait for a trap to be sprung.

But Mary Gambier, most inconveniently, was dead. Or was her loss a convenience, in fact, to Raphael West?

MARY BEING INDISPOSED ON her sopha this morning, and James closeted in his study about his sermon for the morrow, the Austen ladies were free to command the parsonage staff. I ordered brisk fires in the principal rooms, and dressed the mantel with evergreen boughs. Mamma sailed into the kitchen and gave her orders for dinner, which chiefly concerned the freshly killed chickens just procured. Cassandra commenced the baking of mince-pies. The housemaid and cook, being newly returned from a protracted interval of leisure, proved cheerful and ready enough to do our bidding. Cook broke into a lusty performance of "Greensleeves" as she plucked the chickens, and Sarah the maid set James's man—I cannot call him a footman even in pretence, as he was rather a factotum of labour—to chopping more wood. All was light and happiness within; it was quite the parsonage of old. Without, snowflakes began to fall as the candles were lighted.

"Jane," my mother said conspiratorially as we eyed the mahogany table in the dining parlour, "I do not think we can contrive a castle carved out of a block of sugar, but could we not arrange some greens for the centre? And do you think we ought to declare our intention of departing for Chawton on the morrow—as with all the bloodletting at the Chutes, my heart has quite gone out of remaining for Twelfth Night?"

I bent to the sheaf of boughs that James's man had cut for us and carried it into the house. "Tomorrow is Sunday, Mamma. You never travel on the Sabbath."

"Monday, then. Surely that will be long enough for propriety's sake?"

I did not wish to return home yet—I should be disappointed of any chance at solving the puzzle of Mary Gambier and Lieutenant Gage—but I apprehended that my mother was finding her son and daughter-in-law's establishment hard to bear. "Only consider that the children shall be made unhappy. We promised them a fortnight's visit. And you have not yet met with half your old acquaintance in the neighbourhood!"

"It is true that nobody has seen my reticule," she said regretfully.

"Only think how sad for them."

"I do not count Eliza Chute, for she has many fine things, and is accustomed to town bronze."

"Even she admired it, however. But if Mrs. Digweed of Dummer were to espy it, or one of the Miss Terrys, you must be satisfied."

As tho' I had conjured it, a loud rapping was heard at the front door. We waited for the result, the greens for the table suspended in my hands. Presently the housemaid appeared with a parcel, wrapt in butcher's paper and twine.

"Christmas pudding, ma'am," she said briefly, "with Mr. Portal's compliments, and would all the Austens please join them at Ashe Park for dinner tomorrow. Five o'clock. They keeps country hours at Ashe," she added, of her own volition.

"Dinner!" My mother looked to me in doubt. "I do not know what James will say. He does not believe in Sunday travel any more than I do."[10]

"The Portals live but two miles away, Mamma," I said reasonably. "Mr. Portal will send his carriage—he knows that my brother keeps only a gig. And it is New Year's Day. Surely that takes precedence over stricter principles?"

---

[10] Use of a carriage was frowned upon during the Sabbath, which was considered a day of quiet religious contemplation.—Editor's note.

"Do not be telling James so." She fidgeted a little with a candle-stick and a beeswax taper. "I am sure Mrs. Portal would wish to see my reticule."

"How could she not? You know that Papa, were he here, should never hesitate."

And so it was settled. We added the Portals' excellent pudding to our store of delicacies intended for this evening, and set Cassandra to wheedling brandy out of James. It is not quite a Christmas pudding if one cannot set fire to it.

Even Mary found the strength to rise from her sick-bed, on the promise of a gaiety tomorrow.

WHEN MY FATHER WAS alive, New Year's Eve was a time of singing and dancing at the parsonage. The Rector led the festivities, inviting all his acquaintance into these small rooms, and bestowing his sprigs of mistletoe on the young ladies. There was wassail, and roaring fires, and tables creaking under the weight of good things; for no matter how many mouths George Austen had to feed, his benevolent heart was open to every chance friend. I remember theatricals, as well—I wrote some of them myself as a girl of thirteen or fourteen—and one splendid Christmas when all my brothers were at home, they consented to play in a grand production with my beloved French cousin, Eliza de Feuillide. My brothers are scattered and Eliza is in her grave; but I wish that Caroline and James-Edward were treated to similar amusements. If one is forbidden to indulge every sort of silliness as a child, one is bound to do so when grown.

And so this evening I performed a ritual from my vanished girl-hood. As the parlour clock began to strike twelve, I opened the kitchen door to let the Old Year out. Then I hurried along the passage to the parsonage hall, and on the stroke of twelve, threw wide the front door to let the New Year in.

Huddled in her shawl, Cassandra came to stand by me. Snow was falling, and the world looked white and clean.

"There should be a dark-haired gentleman waiting to enter," she said. "For good luck."

I pushed away the thought of Raphael West, and embraced Cassandra. "Never mind, my dear. We have done without him all these years, well enough."

THE EIGHTH DAY

22

GOSSIP

It was I who crept into Caroline's room this morning, with a neat walking dress of bronze-green French twill and a nut-brown wool spencer, trimmed in the same bronze-green. Bonnets being difficult to fashion for a head so small as Jemima's, I had settled for a brown velvet turban dressed with a bronze-green feather, trimmed down from one I had purchased at Burlington House while in London last month. Caroline was already awake, and stared at me soberly from beneath the bedclothes.

"It is a splendid costume, Aunt," she said. "But I do not know when she will find a use for it."

"She should wear it while taking the air in Hyde Park."

Caroline's grey eyes fixed upon mine. "We never go to London. We never go anywhere. The most interesting place I have been in all my life is The Vyne."

"You have been to Chawton," I attempted.

She lifted her shoulders. "Jemima cannot wear her ball gown there."

"You might pretend to be in Hyde Park. Or at the Coming-Out

of an Earl's daughter. With your wit, Caroline, you might travel any-where—and carry Jemima with you. For what do we possess minds, if not to broaden our experience?"

"It is not experience if it is only in your mind," she pointed out. Discomfiting child.

"Perhaps when I next visit Uncle Henry in Town," I said recklessly, "I might take you with me."

"Truly, Aunt?" She sat upright, her countenance all eagerness. "May we visit Astley's Amphitheatre?"

"How could we not?"

"And attend a pantomime at Covent Garden?"

"Uncle Henry's new lodgings are directly opposite Drury Lane."

Caroline threw her arms around me. "I do love you, Aunt Jane. You never make one feel sinful, in longing for pleasure. Or hopeless of ever attaining it."

My heart suffered a queer ache. I might write about love and marriage in my novels; my wit, like Caroline's, could transport me anywhere. But she was right—pretend is not the same as experience.

"Dress yourself warmly for church," I advised. "If you contrive to appear the ideal Rector's daughter, you may win Papa's permission for a London visit sooner than you think."

THE SNOW WAS DONE by the time we exited St. Nicholas's several hours later, but we were chilled to the core. I downed several cups of scalding tea upon my return to the parsonage, before ever breakfast had been laid in the parlour. But the sky began to clear as we finished our repast, and a faint sun shone; everywhere about the eaves of the house came the sound of dripping water.

By four o'clock, when we had changed into evening dress and were assembled in the front hall awaiting the arrival of Mr. Portal's carriage, the coverlet of white was gone and the main road returned to churned mud.

It was a heavy two miles behind Portal's excellent horses to Ashe Park. My brother James rode beside us on his hunter, to afford the ladies more room; and inside the carriage most of us were serene.

"How good it is, to be sure," my mother exclaimed, "to renew old acquaintance!"

Mary sniffed. "And how tedious to be forced to rely on their equipages, for one's social engagements! I wonder that James is not mortified to be indebted to John Portal in this way. A mill owner, to be conveying a clergyman! When James was so superior to John Portal, too, at Oxford."

I exchanged a look with Cassandra. It is true that the Portal family has for many years owned the mills in Laverstoke that produce the paper for Bank of England notes; but I wonder if John Portal has ever entered them. His elder brother lives in Laverstoke, tho' he also owns Ashe Park; and so handsome is the family fortune that John might chuse to reside at Ashe merely for the asking. Mary's petty snobberies are her sole armour against those who possess what she cannot hope to attain; that, and a general sense of ill-usage.

"James ought to keep a carriage of his own," she persisted. "But he will buy hunters, instead! I am sure he does it with the design of vexing me. He would insist I am too material in my concerns, I daresay."

"One hunter cannot run to the same expence as a team, a carriage, and a coachman to drive it," Cassandra observed gently.

"What can you possibly know of domestic economy, Cassandra?" Mary lifted her eyes expressively towards Heaven. "You have never been required to manage your own establishment. You have been a dependent all your life."

"I beg your pardon," my sister returned stiffly. "Mamma and Jane and I live in the strictest economy as a result of Papa's death. Your sister, Martha, contrives on even less. If that is not domestic management, I cannot conceive what is."

"Girls," Mamma interjected. "Pray do not be scolding each other! We are fortunate both in the manner of our conveyance to Ashe Park and of being bidden to dine there at all. Only think what a delightful occasion this is! A gaiety at Christmas, and without the least opportunity for murder, from beginning to end!"

Mary sighed, as tho' already regretting her decision to abandon her sopha. "One always knows what will be served at Ashe, and who will be there. There is nothing in the way of novelty in the country."

"But people themselves change so much," my mother objected, "that there is always something new to be learnt of their characters."

"You possess the happy talent of contentment in your narrow quarter," Mary retorted. "But my understanding demands greater scope for enjoyment—finer sensibilities in my acquaintance. A broader world in which to be known."

I remembered Caroline's unhappy looks this morning. Pray God she had not inherited too much of her mother's temperament. The little fever of envy, once caught, is the ruin of all happiness.

Mary mastered her petulance well enough, however, to appear gracious when once we were arrived at Ashe Park; and the company being increased by a few strangers she had not expected, was moved to behave better than among her friends. Her desire to be well-regarded lent something like animation to her behaviour at dinner.

"Have you heard the excellent news, Austen?" John Portal cried as he handed my brother a glass of Madeira. "Chute means to take out his pack tomorrow."

"But the snow!" James exclaimed.

Portal shrugged and set down his decanter. He is a hearty, handsome fellow with an open countenance and few airs about him. "I had a note from Chute this morning. He says a thaw is already set in around The Vyne, and that his hounds are ready to eat one another alive, so little exercise have they seen. A good casting and a better gallop will be the saving of us all, whether we draw blank or not."

"With this wet, the scent should be breast-high," James mused. "Where is the meet?"

"Sherborne St. John. I've told Lucy she must come and raise a stirrup cup, to see us off."

"Should you like to join me, Mrs. Austen?" Lucy Portal enquired, leaning towards Mary. "I should be happy to offer you a seat in my carriage."

Mary does not think highly of Mrs. Portal, who does not find another's ills so interesting as Mary should like. "I am afraid the effort is far beyond my powers at present," she said weakly. "I was most unwell at The Vyne, as no doubt you have heard."

This was intended as a trailing remark—the sort that elicits vast impatience to learn the whole—but Lucy merely turned to me. "Are you an aficionado of the hunt, Miss Austen?"

"I do not ride—but I should be very happy to watch the Hunt go off," I said. "I will accept a seat in your carriage with alacrity. It is very kind of you to offer it."

"What fun we shall have! I confess I am wild to set foot out-of-doors; the weather has been too confining of late."

At this, my sister-in-law looked positively disgruntled, and left her seat by Lucy Portal in search of more sympathetic ears.

"You must join us, Austen!" Portal cried. "Bring that lad of yours—he'll have an enviable seat and hands, if you've schooled him."

Amidst all James's pomposities I had forgot he was an excellent horseman. He and my brother Henry learnt to ride with The Vyne; when my father could not mount them, William Chute did. They are both hunting-mad to this day.

"My Trooper is not so fit as I should like," James said.

"Let your son sit him," Portal returned impatiently. "The boy's a feather-weight, I daresay."

"True enough—but I haven't another mount so good in my stable."

"I'll lend you Aristo. He's heavy enough for a man of your stone."

"Done," James said, and raised his glass. The two gentlemen moved off in search of others of their fellows lounging about the drawing-room, who might be persuaded to join the Hunt. I glanced about the well-lit and richly-panelled walls, and reflected that my mother was right: how fortunate we were to enjoy a gaiety without the least chance for murder!

Ashe Park is the principal estate in Steventon. I must believe Lucy Portal happy in the command of its numerous elegancies, its comfortable, well-proportioned rooms, its excellent fires, and its expansive park. There were nearly twenty people gathered about her for tea after our excellent dinner, and to review their names and faces was to recall scenes from more than half my life. The Digweeds were there: James, a clergyman who is of an age with myself, and his wife, whom he met in Tonbridge Wells. Maria is generally reported an heiress, and from her dress I may well believe it—she was arrayed as for a ball, and tho' older than James by several years and the mother of five hopeful children, displayed an expanse of bosom that was as startling as it was naked.

I shall have to recommend the stile to Mary, if she persists in contemplation of her own mortality; for with so little in the way of clothes, she might contract a chill, and be carried off within a se'ennight.

Mr. John Harwood of Deane House was also there, along with one of his sisters. Another clergyman—how Hampshire does abound in them, to be sure!—he is a tragic figure, and of especial interest to me, for he was meant to marry my good friend Elizabeth Bigg when at last he came into his inheritance. But on his father's death last year, what should be discovered but that the gentleman had been living far beyond his means—and that his heir was ruined! John Harwood has determined never to marry, but to exert his efforts to clearing Deane of debt, and supporting his widowed mother. His sisters' marriage-portions went with all the rest of his fortune, and the blighting of the Harwoods' hopes has been the talk of the neighbourhood this past year. We must believe that 1815 will see an improvement in them.

"May I assure you, Miss Austen," John Harwood told me at the dinner table, "how very much I enjoyed *Mansfield Park*? The naturalness of all the characters—the sentiments of Edward and Fanny, so admirable in every respect—it is a lesson in the virtues of novel-reading, rather than its ills."

Of course I must feel regard for the tragic fellow; what he lacks in funds, he more than makes up for in taste.

There were also numerous Terrys from Dummer in the room, the ladies quick to praise my mother's reticule. Standing alone, I observed Mr. Michael Terry, who was engaged to James's Anna before she lost her heart to Ben Lefroy this year. Near him were the Wither Bramstons, from Oakley Hall.

I had glimpsed the Bramstons at the far end of the dinner table, and wished them exchanged for their sister, Augusta, who is an eccentric and sharp-tongued lady; she was seated directly opposite myself. At Mr. Harwood's praise of my most recent novel, she uttered a derisive snort. "*Sense and Sensibility* was nonsense, of course, and *Pride and Prejudice* downright vulgar. I expect to like *Mansfield Park* better, Miss Austen; and having finished the first volume, flatter myself I have got through the worst."

Augusta Bramston is happy in being quite deaf. I enjoyed a few choice retorts at her expence, and consoled myself with Mr. Portal's excellent claret.

I had not long been free of the dining parlour and in possession of a settee in the drawing-room, however, before Mary Bramston settled herself beside me with a conspiratorial air. Mrs. Bramston is sister to Thomas-Vere and William Chute; her entire girlhood was passed at The Vyne. She is a dark, lively, stout little lady with strenuous ringlets and blackcurrant eyes, who lives to talk of her neighbours. Of all those dining at Ashe Park, she must be most aware of the nature of our Christmas.

"Miss Austen," she said, pressing my hand with her heavily-ringed one. "Augusta has been insulting you about your books. I am mortified! Pray do not hold her opinions against all of us at Oakley Hall. I thought *Pride and Prejudice* beyond everything great; but your Fanny is too good for me. I prefer Mary Crawford and her rake of a brother. Now tell me everything you can of this unpleasantness at The Vyne. Do you agree with our Eliza, and think Lady Gambier a murderer?"

"Lady Gambier! Not at all!" I returned.

"She quitted Hampshire in her carriage yesterday morning, with that poor creature's body conveyed behind on a hired cart. Her nephew rode beside, Eliza tells me, on his own mount—and only conceive how it snowed! He will contract an inflammation of the lung, I daresay, and then her ladyship will be doubly sorry."

"They were bound for Bath?"

Mrs. Bramston nodded significantly. "To restore Miss Gambier to her grieving mother. Lady Gambier was most insistent that they reach Bath today, for she wished the corpse laid out in the Abbey. She cannot believe, therefore, that the death was self-murder. She would not be seeking Christian burial otherwise. Much less the Abbey!"

It is the most venerable of Bath's many churches.

"Is that not like remorse?" Mrs. Bramston insisted. "Do you not think it certain Lady Gambier cut off the girl's life—and is haunted by guilt?"

"What possible reason can you have for believing so?"

"Why, the laudanum bottle!" Mary Bramston cried. She lifted her pretty hands. "The one discovered near Mary Gambier's body. You must know that it was found to belong to her aunt."

"I did not," I said slowly. "When was this told?"

"Friday evening," Mary Bramston said, "Lady Gambier's last in the house, and one she spent entirely in packing, if Eliza is to be believed. What must her ladyship do, but accuse her maid of having lost her laudanum drops, and turn the whole place on its ear? Louisa Gambier cannot abide a carriage journey, it seems, without she doses herself. Now. What do you make of that?"

I thought it very likely that Lady Gambier's spent laudanum bottle was presently in William Chute's book room. I could not imagine that elderly woman, however, carrying her niece's insensate form through the nursery wing and down the back Chapel stairs.

I said only, "Lady Gambier was very fond of her niece, I believe. She would wish to do everything proper, in respect of the dead. Mr. Chute had no objection to the Gambiers' quitting The Vyne?"

"He could not keep them from a Christian burial, in good conscience, particularly when Mr. West had already gone."

"Mr. West?"

"Did you not know? He took his leave directly the inquest was over."

I was astounded by this piece of intelligence; for the past several days I had been wishing for news of Mr. West's investigations, and had consoled myself in the hope that tomorrow, perhaps, might bring word of them. "He returned to London?"

"I cannot say. Eliza made sure he should send his *adieux* to Miss Austen, if no one else. She declares he has a *tendre* for you, Jane."

"She is quite mistaken." So little did he regard me, in fact, that he had left Hampshire without offering a word of his plans. Did he find no reason now to pursue the murderer of John Gage and Mary Gambier? Had he given up the Treaty as lost to our enemies? Or did he follow a trail in London, of which I knew nothing?

I was suddenly wild to find William Chute and press him for answers.

"Only my brother Thomas-Vere remains at The Vyne," Mrs. Bramston continued. "The three of them must be very dull, rattling around that draughty old place. I believe Mr. West is expected to return, however, when once his business is done—so perhaps I may be invited to meet him after all. I collect Eliza means to go forward with her plans for a Children's Ball on Twelfth Night—and we are all to be invited!"

"I suppose there can be nothing wrong in such a gaiety," I mused, "regardless of the deaths that have occurred. Miss Gambier's family is no longer in residence, and Lieutenant Gage was a stranger to the Chutes. Eliza will be wishing to throw off the pall of The Vyne's recent unpleasantness, and open 1815 in a lighter mood."

"I look forward to making Mr. West's acquaintance. I long to watch him sketch!" Mary Bramston exclaimed. "Is it not marvellous to think of my brother William, enshrined in a Parliamentary portrait? Thomas-Vere and I should never have credited it when we were children together in the nursery, I declare. William was always so slow at his lessons!"

Mr. Wither Bramston then approached, to save me from the necessity of a response, and asked after my brother Henry. I was able to assure him that the new lodgings in Henrietta Street were exactly to a single gentleman's liking, and that Henry's latest horse looked very promising at Newmarket. But I confess my mind was far from the trivialities of the conversation; I was pursuing in thought the elusive figure of Mr. Raphael West, and his guarded movements.

Our party broke up soon after. Lucy Portal was pressing in her invitation to all the Austen ladies, to ride out in the Portal carriage and watch The Vyne Hunt go off; and this second opportunity was not lost on Mary. She had been consulting with her husband, and saw the wisdom of acquiescing in general enjoyment. To be spending an entire day alone, with only her daughter about her, was to be foregoing an ideal stage for her powers.

THE NINTH DAY

2 3

HUNTING WITH THE VYNE

Monday, 2nd January 1815
Steventon Parsonage

"Aunt Jane!"

The whisper was urgent enough to penetrate even my brain, clouded with sleep. I lifted myself from the pillow and looked confusedly to the door. A small figure shivered there, in a dressing gown too short in sleeves and hem.

"What is it, Caroline?"

She took this for an invitation, and bounded across the room to my bed. "Neither of the faeries came as usual this morning. I awoke early, and waited; and when it seemed as tho' Jemima and I must be forgot, I came to see if my aunts were already at breakfast. But only think! It is past seven o'clock, and you are both still abed!"

"We were out rather late last evening."

"At the Portals', I know," she said wisely. "I do not like Ashe Park so well as The Vyne. I regard The Vyne as the finest place I have yet seen."

"Nonetheless, one must have variety," I said sleepily. "Only think if it were always The Vyne, and only The Vyne. Are you here for your present? Aunt Cassandra was to deliver it today." It was a jonquil-coloured carriage dress intended for the very airing in Hyde Park Caroline had recently despaired of.

"I am not only come about Jemima," she said, and tugged at my arm urgently. I lifted the bedclothes and admitted her to the warmth; she was like a small bundle of frozen twigs, huddled against me. "James-Edward says he is to hunt today with Papa. And that you and Mamma are all going to see them off, in Mrs. Portal's carriage. Is it true that I am to be left entirely alone?"

I had not considered of this. No doubt Mary had ignored Caroline's abandonment as well.

"There is Cook," I said doubtfully. "And Sarah."

"Tosh," Caroline said firmly. "You would console me with servants, when you are all gone to Sherborne St. John to be happy? It is most unkind. And at Christmas."

I sighed. "I shall speak to Mamma."

"You are good to me, Aunt." She snuggled down in the covers. "I had been wondering when Jemima might wear her handsome riding habit. To lift a stirrup cup with The Vyne is to be wearing it to some purpose!"

JAMES PORTAL'S STABLES ARE among the finest in North Hampshire, and it was gratifying to set out behind a neat pair of steppers in the bright winter sunshine this morning. Lucy Portal was all that was cheerful and welcoming; we Austens were in spirits; and if Mary was not, she had the good sense to disguise it from her hostess. We made sure to place her beside Lucy, on the seat facing forward, conveniently close to the squabs and the window, so that she might doze or seek fresh air if she fancied herself sick. Cass, Mamma, and I sacrificed our comfort and sat with our backs to the coachman—we had barely enough room between us to accommodate our stays—and tho' this gesture was ignored by Mary, for whom it was chiefly intended, we were nonetheless conscious of virtue.

Caroline, upon arriving at Ashe Park, was invited to spend the day with the daughters of the house in the nursery wing; and this answered so well her desire to exhibit Jemima, that she jumped down without a backwards glance. I felt a twinge of relief; Mary was fractious child enough to manage, for one pleasure outing.

It is ten miles from Ashe Park to Sherborne St. John. The gentlemen rode beside our carriage, James-Edward sitting his father's hunter and looking austere, in his effort not to look sick with excitement. My brother was astride the aptly-named Aristo, a beautiful chestnut gelding with powerful flanks and shoulders; it was a mark of John Portal's trust and affection that he had lent such a mount to James. Being lighter than my brother, he rode a showy dappled grey mare with a mouth so sensitive her head was constantly on the twitch.

"What a fine day for a gallop," Lucy Portal observed.

"Do you hunt, ma'am?" my mother enquired.

She coloured faintly. "In the general way. But I am at present . . . indisposed. I hope to return to the field next winter."

When another little Portal should be safely established in the nursery.

"Eliza Chute will be chasing with the men this morning," Mary observed. "Never having occasion for an indisposition in her life."

It is possible Mary intended merely to refer to Eliza Chute's excellent health; but the suggestion that Eliza had declined to bear children because she preferred to gallop, could not be ignored. I observed Lucy Portal's eyes to widen.

"Do not be waspish, Mary," my mother suggested serenely. "It cannot recommend you to your friends, and must provide fodder for your enemies."

"I should be glad, indeed, to know that Mrs. Chute is recovered from the shocks of this past week," Lucy hurried to say, "and that all your party was no worse for having been treated to such unpleasantness."

The good manners that had prevented her from broaching the subject of murder at her own dinner table, were no impediment to canvassing the subject in the intimacy of a coach. And that swiftly, perfect accord was achieved between Lucy Portal and Mary. All that could be heard on the subject by one, and all that could be told on the part of the other, swiftly ensued; and the three of us who shared the facing seat, uttered not a word. It is possible that our thoughts on The Vyne were less easy to convey than Mary's—for our concerns must always be for others, and not solely ourselves. I was treated once more to a novelist's valuable lesson, however—in apprehending that one's perception of plot and character are influenced entirely by one's own experience. To hear Mary tell the story of our Christmas at The Vyne, one would have thought that she was hounded by violence from first to last—perceived more than anybody of the nature of the probable murderer—and barely escaped with her life. It was a lesson in writerly humility. We are each the heroines of our own lives.

SHERBORNE ST. JOHN IS pretty enough, with its venerable church, St. Andrew's; its neat village green, surrounded by cottages; and its single publick house, the Swan. This is nearly two hundred years old, and has witnessed the gathering of The Vyne Hunt for a number of decades. This morning the scene was all animation—with any number of our acquaintance mounted upon horses of varying strengths and mettle. Most were gentlemen, in leather breeches and top boots, with frequently a pink coat to be seen; but a few of the dashing riders were female, their long skirts fanned charmingly over their mounts' backs. I espied Eliza—her habit was garnet-coloured wool, with black frogs, and a curly-brimmed beaver. She must have espied me at exactly the same moment, for she raised her whip in her gloved hand.

"There is Sir William Heathcote," my mother exclaimed, as she gazed out of the carriage window. We had pulled up near the lower end of the green, due to the press of horsemen before us. "All the way from Hursley Park—and at his age too!"

I saw Cassandra suppress a smile; Sir William was nearly ten years younger than Mamma.

"He looks very well," I observed, "and has an excellent seat. For an elderly fellow."

"I believe that the baronet is a guest at Beaurepaire," Lucy Portal said. This was a very ancient manor near Sherborne St. John owned by the Brocas family, who fought with the Black Prince at Poitiers and Crécy. "I invited them to dine with us last evening, but they very properly declined a journey of ten miles, on an evening without a moon. See, there is Sir Bernard Brocas, on the black gelding, beside his friend."

I ignored the Brocas baronet, but eyed Sir William with interest; it was his son of the same name who had married—and widowed far too young—my dear friend Elizabeth Bigg. She had returned to her girlhood home of Manydown some five years ago—and there she must remain, now that dear John Harwood is too ruined to marry her.[11]

We quitted the coach and stepped down onto the sparkling grass

---

[11] The Bigg-Wither family of Manydown House, six miles from Steventon, had some of Jane's oldest friends. She briefly accepted the hand of Harris Bigg-Wither, Elizabeth's younger brother, in marriage in 1802, before regretting her decision and breaking off the engagement. Jane was five years older than Harris, who was described as ungainly and prone to stuttering.—Editor's note.

of the village green—where the snow had fallen yesterday, was this morning the remains of a black frost, and the air was decidedly chill at our noses. The gentlemen of our party dismounted and walked their hunters slowly into the throng, hailing their acquaintance; I saw James throw his arm round his son and present him with pride to numerous fellows. This was something like a schoolboy's holiday from Winchester!

"Tally-ho, Austens!"

Eliza's animated voice, carrying across the green. She was on foot, her long train looped over her arm, and slightly breathless from negotiating the crowd. "Mrs. Austen, I have not time to do the pretty as I ought—but allow me to beg you most earnestly to join us, along with all your party at Steventon, on Twelfth Night for our Children's Ball."

"You mean to go forward?" my mother cried, clapping her hands. "I am so glad I did not undertake to quit the parsonage this morning. I should have missed all the fun!"

"Nonsense! Your beautiful cards of invitation had all gone out already; and we are owed a little enjoyment, I think, after all our trials," Eliza retorted robustly. "I depend upon you coming to us tomorrow and staying the next two nights—for we have all our arrangements to consider, and will require considerable preparation. Jane must advise me on Characters—and Cassandra will be wanted about the costumes. Mary, of course, may offer her suggestions as to our menu."

This last trailed away on an uncertain note, as tho' Eliza had only just recollected Mary's presence.

We offered our eager thanks and promised our assistance.

"Do not forget to bring James-Edward and Caroline," Eliza called over her shoulder. "I should not have Jemima miss our revels for worlds!"

And then, through a parting in the mill of hunters and horseflesh, I saw him. Mr. Raphael West.

He was holding the bridle of a pretty little mare with an Arab head, who stood docilely enough by his side. Not far away was William Chute in his Master's garb, and a few paces behind, holding the reins of two more horses—Mr. Benedict L'Anglois. I supposed one could not be a truly first-rate secretary, unless one could ride to hounds.

A lady on horseback passed between us then, veiling the grouping from my sight. Mr. West, returned so soon from his business! And ready, apparently, to gallop through coverts in search of a fox! It did not appear that intrigues of French spies claimed too much of his time; and had there not been the memory of the bodies in the Chapel, I might have believed he invented the whole, to pass a tedious interval among spinsters in the country.

Another instant, and I found that he was bowing in front of our party, his horse left in charge of L'Anglois.

"Mrs. Austen," he said cheerfully. "Mrs. James Austen, and Miss Austen, Miss Jane Austen—I do not have the honour of knowing your friend."

Mary smoothly intervened here, and made Mr. West her gift to bestow upon Lucy Portal; and our acquaintance from The Vyne as well as the celebrated painter Mr. Benjamin West's son, were offered for her delectation. Mrs. Portal dimpled at West and curtseyed. "The honour is mine," she said gracefully. "I have long admired your father's genius."

How tedious it must be, to be welcomed always for one's father's sake.

"You ladies do not ride?" His gaze and his politeness were general; those probing eyes barely grazed my countenance.

"Only the gentlemen, sir," Lucy replied.

"Then I shall hope to find you later, established in the Swan," he said gallantly, "when we have galloped back, shivering and hopeless. No fox worth his pelt will poke his nose out-of-doors, on such a freezing day! Mrs. James Austen, I must beg you to hurry inside, or you shall certainly catch your death!"

Sensible of the compliment he paid her, Mary walked immediately in the direction of the publick house; a servant stood in front of the entrance with a steaming cauldron of stirrup cup.

"Jane," he muttered low when I would have passed with the others.

I saw Cassandra glance over her shoulder, and then walk on.

"Mr. West."

"Do you think it wise to quit the protection of your brother? Anyone might strike at you in this crowd. It should be as nothing to run you down with a horse, and claim an accident. Promise me you will not stir out of the Swan alone until the gentlemen of your party are returned."

I lifted my brows at him coolly. "You persist in believing me an object of violence, sir? I wonder, then, that you chose to quit the county these past several days."

"I thought you safe in Steventon—and went in pursuit of certain information I would gladly share, when once this fox is run to ground. Look for me at the Swan."

He touched the brim of his hat and wheeled away; William Chute was already mounted, and the hounds had been let slip from the carts in which they had been carried the three miles to Sherborne. They set off in a tightly coursing pack through the main street of the village, William Chute following behind. In a beautiful stream of colour and motion, the rest of the riders urged their horses after the Master of The Vyne, towards the open country and coverts beyond.

I flinched suddenly as a horse shied too near my head, and jumped back from the verge of the green. *Anyone might strike at you in this crowd.* Raphael West's words echoed in my ears like a prediction.

I glanced up—Benedict L'Anglois, an expression of consternation on his handsome countenance as he struggled to control one of Chute's high-spirited hunters. Perhaps he did not hunt so very much, after all. "Your pardon, Miss Austen!"

I waved my acknowledgement, and hurried to join the other ladies at their stirrup cup.

2 4

CUT DEAD

Monday, 2nd January 1815
Steventon Parsonage, cont'd.

We were a merry party in the Swan's snug side parlour that wintry January morning. Any number of ladies had driven out to see their gentlemen trot off in negligent stile behind William Chute, and tho' some might turn round directly and seek the comfort of their homes, those who lived too far distant were resigned to stay until the Hunt should return. The Swan's affable proprietor, Mr. Gigeon, supplied us with milk punch, rashers of bacon, custard tarts and apple pastries, cheese from Cheddar and Frome, and slices of his own smoked ham. Those of us who had endured a lengthy carriage ride to reach Sherborne St. John were only too happy to sample Mr. Gigeon's fare; and when his lady appeared with venison pie, hot from the oven, our happiness was complete.

"I do not intend to ask after brawn," my mother confided as she sampled a custard tart. "I am sure the Swan's must be superior; but I shall be treated to it upon another occasion, perhaps."

A fire roared in the hearth; our situation was entirely private from the general run of the publick house's patrons; and a dull sunshine picked out the lead in the old inn's windowpanes. I seated myself

264 · STEPHANIE BARRON

on a settee near Cassandra whilst my mother renewed acquaintance with some friends from Deane, where the Harwoods lived. John Harwood, it seemed, had sold his father's string of hunters—he could no longer support a stable, and was not to be found among the handsome company that had ridden out this morning. It must be gall and wormwood, to continue in a neighbourhood where one had been accustomed to figure as squire—and to have the entire world talking over your misfortunes.

"Were you happy to see Mr. Raphael West, Jane?" Cassandra enquired, breaking in upon my reflections.

I toyed with a slice of bacon. "No more than yourself, my dear. He is an engaging acquaintance, to be sure—with so much knowledge of the world, and of the people in it."

"I wonder at his remaining in Hampshire so long," she said slowly. "Surely it cannot require much more of his time, to capture William Chute's likeness? His talents are so great—his hand so swift. I should labour a fortnight to express on paper what he achieves in a quarter-hour."

I turned my head aside, so as not to appear to scrutinise my sister too closely. Cassandra has mourned her long-lost love, Tom Fowle, nearly twenty years—since his needless death of yellow fever in Santo Domingo. To my knowledge, she has never seriously entertained an attachment since. To her, Tom's memory is sacred; her heart went into a tropick grave. Was it possible that her connexion with Raphael West—a man whose first love was also gone, and who shared her love of Art—had awakened a flame in the embers of Cass's heart?

I could not follow the thought too nearly; it suggested the possibility of pain. I said only, "Mrs. Bramston informs me that Mr. West has lately been in London. He is only just returned to The Vyne from business there. I confess I am surprized he should chuse to reenter a house and a situation from which he was lately freed—but there is no accounting for the tastes of gentlemen, to be sure."

"If he lost several days in his journey, perhaps he does require further poses of William Chute. There can be nothing else of importance to call him back here," Cassandra said evasively.

Did she look to me for reassurance? Did she wish me to declare as boldly as my character might, that Mr. West had formed an attachment to shy, principled, retiring Cassandra and her tentative sketchbook—or to declare, rather, that he had returned to Hampshire for me?

I could neither support nor crush her hopes so entirely. I did not believe either conjecture to be true. I sensed in Raphael West a single-minded purpose, beyond the petty interests of those around him. He reminded me more strongly than any I had encountered since Lord Harold's death, of that steely gentleman. Like the Gentleman Rogue, West's intellect was engaged in a higher and more deadly game than mere courtship. He treated with the fate of Nations, and the men who would rule them. What were affairs of the heart, but indulgent distractions?

I would never set myself up as rival to Cassandra. It was a fond saying of my mother's, when both of us were young, that if Cass were to be taken to have her head cut off, I would be clamouring for the treat, too. —So much did I always adore my elder sister. I will never have her goodness—I am cursed with a sharper mind, a more restless spirit, an unendurable dissatisfaction with the inequities of life. Cassandra is one of the Blessed. I should leave her in her little fever of happiness over Raphael West, and let time work the necessary correction.

AFTER AN HOUR OR so of lingering within doors, our group of ladies—some eleven in number, counting the folk from

Deane—began to surfeit of food and indolence. My sister took out her sketchbook to capture the scene in charcoal. My mother unearthed her netting—she had embarked upon another reticule, a diminutive one intended for Jemima. I strolled to the window and gazed out upon the monochrome of January. A churned stableyard; the dark etching of elm and oak against a livid sky. I wondered whether I might hear a hunting horn or the baying of distant hounds, if I ventured out-of-doors—but no doubt the pack was miles distant by now.

"Should you like to take a turn along the lane, Miss Austen? The ground is rather dirty, but after so long an interval in the carriage, I confess I am wild to be in the air."

Lucy Portal. *Wild* appeared to be a favoured word; and it captured the impulsive nature that shone from her open countenance. "I should be happy to. But are you well enough?"

"Perfectly—else I should not have suggested the scheme."

If her indisposition was pregnancy, she was not very far along. I reached for my spencer, gloves, and bonnet, and told my mother I should return presently. I half-expected Mary to force herself upon us, but discovered that she was dozing in a chair by the fire. Cassandra lifted her finger to her lips in an appeal for silence. Lucy and I crept out of the side parlour.

She sighed with relief once we had gained the road in front of the village green. "There appear to be a few shops over there," she said, gesturing vaguely, "but I confess that to be shopping is not at all what I intended. I want a brisk interval of exercise, which no amount of dawdling in front of milliners' windows may supply."

I declared myself of her opinion, and so we set off in the direction the Hunt had taken that morning, towards the open country beyond the village.

"I am glad you were so good as to accompany me, Miss Austen, for I intend to interrogate you."

"Indeed?" I returned politely.

"Ever since Mrs. James Austen let slip this morning that poor Miss Gambier is believed to have been murdered, I have been on the fidgets! You must know that we passed much of our girlhood together."

"I did not. I am very sorry for your loss." Of course Mary must be saying what she should not, in canvassing the sensation at The Vyne. I had barely overlistened her conversation in the carriage this morning, but her indiscretion could not surprize me.

"Miss Gambier was forever visiting Freefolk Priors, while old General Sir Mathew leased the manor from my husband's father, Harry Portal. Miss Gambier's mother was the General's niece, you know."

"I had forgot Mr. Portal's father owned the General's house!" I exclaimed. "And so your husband grew up there, before it was let?"

"In the old place. The manor at Freefolk Priors has since been pulled down. When the General died, John's father built Laverstoke House new upon the site. John's elder brother, William, lives there now. But I persist in thinking of the place as it was in the Mathews and Gambiers' day. Which, of course, is my own!"

"You grew up in the same neighbourhood, I collect?"

"In Whitchurch, but a mile distant. I met my husband at the Basingstoke assemblies."

They had much to answer for, those balls—James had fallen in love with Anne Mathew, the General's daughter, at one of them.

"I fell out of my acquaintance with Mary Gambier," Lucy Portal continued, "once I married. Our paths lay apart. But I was fortunate enough to discover her living in Bath about a year ago—we took a house in Laura Place, you know, while Ashe Park was being refurbished—and should have been happy to renew our friendship."

"She was not?" I asked.

Lucy hesitated. "I should say rather that she was changed. The open character I recalled from our youth had become guarded and opaque. To call her aloof must suggest a conscious revulsion from my overtures; say rather that she barely noticed them. She appeared to me as one who had, in some measure, renounced Society and all its pleasures."

In the distance I caught the faint sound of baying. The pack was in full throat; the fox must have broken. Even now the bright stream of horses and riders, vivid spots of colour in the landscape, must be coursing after the Master.

"I should describe Miss Gambier in much the same terms," I said. "Her character appeared as a puzzle. She was often on her knees in The Vyne Chapel—but given what occurred there last week, this is hardly wonderful."

"Mrs. Austen suggested there was an attachment between Miss Gambier and the messenger who was killed."

"So it appeared," I said carefully. "Can you tell me, Mrs. Portal, whether there was any mystery surrounding Mary Gambier, when you met her in Bath? A whisper of scandal, perhaps, or a rumour that persuaded her to avoid Society?"

She shook her head. "If Mary suffered from idle talk, it was not on her own account."

"Her brother's, perhaps?"

"Edward!" Lucy smiled indulgently, as one who has known a man first as a troublesome boy. "He was at Oxford that year, I believe—and must have persecuted only his tutors. No, Miss Austen, I refer to Lady Gambier. There are many in Bath who refuse to receive her."

My footsteps slowed. "She is a difficult personality, to be sure. But . . . to cut her dead? Whatever for?"

Lucy Portal might have answered me. But at that moment, the clatter of a horse, galloping flat-out, assailed our ears. We turned as one and gazed up the lane towards the coverts. I did not recognise the rider at first, but then Lucy clutched at my arm.

"Your nephew, Miss Austen," she said. "And in a tearing hurry. Whatever can be wrong?"

I think we both expected James-Edward to pull up his horse and speak to us as he approached, but to our surprise he did neither. He was clinging to Trooper's neck like a monkey, and if I had not known what an excellent rider he was, I should have suspected the horse of running away with him. His mouth was set in a grim line as he swept past, and his gaze did not swerve from his object. Indeed, it is probable that Lucy and I were invisible to him.

Without a word we gathered our skirts and hastened back the way we had come. We were in time to meet James-Edward at the door of the Swan, already remounting his horse.

"What is it?" I cried, as he turned Trooper impatiently back towards the open lane. In the stableyard behind, an ostler was harnessing a team to a cart.

"An accident," James-Edward said, his eyes on the cart.

I realised with foreboding it was meant to follow him—and take up a body.

"Who?" I demanded.

"Mr. West. He was thrown from his mount, and took a nasty knock on the head."

"His neck is not broken?" Lucy Portal faltered. Of all injuries on the hunting field, it must be the most dreaded.

"Or his back?" I said.

James-Edward lifted his shoulders. "Who can say? He is insensible. Papa could not rouse him. Mr. Chute sent me back for the surgeon—but he is attending a birth at Monk Sherborne, I'm told. We shall bring Mr. West back here in the cart."

"Better than lying in a field," Lucy said.

I attempted to nod. A cold desolation spread through me.

MRS. GIGEON, THE PUBLICAN'S wife, ordered a fire lit in her best bedchamber and set cans of water to heat on the kitchen hearth. A stable lad was sent on horseback to Monk Sherborne in search of the surgeon—a man named Price—and an air of urgency overtook the Swan. For those of us who were acquainted with Raphael West, and forced to wait in idle suspense, the interval before the cart's return was an unhappy one. The folk from Deane might gossip and smile, while those who had been intimate at The Vyne must collect in silence by the parlour window.

"An accident?" Cassandra muttered. "Oh, Jane—"

I clasped her fingers in my own. "I cannot help but think of Madam Lefroy."

Ben's mother, Anne Lefroy, and my own dear friend—who died from a similar fall from her horse nearly ten years ago.

"I daresay it is another of these murders," my mother supplied philosophically, as tho' she referred to comets coursing unexpectedly across the night sky. "It is too much to believe that Providence would strike from caprice, when the Chutes have already borne so much!"

"Do we know how the fall occurred?" Cassandra asked.

Mary might be of importance, here. "James-Edward says that Mr. West was crammed before a fence, and thrown."

"Crammed?" I repeated. "By whom?"

"James-Edward did not say. I suppose he did not notice. It may have been more than one rider, perhaps."

Cramming was the bane of good horsemen—when less experienced hunters, or wilder mounts, forced their way too close to one preparing to leap over an obstacle. It might well have been a chance encounter, such as should occur on any hunting field.

But my heart argued it was not.

He had warned me to guard myself. He had feared that I would be an object of violence. When in fact . . .

"If only he had stayed in London," I muttered.

"Girls," my mother cried, "James is come!"

I leaned over her shoulder—Mamma is shorter than I by several inches—and stared through the frost-rimed windowpane. My brother led a sort of cortège, with William Chute at his side. Behind them came the Swan's cart, driven by its chief ostler, and bearing within— God knows what tragic figure. As I watched, James pulled up Aristo and dismounted, handing the reins to a stable lad.

We hastened as one to the door. James had jumped into the cart and was lifting Raphael West's shoulders. Despite myself, I winced; if the spine should be damaged—

William Chute was at his feet, and had grasped West's ankles. The stable lad hurried to support the midsection, and slowly—slowly— our friend was eased from the bed of his conveyance.

I waited until the men should have turned with their burden, to face the Swan's front door—saw his white face and shuttered eyes, the way his head lolled helplessly on one shoulder—and felt ill. I stepped backwards, into the hall. Cassandra started forward.

She knew nothing, of course, of his true employment—nothing of the restless spirit that urged him to direct his wit against the enemies of the Crown. Nothing of the Secret Funds, or his constant exposure to danger. She knew only the sensitive hands that captured the world on paper as surely and swiftly as an angel, and the probing gaze that saw into one's very soul.

William Chute eased his burden into the Swan's foyer. The other two men followed him across the threshold. I could not help but recall a similar group of bearers who had laboured under my eye, carrying John Gage's body back into The Vyne. The two scenes possessed a fearful symmetry.

"How very ill he looks, to be sure," Mary whispered audibly as Raphael West was carried above-stairs. "They say that three times is the charm, poor fellow. I suspect he shall not last out the night."

THE TENTH DAY

2 5

HOLDING VIGIL

Tuesday, 3rd January 1815
Steventon Parsonage

I did not sleep at all well last night. Upon our return at dusk to Steventon in John Portal's carriage, I had believed myself utterly drained from the emotions of the day; so exhausted that a little soup was all I could stomach, before bidding my equally enervated companions *adieux*, and hastening to my bedchamber.

But sleep would not come to ease my troubled mind. Scenes of the previous hours would intrude, and with them the speculation so natural to one anxious for Raphael West's survival. I was constantly on the twitch for a knock at the door, during the late hours of night and the early hours of this morning—for James had remained at Sherborne St. John, in the event that final absolution was requested.

He was still insensible when carried up to the Swan's bedchamber. William Chute and my brother removed his clothes and dressed his inert form in one of Gigeon's nightshirts. He was kept warm, and a little brandy placed between his lips, and hartshorn tried under his nostrils. He did not stir, even when the contusion at the rear of his head was bathed with warm water, and a poultice applied. The skin had not been broken, and there was no blood to be seen, but the reports we received in the side parlour were guarded.

"He did ought to have come around by now," Mrs. Gigeon observed when an hour had passed, "unless it be that that there skull is cracked. My sister knew a man once, knocked down in the street in Lunnon, who stood up—got into his carriage—drove back to his grand house—and died in his Saloon a bit later. There's no telling, with blows to the head."

It was full three o'clock before the surgeon arrived from his troublesome labour, and tho' our relief at his appearance was immense, he did little more than palpate the scalp. Mr. Price opened West's eyes, which appeared to see nothing; listened to his heart; and felt for a pulse—which he proclaimed to be tumultuous. He then bled him a pint, and ordered that he should be called, no matter what the hour, if there was any change.

James told us all this when he came down to bid us farewell. Mr. and Mrs. Portal, tho' considerably moved by our friend's fate, could not entirely share our anxiety—Raphael West being a stranger to them. They were naturally eager to be getting home to their children.

"Go with them, Mary," James ordered. "Chute has sent word to The Vyne. He and I shall remain, to do all that body or soul may require."

With this we were forced to be content.

It was a silent and dull ten miles, back to Ashe Park. I stirred myself only once, to enquire of John Portal whether he had witnessed the accident. He had not. He had jumped the hedge well before Mr. West, and had turned back with Chute when another hunter blew his horn. Considerable confusion then reigned. He had heard something of cramming. He considered it impossible to know who was responsible.

Only little Caroline chattered the remainder of our journey to the parsonage. Jemima, it seemed, had been a great success in the Portal nursery.

THERE CAME NO SUMMONS, no word in the night. I must have slept at last, for the morning light at the window awakened me. I lay there an instant, conscious of a great oppression looming at the edge of my mind. And then I remembered. Did no news mean good news—or bad? Was West unchanged—or beyond all care?

I rose from the bed and donned my dressing gown.

The addition to Jemima's wardrobe today was a diminutive Paisley shawl, cut from a real one that my brother Frank had brought as a present from India, years ago. Appropriate for a winter day when Caroline and her doll should be fettered within doors, pacing the floors as women so often must—or hemmed in by sopha cushions, with only books and needlework to hand. It should never have been appropriate for me to remain behind with James at the Swan, but I was certain I should waste every hour of this unfortunate day, in waiting for intelligence of the patient.

Cook was bustling about the kitchen, tho' no sign of her mistress could be found. My mother, like Cassandra, was still abed. I fetched my own teacups and pot and carried them on a tray back upstairs to wake Cassandra. We deserved a little Vyne indolence to comfort us this morning.

JAMES APPEARED, LOOKING QUITE weary, at a few minutes past eleven o'clock. He came in through the rear of the house, from the stables, so we did not know immediately that he was home. I had been endeavouring to work at the negligible pages of my latest story—my frivolous madcap Emma is about to have her nose put out of joint by a proposal from the odious Mr. Elton—and found the effort ill-advised. When one's mind is darting with anxiety, it must be impossible to string three coherent words together. Add to this the vexation of a poorly-mended pen, which drove me out of the parlour in search of a knife. In the passage I encountered James, entering his book room.

I stopped short. "What news?"

"There has been no change."

"He is still insensible?"

James nodded listlessly. "Price believes the case is not hopeless— but it shall be as God wills. Chute intends to remove him tomorrow to The Vyne."

"His unfortunate father has been informed?"

"I believe Chute intended to despatch an Express to London."

I clasped my shaking hands and raised them to my lips. "I shall tell Cassandra."

"Jane—"

"Yes?"

"We are still bidden to The Vyne tomorrow for this foolish Children's Ball. Eliza means to go forward, Chute says, as half the county has been invited. Perhaps by then West will have come to his senses. You need not entirely despair."

I nodded, unable to speak. Kindness from James was altogether unexpected. We were not in the habit of offering each other sympathy.

I left him to the solitude of his book room, and went to find my sister. How many hours remained, before I might once more enter The Vyne, and look with my own eyes on one who might, even then, be gone?

THE ELEVENTH DAY

2 6

SKETCHING THE TRUTH

Wednesday, 4th January 1815
The Vyne

T he Yule log, to Caroline's delight, was still burning in the
Staircase Hall—tho' considerably reduced in girth and grandeur. She took Jemima to it immediately, so that the doll should
not suffer a chill in removing her wraps. Today Jemima was arrayed
in a pale green spencer over a gown of Irish linen, worked with
green crewels—run up from scraps Cassandra had kept from one of
her own gowns, years ago. I had searched half of London for those
lengths of linen, I recalled; and now the dress was fit only for the
rag bag. Caroline, however, reveled in the fanciful crewels nearly as
much as Cassandra once had.

We collected near the fire, awaiting Eliza. The taciturn Roark had
gone to inform her of our arrival, while footmen carried our things to
our familiar bedchambers. Our party was in general subdued, with
the exception of Mary—who seemed conscious only of the promised
Children's Ball, and her own daring in defying her husband's wish
not to attend it.

"Ah, the Austens!" Eliza cried, advancing upon us with her
hands outstretched. "How happy I am in my good friends—and how

excessively grateful that you have come, to lighten a little the air of gloom in this house!"

"How does Mr. West go on?" my mother asked immediately, as she removed her gloves and bonnet.

"He is unchanged." The twinkle of welcome fled from Eliza's countenance. "Mr. Price has been to see him, and has bled him again. There is no fever, and no sinking of the pulse—but no sign of consciousness, either."

"His poor father," my mother murmured.

"William has had a reply to his Express to London. The old gentleman is much grieved—this news, coming hard on the heels of the death of his beloved wife, is dreadful! He is far too frail, however, to make the journey into Hampshire at this time of year. We are aware that Mr. West also possesses a daughter—but we do not know her married name! It is most vexatious—"

"Indeed," Mary interjected, "for if Mr. West dies, you will be forced to bear all the expence of conveying his corpse to London. I wonder that his father did not consider of it!"

This observation had the power to strike us all dumb. Thankfully, Eliza suggested we seek refreshment in the Saloon, and we hastened to avail ourselves of William Chute's Madeira and claret.

The Master of The Vyne Hunt looked tired almost beyond recognition. In my preoccupation with his more immediate troubles, I had ceased to consider the weight of anxiety caused by the continued loss of the missing Treaty, as well as the unexplained murders. I expressed my concern for his health, but Chute brushed this aside affably enough.

"I cannot mend what I cannot help," he observed. "We shall procure another copy of the signed Treaty. Castlereagh is to return to London in February, you know—the Duke of Wellington is to take his place in Vienna—and my burdens in Parliament will be considerably eased. It is just as well, now that Ben has left me."

"I beg your pardon, sir?"

"Mr. L'Anglois," Chute said. "He has reconsidered of his decision to remain in England."

I glanced about the Saloon, and indeed, there was no sign of the secretary.

"A letter arrived from Paris the very morning of our Hunt," Chute continued. "The Comte d'Artois was most pressing in his desire for Ben to join him—and I cannot blame the fellow for wanting to be away. I suspect he had a *tendre* for Miss Gambier, you know. His spirits have been very low since her death. He took it hard."

I recollected L'Anglois's white face and stricken looks as we discovered the body lying by John Gage's bier. His effort to engage Miss Gambier with sheet music from France. I had suspected an attachment. With the lady in her grave, there could be nothing more for him in Hampshire—perhaps nothing more in England. My own brother Charles had found balm for suffering, in flight.

"He waited only to see West safely returned to The Vyne," Chute concluded, "before he bid us farewell this morning. Such a competent fellow. It shall be long and long before I find another like him."

"What is your opinion of Mr. West?" I asked in a lowered tone. "Has no one said how the accident on the hunting field occurred?"

Chute shook his head. "L'Anglois saw West's horse crammed—but was too unfamiliar with the neighbourhood to recognise the rider. West had stopped but a few moments before to sketch the scene, I believe, and most of the field had gone on before him. Certainly no one has admitted to the fault."

"He had his sketchbook with him?" I exclaimed. "Where is it now?"

"In his room." Chute furrowed his brows. "Should you like to see it, Miss Jane?"

"Very much," I replied.

MY HOST ENDEARED HIMSELF further by keeping his intentions from the rest of our party. He moved among his guests with frank good humour, chaffing James-Edward on his excellent seat and admiring Jemima's costume. He complimented Mary on her good looks, and brought a blush to my mother's countenance by saluting her cheek. On the ostensible errand of replenishing our glasses, he exited the Saloon, and not ten minutes later bent to inform me, in a subdued whisper, that the sketchbook was now in his book room. I might be private there. From all this I concluded that William Chute regarded me in some wise as a co-conspirator, and thought discretion our friend.

I AM UNCERTAIN WHAT I thought to find in looking through West's drawings. The mounted rider who had caused his injury? That should not be possible—the horseman had presumably come upon him from behind as he was in the act of jumping the hedge, not while he was at rest, with charcoal in hand. I sought the sketch-book because I wished to know West's mind—and being injured, it was more than ever barred to me. Were I in similar circumstances, I should hope my friends would think to consult my journal. West's sketchbook was his daily record, his visual memory.

The initial pages were unfamiliar: scenes of domestic life, of a young woman with her head bowed over a book. His late wife? Or his daughter? Someone else who was dear to him?

These pictures gave way to studies of draperies on a classical figure; of a cuff and a wrist and the fingers of a male hand; of a

Gypsy grouping beneath the spreading branches of an ancient oak; the lineaments of a horse, and the remnants of a tavern meal scattered upon a table. There was a series of sketches in charcoal that must tighten my throat with wonder—a human forearm, with its inner structure of muscle and bone revealed. How had he seen this? Was it imagined, or real? Had he lifted the skin of a man or—I swallowed convulsively—a corpse?

But I was taking too much time. My absence from the Saloon should be noted.

I paged hurriedly through the various studies of William Chute, recently taken, until I reached the last sketch I had glimpsed—the one of Amy Gage and her son in the Angel Inn at Basingstoke.

So vivid was the image of the woman—the page summoning her to life—that my eyes widened a little. I turned to the next drawing. This was the likeness of the boy alone—a soft and angelic portrait. How had West obtained it? He had written one word beneath: Jem. It was the sort of name Mrs. Gage might chuse, when a more genteel woman should insist upon James.

I studied the boy's features. I could not find John Gage in them; but I had known the Lieutenant so briefly, my memory of him had begun to fade.

Next there was a sketch I recognised—of the Portsmouth Naval Yard. Masts strove for pride of place, while figures in uniform hurried by. West had gone to Portsmouth as well as to London, then. I considered this bit of intelligence. He had referred to a French spy, taken in the Bosun's Whistle. He had sought some evidence of connexion between Amy Gage and the traitor. Had he found it?

I turned eagerly to the next sketch—but it was a series of ledger entries rather than a picture. I peered closer, my eyes weak in the light cast by the book room fire. It appeared to be a baptismal register—with the usual names and dates. Lieutenant Gage and his wife, Amy, had baptised their son, James, on the sixteenth of March, 1813, in the Portsmouth Garrison Chapel.

"They were truly married, then," I murmured to myself. "Poor Mary Gambier."

I turned the page, and saw a copy of the Naval List for 1811. Admiral Lord Gambier had been assigned to the Atlantic Station; his first lieutenant, John Gage.

The final leaf in Raphael West's book was another copy of a ledger—this time, from St. Martin-in-the-Fields, London. I searched the list of names for one I might recognise.

And naturally, I found it.

John Gage, bachelor, resident of Greenwich, holding the King's Commission in the Royal Navy, had married Aimée L'Anglois, spinster, late of Montreal, on the first of March, 1813.

A mere fifteen days before the baptism of their child, who—judging by his present appearance—must even then have been a year and a half old.

I stared at the sketchbook lying open in my hands. L'Anglois. And her Christian name spelled in the French stile, as befit a girl from Quebec.

How had she come to be in England? How had she met John Gage? What was her relation to Benedict L'Anglois? Sister? Cousin? Cast-off wife?

And was Lieutenant Gage's murder in fact a personal matter—a crime of passion between two men, divided over a single woman?

I shook my head in vexation.

Then why steal the Treaty?

Or kill Mary Gambier?

The sound of footsteps on the stairs persuaded me to close the sketchbook and return it to Chute's writing table. But I had only just achieved the book room doorway when William Chute appeared, Lord Bolton on his heels.

"Miss Austen," Chute said. "You remember his lordship."

"Perfectly." I curtseyed.

"He has come to talk over this sad affair of West's. Have you looked into that sketchbook?"

"I have, sir."

"Did you discover anything of interest?"

"That it is most unfortunate you allowed Mr. L'Anglois to quit The Vyne."

"Hey?" Chute frowned. "You must explain. Pray take a chair, my lord. Sit down, Jane."

I sat. I opened the sketchbook to the critical pages. I allowed William Chute and his neighbour ample time to study them. I waited. The expressions on the two men's countenances were puzzled.

At last, Chute sat back in his chair and stared at me pugnaciously.

"I deduce that the widowed Mrs. Gage is a connexion of Ben L'Anglois," he said. "You will remember L'Anglois, Bolton—my secretary. He left us for Paris only this morning. He is to rejoin his patron, the Comte d'Artois, at the Bourbon court."

"I see," Lord Bolton said.

I doubted that he saw very much.

"But his having the same family name as Mrs. Gage does not make him the Lieutenant's murderer," Chute continued. "If anything, it makes the two men family."

"Then why did Mr. L'Anglois not acknowledge as much, when they were seated here at the same dinner table?" I enquired. "Why fail to mention his family, once Lieutenant Gage lay dead?"

"The same may be asked of the Lieutenant," Chute countered. "He did not own a relationship."

"He may never have learnt your secretary's true name," I suggested. "Recollect, Mr. Chute, your wife was forever calling him Mr. Langles."

Chute grimaced.

"Mr. West went to Portsmouth," I continued, "because he knew a French spy had been taken there. He knew Amy Gage lived there. He was attempting to find some connexion between Portsmouth and this house—and he found it, sir, in Benedict L'Anglois."

"That is nowhere shewn in these pages," Chute said stubbornly. "West discovered the record of the Gage marriage, and their child's baptism; well and good. That says nothing to the point of murder."

"Unless Mrs. Gage was first Mr. L'Anglois's wife," I suggested. "In which case, her second marriage is bigamous."

Chute snorted. Lord Bolton looked intensely uncomfortable. I imagine that a lady as wanting in propriety as myself has rarely come in his lordship's way.

"You will observe that the marriage occurred only two weeks before the child was christened, in London," I added.

"But from the Naval List, we know that the Lieutenant was serving on the Atlantic Station for some time," Chute said.

"The usual port of call is Halifax, I believe," Lord Bolton contributed. "Is it possible Gage met his wife while on shore in Canada?"

"Most probable," I agreed. "But why wait to marry, years after the child's birth?"

Chute lifted his shoulders. "Perhaps Gage was forced into it! Admiral Gambier is everywhere known as a pious and religious man. He should not scruple to enforce a marriage if he thought Gage had wronged the girl. She may have brought the Admiral her grievance.

He may even have carried the bride to England, and seen the marriage performed."

"—then punished Lieutenant Gage by refusing to advance his rank," I mused. "I thought the Lieutenant ought to have made Master or even Post Captain by this time. But if Admiral Gambier disapproved of John Gage's conduct, the case becomes clearer."

"We shall not know for certain, without we question his widow." Chute sighed.

"Indeed. Tell me, Mr. Chute—do you know where Benedict L'Anglois grew up?" I asked.

"In Canada," he admitted heavily. "I discovered that fact among his references. His mother is English, but he was educated in Paris."

"Hence his command of languages. He must have been invaluable to his Bourbon patron," I said. "Or to whomever else paid him."

If Chute caught my meaning, he did not betray it. "The Comte d'Artois employed him for seven years," he said. "Before that, he was in Paris. It must be many years since he crossed the Atlantic."

"Perhaps he married Amy too young," I suggested. "Perhaps she thought him dead—and he allowed her to believe it so."

"But even if we grant that L'Anglois and Mrs. Gage are related," Chute said, "wife, sister—that does not account for the murder of Mary Gambier. L'Anglois was absent from The Vyne when it occurred."

"I know. It is all wrong!" I admitted in frustration, "starting with the child."

"The child?"

"Jem, I think Mr. West called him."

Chute turned to the sketch.

"Recall the charades on Christmas night," I persisted. "Natural son. The riddle that so offended Mary Gambier."

"Jem is certainly that."

"But why should the barb strike at her? And why must her aunt nearly faint?" I rose from my seat and began to pace restlessly before the fire. "Why should Mary be murdered, because Benedict L'Anglois is a cuckold? Why draw her figure as a crucified martyr? And God in Heaven, Mr. Chute—why steal the Ghent Treaty, if all this violence is due to an affair of the heart?"

It was Lord Bolton who answered.

"To make a personal murder appear to be a political one," he said.

"If personal," I mused, "the grudge ought to have ended with John Gage's death. But the violence continued. Miss Gambier is dead, and Mr. West lies insensible, after his accident yesterday. Mr. L'Anglois claimed to have witnessed the cramming of Mr. West's horse. Is it so unlikely that he crammed Mr. West himself—with the intent of silencing him?"

"Because of these sketches?" Chute demanded. "How could Ben know of them?"

"Perhaps he was merely afraid of what Mr. West might suspect," I said. "Mr. L'Anglois knew Mr. West had gone to London; he saw Mr. West return to The Vyne. The more a murderer's suspicions swell, the more violence he commits."

"Ben must be found," William Chute said brusquely. "We cannot go on accusing him of the most hideous deeds, without he is allowed to answer for them. It is not the way of Justice."

"I am of your opinion, Mr. Chute," I said. "I should dearly love to hear Mr. L'Anglois explain himself. Send word to the principal Channel ports, by all means—and see if you may secure him."

27

CHARACTERS

Wednesday, 4th January 1815
The Vyne, cont'd.

"Jane," Mary said indignantly, "it is not to be borne! Here I have gone to all the trouble of searching out my sister Martha's receipt for Brandy Pudding"—Martha is by far the best cook of the three Lloyd sisters—"and Eliza refuses to entertain the notion of a flaming sweet! She is all for the fashion that is so much the rage in London."

"What is that, Mary?"

"Twelfth Night cake." She uttered the final word with loathing. "I do not know what we are come to, if one cannot eat pudding on the fifth of January."

"Given the number of place cards I am writing out," Cassandra said in a harassed voice, "we ought to have several of both. Surely Mrs. Chute will offer more than one sweet?"

"That is an excellent notion," Mary replied. "I shall tell her it is my sisters' opinion that cake alone shall not do. Eliza cannot stand firm against all the Austens."

She hurried off, triumphant for once in her association with our family.

292 • STEPHANIE BARRON

"We should be happy, I suppose, that she has so much energy." My mother sighed. "It appears to thrive on opposition. Jane, dear, do you think James will consent to figure as the Lord of Misrule? For you know he does not in general approve of orgies."

"I hardly think a Children's Ball may be called an orgy, Mamma."

"Perhaps I have got the word wrong. Only, on the last occasion when we discussed the matter, your brother was most decided in condemning every form of Twelfth Night masquerade as a . . . a . . ."

"Saturnalia," I supplied. "Appoint James-Edward Lord of Misrule, Mamma. Twelfth Night is an occasion for liberty—and putting sons in command of their fathers."

"I sometimes wonder what my dear husband would chuse to say about James," my mother mourned. "He seems most averse to innocent enjoyment. As tho' joy were the stepchild of Evil. For what else did Providence intend us, my dears, if not happiness?"

"James would argue, suffering," Cassandra supplied.

"James has got it all wrong," Mamma said firmly, and wrote James-Edward's name under Lord of Misrule.

Topsy-turvy is the only order of the day—or night, as it happens—on the Eve of the Epiphany. My brother is not far wrong in seeing Twelfth Night as a threat to decency. For women are expected to dress as men, and men, as women. Children hold court at the Children's Ball, with their parents as toad-eating subjects. Servants are permitted to sauce their masters. Grooms may kiss the Lady of the Manor—provided they present a sprig of mistletoe.

Caroline was bursting with ambition to figure as the Twelfth Night Queen. It was probable, however, that the honor should go to Miss Wiggett, as the daughter of the house, with our Caroline as Lady in Waiting. She must be content to tend to Miss Wiggett's train, as I had informed her sternly. Caroline promised to be good, tho' with a sulky air; I do hope she has not taken a lesson from her mother, in the speediest way to seize attention.

"How many of our neighbours has Eliza invited?" my mother enquired.

"Sixty-six." Cassandra supplied. "And that does not include the children."

It would be a rout. A fearful squeeze, as they are wont to say in London. Eliza had determined that only the Stone Gallery would do for our ballroom; this ran along the west side of the house on the ground floor, just beyond the billiards room and directly below the portrait-filled Oak Gallery. It had previously figured as a lumber-room, and was characterised by ancient chests, decaying hobby-horses, quantities of broken furniture, and the occasional rusted garden implement. James and Thomas-Vere had been set to superintend the removal of this motley to the garrets; a team of four labourers were tasked with the heavy lifting.

"If only Mr. West might be well enough by tomorrow to attend!"

My mother threw out this hope in all innocence, but neither Cassandra nor I knew how to answer. We were, at present, somewhat at odds. Cassandra was determined to figure as a heroine. She had insisted upon being conveyed to Raphael West's bedside, and proceeded to bathe his forehead with lavender water, until Mr. Price, the surgeon, banished her from the sickroom.

Mr. Price declared the swelling at the rear of his patient's head to be lessening, but his condition otherwise the same. He had forced a paregoric draught down West's throat, and urged that pork jelly be administered by spoonfuls to keep up the patient's strength. For this duty, Cassandra immediately volunteered; but Eliza would not hear of her sacrificing herself in this way. She had not come to The Vyne to minister to the sick. Mr. West was being nursed by Miss Wiggett's old nanny, who, now that the governess held pride of place in The Vyne schoolroom, had nothing to do but darn socks and mend rents in Miss Wiggett's gowns. Mr. Price reposed complete confidence in Sackett, as she was called, and thought that nothing could be more promising for Mr. West's recovery.

With this—and with the lesser rôle of inscribing place cards— Cassandra was forced to be content. It was as well she knew nothing of my conference with William Chute and Lord Bolton in the book room. The knowledge that I had examined Raphael West's sketchbook without his consent should certainly have roused her indignation.

IT WAS BUT AN hour before dinner by the time we had completed our preparations. Thomas-Vere and I had laboured gamely over the composition of so many characters—some thirty-five couples, male and female. Only those we purposed to take ourselves—meaning The Vyne household—were assigned. I was Miss Candour, and must tell everyone frankly what I thought of them. Thomas-Vere was Sir Macaroni, a rôle he should fill to admiration (he intended to borrow a pair of Eliza's heeled French slippers and mince about the Saloon). James was to be The Archbishop, so that he might look his disapproval at the proceedings without offending the guests; William Chute was the Gamekeeper, and might walk about with a fox's mask or a pheasant in his pockets. Eliza was Mrs. Topnote, the celebrated Italian soprano, and must sing for her supper; my mother was Lady Lavish, as befit one who possessed such a handsome reticule. Cassandra we stiled as a Greek Muse, so that she might carry her sketchbook. Mary, we had by common accord, deigned Duchess Highinstep, so that her patronising airs might be taken for a game, and not in earnest.

The majority of the characters, however, were intended to be proffered at random to guests as they arrived in the front hall. Thomas-Vere should have charge of the gentlemen, and I, the ladies. The children—some couple dozen were expected—should form the Queen's Court. Miss Wiggett and James-Edward were to be Queen and King of Misrule—and little Caroline was to wear a splendid faerie-gown of tulle, as Lady in Waiting.

She had spent the better part of the afternoon in the kitchens, watching Eliza's French cook create the intricate decorations for the Twelfth Night cake. These were formed of sugar paste, pressed into boxwood moulds, the shapes then being used to form fanciful royal crowns. The confection itself was a light fruit-cake, made with yeast so that it should rise, and covered all over with a heavy paste icing. It was the most remarkable shade of pink; I suspected it had been coloured with cochineal. The last of the sugar paste crowns and scalloped edging had just been applied as we were mounting the stairs to dress for dinner; Caroline tripped up to the schoolroom behind Miss Wiggett in considerable excitement.

"You go ahead, Jane," Cassandra said as we achieved the landing. "I shall just stop a moment to enquire of Sackett whether Mr. West requires anything. Poor man, he shall be entirely forgot in all these preparations for the ball!"

"He is in excellent hands, Cass," I replied. "Indeed—"

I broke off at the sound of a coach and horses pulling up before the South Porch, and moved to the landing window that I might have a clear view of the scene below. Cassandra silently joined me. Eliza had said nothing of any arrivals this evening.

The carriage was a handsome landau pulled by four horses. The sidelights revealed a crest on one panel—but in the dusk it was impossible to decipher. Had Lord Bolton returned?

A liveried footman jumped down from the landau's rear seat and opened the carriage door. A gentleman stepped out, and turned to take the hand of a lady within.

Both were arrayed from head to toe in black: deepest mourning.

"Edward Gambier," Cassandra whispered, "and her ladyship. What can they possibly mean by attending a ball?"

We stared at one another, perplexed. Neither of the Gambiers should be within a mile of a Twelfth Night celebration in their present bereavement. "Perhaps they have no notion a revel is in view," I said weakly.

"Then why are they come back, Jane?"

"Perhaps they mean to accuse one of us of murder."

I WAS MORE FORWARD in my dress than my sister, and thus descended to the Saloon to await the dinner bell alone. I suspected Cass of dawdling in the upper passages in the hope of meeting the nurse, Sackett, and found myself yearning for a return of her usual good sense. There have been moments in the nearly forty years I have known Cassandra when I wished her more spirited—more open to experience and novelty—less preoccupied with what was correct than with what was enlivening. But if her present infatuation with Raphael West must be taken as a sign of the latter, I must be more circumspect in my wishes.

"Miss Austen," Edward Gambier said with a bow as I entered the Saloon. "I daresay you did not expect to meet again so soon."

"That does not make the event any less desirable," I returned, extending my hand to him. "Rather the reverse."

"You are very good."

He was less smiling and jovial than I remembered; not to be wondered at, now that he had known his sister's loss some days. Grief is more likely to tighten its hold in the first week, when disbelief has given way to the horror of acceptance. I noted his bleak eye and haggard appearance, and pitied him.

Thomas-Vere Chute then entered the Saloon, to exclaim over Edward Gambier's presence. I concluded that not only the Austens remarked upon the sudden arrival.

"The obsequies in Bath were exactly as one should hope?" Thomas-Vere enquired in a lowered voice.

"Indeed. Tho' my poor mother is now prostrate at the grave. I should not have left her, indeed, did my aunt not command my support. Between the claims of two elderly ladies, how is one to chuse? Neither ought to be denied."

Except that one had a fortune to bestow.

I met Thomas-Vere's gaze. He lifted his brows slightly; he, too, was as puzzled as I.

"Your aunt accompanied you here?" I enquired, with a false air of surprize.

"Yes. She is greatly fatigued from our journey, however, and takes dinner in her rooms."

"If you chuse to do the same, Mr. Gambier, no one should blame you."

Edward Gambier gave me a wintry smile. "I find that I require the balm of Society, Miss Austen. I have a difficult task before me, and must take solace in the support of my friends."

Good lord, did he indeed intend to accuse one of us of murder?

"You may count me among them, sir. But surely you do not refer to our Twelfth Night ball tomorrow evening?"

"Ball?"

William Chute appeared in the room, my mother on his arm, and advanced upon us. "Gambier! I did not for the world expect you! To what do we owe this pleasure, my dear fellow?"

Edward Gambier knit his delicate brows. "To my uncle, sir. Admiral Lord Gambier. Did he not communicate his intention of descending upon The Vyne tomorrow?"

"If he did, the communication was mislaid," Chute retorted tartly. "But no matter. He is very welcome, to be sure. What is one more, when a hundred are expected?"

"A hundred?" Gambier repeated blankly.

"For the ball," I supplied.

"Good God, I had no idea." He accepted the glass of wine Chute offered him, and tossed back half of it. "My uncle has not yet learnt of Mary's death."

"Dashed awkward," Thomas-Vere said.

"He wrote to us in Bath," Gambier persisted, "that he intended breaking his home journey here, Mr. Chute. At The Vyne. He means to present you with a copy of the Treaty of Ghent. You are sure you have had no word?"

Realisation overcame me. Benedict L'Anglois. He had received the Admiral's communication, and opened it in the way of secretaries scouting their employer's correspondence. Rather than meet the Admiral—he had bolted.

"My aunt's letter breaking the news cannot have reached him before he left Ghent," Gambier went on. "In good conscience, we could not allow my uncle to learn the intelligence of Mary's end from mere acquaintance. He was excessively fond of her. We came post-haste to arrive before him, so that he might hear the dreadful truth from our lips."

"I see," Chute said drily. "We must hope the Admiral is a little delayed in his journey, lest the revelries in this house tomorrow appear in exceedingly poor taste. Let me refill your glass, Edward—you have need of it."

THE TWELFTH NIGHT

2 8

THE UNEXPECTED GUEST

Thursday, 5th January 1815
The Vyne

Cassandra insisted upon taking a turn with Sackett at sitting up by Raphael West during the night. When I closed the bedchamber door, there she was, gently lit by a shielded candle, a few feet from his bedside. If West did not instantly offer for Cass's hand in marriage upon regaining his senses, there was no justice in the world; and I attempted to be sanguine about it. I had long since given up any pretensions to his interest I might have entertained. I was unwilling to fight my sister for happiness. What man could resist the mixture of sweetness and devotion Cass presented? Regardless of the fact that she should be two-and-forty in a matter of days? He was some years older than that himself.

I was wakeful much of the night, being alone in our bedchamber. In the early hours of morning, Cass crept into bed, and I was able to sleep a little. It fell to me, however, to deliver young Caroline's final gift of the Christmas season—Jemima's Twelfth Night costume.

This was a diminutive domino robe and mask Cassandra and I had fashioned out of a startling shade of pink silk. It was designed to fall in rustling folds over the doll's head and gown, sweeping to her feet, with intriguing almond-shaped openings in the black eye mask. This was the usual garb worn by fine ladies who condescended to appear at publick masques; and no rakish beau should presume to know Jemima's identity, in the midst of the Children's Ball. Caroline might clamour for a matching domino, but she must be contented with faerie tulle.

As I returned from the nursery wing along the upper passage in the weak light of dawn, my hair hanging down my back, I was startled to discern a wraith-like figure wavering in a doorway ahead of me. I stopped short and peered through the gloom. It was Raphael West.

He had one hand on the doorjamb and the other pressed to his eyes. His head undoubtedly ached. But he was upright—God in Heaven! How had he managed it?

He stepped forward, and swayed.

I ran to him, catching him under the arms as he fell. He was exceedingly heavy for one of my weight, but I was not overpowered.

"Raphael," I said urgently. "Raphael."

He opened his eyes, sense swimming in them, as unfixed as stars in the night sky.

"Jane," he said wonderingly, and touched my cheek with his fingers. "A dream. I have such dreams—"

"No," I said. "I am here. Where is Sackett? Where is—"

He lifted my chin with one finger, and set his lips on mine.

He acted as all dreamers do, as tho' under the compulsion of a greater god. I was party to the spell, for I did not protest or break his hold; I merely swooned beneath him, conscious of a wetness on my cheeks where tears of thankfulness slipped down. I was thankful for his life. For the sense that had returned to him. For this benediction at his hands. When at last he released me, his dreaming gaze still not entirely of this world, I said only, "You must go back to your bed. You had a fall on the hunting field some days since. You require your sleep."

He nodded once, turned, and immediately threw himself down on the bedclothes. I closed the door as quietly as possible; I do not think he was sensible, even then, that I was there.

It was only as I moved back towards my own room that I saw my sister Cassandra outlined in the doorway. How much had she witnessed? I stopped short, stricken; but without a word, she turned away. In her countenance I detected something of a bird who knows its wing is broken beyond repair.

It was Sackett who delivered the news of Raphael West's awakening. She had witnessed his eyes open at dawn, and had immediately descended to the kitchens to prepare beef tea. It was during this interval that I discovered him wavering in his doorway; and upon Sackett's return, West was once more asleep. He remained in that state—healing, restorative sleep, rather than the insensible state that had prevailed for days—until Mr. Price arrived at ten o'clock, and testily woke him.

"You are recovered, sir," he declared as he examined West's eyes. "Do you recall anything of the Hunt morning, and your fall from your horse?"

"I do not," West replied. "The moments leading up to it, and everything after until this hour, are as a blank."

He was unlikely, then, to remember my face upturned to his, or the waking dream that had been our kiss. I mastered a feeling of disappointment, and resolved never to think of it again.

Price insisted on bleeding his patient, and at last the beef tea was offered. West informed poor Sackett that it was the merest swill, and demanded steak and ale. William Chute was only too happy to accede to the request.

"We shall let him recover his strength, Miss Jane," he confided to me, "before we tax him with the sketchbook. I should hate to learn that he has forgot all he discovered in Portsmouth and London, along with his memory of the hedge at Sherborne!"

West was asleep again by noon, the bleeding having enervated him. In returning to my bedchamber in search of a needle and thread—Mary would demand a headdress of feathers for her rôle as the Duchess of Highinstep, and nothing would do but I should fashion it—I discovered Cassandra curled under a shawl in a tragic mood, staring into our fire.

I knelt down beside her chair.

"Do not look like that, Cass," I pleaded. "What you observed meant nothing. He was half-alive, half-dreaming. He did not even know I was real."

"He knew," she said, in a barely audible voice. "He loves you, Jane."

"Nonsense." I was as brisk as tho' she were young Caroline. "I suspect Mr. West loves nothing so much as his art; and that is just as well. It shall never disappoint, as a flesh-and-blood lady should."

"Do not sport with me. If he asked for your hand, you should be gone in a thrice."

"And leave you? Never." I grasped her shoulders. "We are both of us too old to be thinking of setting up our own establishments, Cass. And besides—the question does not arise. He has no memory of that meeting in the passage; it is but a part of the whole insensible period of the past few days. I do not regard it; and you should not, either. I am certain Raphael West does not."

She held my gaze searchingly. "Truly, Jane?"

"Truly. We shall leave The Vyne tomorrow, and he shall return to London. Life shall go on as before. We shall remember him as a man thankfully delivered from peril, when others were not—and be content in the knowledge that he lives."

She heaved a sigh, and held my hand between both of hers.

I left her then, to compose herself—and endeavoured to follow my own advice with as much grace.

IF MY HEART HAD been lighter this evening, I might have played at Candour in better spirits. To be witty without giving offence is an art I have not entirely achieved; and I began to regret my choice of character, from a fear of abusing everybody. I should rather have represented Policy, or even Hypocrisy—and gone about with fulsome compliments for all. As it was, I constrained myself to say only what was both honest and inoffensive—and thus, said very little at all.

Half the Kingdom, it seemed, had travelled through the cold to grace Eliza Chute's Stone Gallery on Twelfth Night. Thomas-Vere and I stood at the foot of the staircase in the entrance hall, in the dying warmth of the Yule log, with baskets in our hands and masks covering our eyes. The effect was of a highwayman and his jade begging alms, but I did not care. The disguise allowed me to feel other than I was. Anonymity may be a powerful drug; it is as well we do not taste too much of it in our daily lives. As the guests entered in pairs and in groups, Sir Macaroni and Miss Candour offered their baskets of male and female rôles; the guests chose at random, and went on to assume their characters in the heat and chatter of the Great Drawing-room. Wither and Mary Bramston were among the first to arrive, as befit those in some wise attached to The Vyne; she penetrated my mask immediately, and asked whether "that poor artist fellow was dead yet."

"Unfortunately not," a voice above us on the stairs said quietly;

and Raphael West, arrayed in his most correct evening dress of black coat and white shirtfront, with his cravat splendidly tied, descended the final few steps. "Raphael West at your service, ma'am," he said to Mrs. Bramston, and bowed low over her hand.

She had sense enough to colour as she murmured her pat phrases of congratulation on his recovery, and forgot entirely to draw a character, returning to do so once West had safely moved on.

"Do not trouble to take a card, my dear fellow," Thomas-Vere enjoined as West approached him. "We did not provide one for you. You were to have died well before this evening's gaieties—and have confounded all expectation. You shall do very well as The Beau, however, for a more elegant turnout is not to be found in the drawing-room. Everyone will know at a glance that you are meant to parade as Brummell."

"I shall not offend your dignity by enquiring if you are well enough to stand," I said. "Do not be making a fool of me, therefore, by falling over into a swoon."

"What is your own rôle, Jane?"

"Candour. I am meant to expose the nakedness and expence of half the ladies, and abuse the figures of all the men."

"I can think of nothing more suited to your talents." He bowed.

I grimaced at him. "Am I such a shrew?"

"Nay; a powerful voice for Justice. Is it true that Lady Gambier has consented to join us?"

Thomas-Vere let out a snort. "I had thought she would keep to her room in strictest mourning. But perhaps she drew Melpomene as her rôle—the Muse of Tragedy—and means to play it for the crowd."

Throngs of happy guests, in their most brilliant finery of the season, passed to and fro in the Staircase Hall and the

Saloon, the drawing-room and the dining parlour; but all these were behind our position at the foot of the stairs, and I could see nothing of Lady Gambier. Edward Gambier I knew to be present—he was as simply arrayed as Raphael West, but his cravat was black instead of white.

"When all this is over," West murmured while Thomas-Vere was engaged in offering a card to John Harwood, "I must speak to you about my researches in Portsmouth and London."

"My duty as Candour compels me to admit that I have looked into your sketchbook," I said. "William Chute has done the same."

He frowned.

"You forget," I warned. "It was feared you would die. We thought it imperative to know why someone wanted you silenced. Ah, Mrs. Portal! How ravishing you look in that singularly-coloured gown!"

I presented my basket and offered Lucy the rôles; they were dwindled, now, to but a handful. A few minutes more at my post, and I should be released to what enjoyment in Twelfth Night I could find.

"Then you have seen pieces of the puzzle," West said. "But we shall talk of this tomorrow."

He bowed, and moved around the staircase into the crowd.

"That was Mr. West, was it not?" Lucy Portal observed. "I am happy to find him recovered. It was a dreadful moment when we were interrupted in our walk, by the passage of your nephew's horse—on such an errand!"

Her words recalled a question that had lingered in my mind. "Mrs. Portal," I said when she would have moved on, "you may be surprised to learn that your old friends the Gambiers are within."

"The Gambiers?" she repeated. "At such a time? And in deepest mourning?"

"Their arrival was unexpected. But it brought to mind a matter you mentioned on our Sherborne walk. You said that Lady Gambier was not generally received in Bath society. I have been wondering what you meant."

Lucy smiled at her husband. "Go ahead, John—I shall be with you in a moment. I meant, Miss Austen, that many in Bath were inclined to cut Lady Gambier in favour of her husband, the Admiral. You know that the two are estranged?"

"I did not," I said.

"The Admiral is everywhere admired, as much for his propriety as a Christian, as for his record of service," she said. "But having brothers in the Navy, you will know this already. Lady Gambier's coldness to her husband has excited much comment; he is generally to be pitied."

"That makes matters plain. Thank you for your candour, Mrs. Portal."

She dimpled, and plunged into the throng.

"Well, Miss Austen, I believe we have earned several glasses of my brother William's claret cup." Thomas-Vere set down his basket and offered me his arm gallantly. I tried not to stare overlong at the spectacle of his hosed feet, encased in a pair of Eliza's heeled slippers. I held my masked head high, instead, and prepared for enjoyment.

IT WAS A REMARKABLY pleasant evening. James-Edward and Miss Wiggett were charmingly coupled as the King and Queen of Misrule; their court enacted a series of tableaux, to the general admiration of their parents, and quitted the drawing-room for a juvenile feast above-stairs, complete with an entire Twelfth Night cake.

My mother was discovered in a comfortable coze with the elderly Sir William Heathcote, who proved the ideal escort for Lady Lavish.

Mary was happy in avoiding the Archbishop and his frowns, by dancing several dances with Mr. Harwood, who must regard the rector's wife as the safest object of a ruined young man's affections. Lady Gambier held pride of place near the fire, where she clutched a handkerchief and spoke to nobody. Cassandra solaced her disappointed hopes by sitting quietly in a window embrasure and sketching the colourful company; I observed Raphael West to join her there, and gently offer his opinion of her drawing, which brought a blush to Cass's careworn cheek and a brighter light to her eyes. He had no notion she nursed a *tendre* for him, of course, and behaved only as a gentleman ought; but I silently blessed his good manners and sensibility.

I had been whirled about the Stone Gallery myself on two occasions—once by Thomas-Vere and a second time by my nephew, James-Edward. I had refreshed myself with pasties and Naples biscuit and William Chute's champagne. The hour wanted but a few minutes until eleven o'clock, and some of our guests with children in their keeping had begun to make their *adieux*. Eliza, wrapt in a sable stole, had taken up her post near the South Porch to press their hands in farewell. She looked contented and at peace, as tho' the unpleasantness that had marred The Vyne were at last banished.

And then, among the welter of carriages drawing to the South Porch door to carry away the departing guests—one arrived, and drew up at the door.

It was a post-chaise, not a private carriage, and the postboy so chilled at this hour of the night that the occupant opened the carriage door himself. He stepped out, fitting his tricorn hat to his head, his cloak swirling about him.

"Oh, Lord, Jane," Eliza breathed as she clutched at my arm. "It is the Admiral. I had hoped we should not see him here until morning."

I did not reply; my gaze was riveted by the figure descending from the carriage behind Lord Gambier.

Amy Gage.

In her arms she carried her son.

The Admiral guided her through the maze of carriage wheels at the door and hurried into the foyer, sweeping off his cloak. "Mrs. Chute, ma'am? Well met. You had my letter, I hope? Had no notion we should be interrupting a rout!"

"Admiral," Eliza said breathlessly. "You are very welcome. Pray come into the warm. And . . . your companion?"

"Well," said Edward Gambier behind me. "If it isn't Dismal Jimmy and his bit of French muslin. I didn't think you would try it on, sir, in a house where your wife was staying—and before half the county, too!"

29

MISS CANDOUR MAKES HER CASE

Thursday, 5th January 1815
The Vyne, cont'd.

Jimmy. Jem. The boy was named for his father—and it had never been John Gage.

Much that I had not understood, fell into place as a latch slides into a hasp. But this was not the time or place for brutal declarations; Eliza had already suffered indignities enough.

"What brought you to Hampshire, Edward?" Lord Gambier demanded in bewilderment.

"Not only I, sir, but my aunt as well," Edward returned grimly. "She is even now in the drawing-room, if you wish to know which room to avoid."

"Let me escort you upstairs," I suggested to Amy Gage, "so that you might turn your child over to Nurse. She is an excellent woman and will know just how he should go on; and he will enjoy the company of my niece—a trifle older, to be sure, but ready enough to comfort the boy, should he be wakeful in the night."

"By all means, Jane," Eliza said thankfully, "and pray require Nurse to make up a bed for this young woman in the schoolroom as well, so that she might be near her son."

I extended my arm to Amy Gage, who was shivering in the draughts of the foyer, and said over my shoulder to Edward Gambier, "A little conduct, sir, if you please. You owe your hosts some civility, if not your uncle. Pray carry him up to the library and provide him with brandy. You may give him a piece of your mind there."

Edward had the decency to look abashed, and nodded. "You're correct, of course. I forgot myself. Sir—if you would be so good as to follow me above-stairs."

Our little cavalcade hurried off, without half the county, as Edward had suggested, being aware. The child was starting up a wail of exhaustion—the journey from Portsmouth was a long one— but Mrs. Gage muffled him with her cloak. In short order he was established by the schoolroom fire, being petted by Nurse and fussed over by Jemima and Caroline. Amy Gage gave me one grateful look, and I left the small party to its own devices.

"Who is that girl, Jane?" Eliza asked as I once more descended the stairs.

"Lieutenant Gage's widow," I supplied.

"Then I do not understand anything at all," she said, and threw up her hands.

IT WAS NEARLY AN hour before the last of the Twelfth Night guests had departed The Vyne. As the rest of us mounted the stairs in search of our beds, Edward Gambier came to the library door.

"Aunt Louisa," he said. "My uncle is here. I have told him about Mary."

Lady Gambier was being supported up the stairs by my mother— despite the fact that Mrs. Austen was the senior of the two women by roughly fifteen years. She achieved the landing as her nephew spoke, and raised her head to stare at him.

"Very well," she said. "We have achieved our purpose. We return to Bath in the morning."

"Do you not wish to speak to him?" Edward asked.

She hesitated. "What is there to say?"

"You might comfort him in his distress."

To my horror, her ladyship managed a wintry little smile. "Let him have his fill. It may be some recompense for the injuries he has done to me."

She turned away from the library door. The rest of us collected on the landing—my sister and brother, Thomas-Vere, Mary, the Chutes, Raphael West—stared after her.

"No," I said firmly. "It will not do, my lady. It is not justice to your niece—and what is left to any of you, now, but Justice?"

She turned her basilisk stare upon me and said, "You are impertinent, Miss Austen. It is both vulgar and unbecoming. Much may be forgiven youth—but not a woman of your age."

"Call me Candour," I suggested, "for I mean to speak the truth, Lady Gambier. It has been sadly lacking—both in your family, and in this house. Mary Gambier died for want of truth, and you carry that on your soul."

Her face coloured, then went dead white. I thought she might swoon. Edward Gambier leapt forward and supported her.

"Bring her into the library," William Chute ordered, "and lay her upon the sopha."

Edward did as he was told. We all followed—even James the Archbishop, who might have been expected to urge privacy.

The Admiral looked up as we entered, and rose from his seat by the fire. He was an imposing figure of a man, despite his weathered countenance and thinning hair—a number of years younger than his wife, and more youthful in health and vigour. Where she had retreated into age, he had defied it; and their worlds seemed similarly parted.

"Good evening, Chute," he said courteously; but his eyes bore about them the signs of weeping. "Edward has told me of the tragedies you have witnessed here. I learnt of Gage's death, of course, from your letter—but no word . . . no word—"

He put his face in his hands. After an instant, he recovered himself.

"I do not know the rest of your party."

Chute made the introductions.

Eliza ministered to Lady Gambier with a vinaigrette.

"Her heart is not strong," Edward said. "Aunt always looks the Tartar—but the least shock might carry her off."

"It is a wonder your sister's death did not do it," Eliza murmured.

"But that was no shock to her ladyship," I observed. "Was it, Edward?"

He stared at me, and rose from his position by the sopha. "What did you mean, when you said Aunt Louisa should have Mary's death upon her soul?"

"I meant that your sister need not have died, had she not been burdened with your aunt and uncle's secret," I returned.

"Not another word!" Lady Gambier cried hoarsely from her supine position. "I forbid it."

"And you, Admiral?" I enquired. "Would you have your family fester in continued doubt, now you have already lost your dearest girl?"

He shook his head. "Not for any price."

"Why did you bring Mrs. Gage to The Vyne?"

"I discovered her in Portsmouth upon landing there two days ago from Ghent," he said. "Gage's death left her in desperate circumstances. There was nothing to keep her in Portsmouth any longer.

I intended to carry her and the child to Bath, where she might find employment—as a seamstress, or in service. That is all."

"And how did she come to be married to John Gage?"

The Admiral studied me a moment. "I arranged the marriage for their mutual benefit. Mrs. Gage received the protection of the Lieutenant's name, and the Royal Navy—and Gage . . . earned my gratitude."

"And the promise of eventual advancement, I presume?"

"He should have had his next step this year."

"That plum must have palled in his mouth, however," I suggested, "once he met your niece in Brighton last summer."

"Fool," Louisa Gambier muttered from her sopha. "He should not be talking so. He should not have thrown that sailor in her way."

"John Gage fell in love with Mary Gambier," I said carefully, "at the very moment he might have earned the step that should enable him to marry her—only he was married already, to a woman he did not love! Tell me, Admiral—who is Jem's father?"

There was a brief silence. "I am," he said.

A little sigh ran through the room.

"Good God, sir!" Edward Gambier cried. "Dismal Jimmy, of all people in the world, to have got a by-blow! It might almost be cause for laughter—were it not gross hypocrisy!"

"You cannot say anything to me that I have not said to myself," the Admiral retorted. "A period of madness—of heedless judgement in a distant port . . . and then I, who never had a son, am suddenly the father of a natural one—and dare not acknowledge him!"

"The joke of Providence," Edward observed bitterly.

"Or of Benedict L'Anglois's charade," I suggested. "He was excessively sly, Christmas night, in circulating his riddle—which the Gambier ladies could not fail to notice."

Edward held up his hand. "Of what concern is our family scandal to such a man? What can a child of two or three have to do with Gage's murder? Much less Mary's?" He wheeled upon me. "Do you merely satisfy your desire to know our family secrets, Miss Austen—or is there a purpose to your interrogation?"

I might have answered, but Raphael West spoke for me.

"It is not only Miss Jane who is concerned with Justice," he said. "I am a guest at The Vyne in part to paint its owner—but also on behalf of the Crown. Mr. Chute, you see, has been harbouring a French spy. It was to seize him that I came into Hampshire."

Eliza let out a little cry. "William! Whom have we been harbouring?"

"Poor old Ben. He's a wrong 'un, I'm afraid."

"Mr. Langles!" Eliza moaned. "But he was always so polite. So very distinguished, seemingly."

"What Frenchman is not, my dear?" Mamma offered kindly.

"Explain yourself, West," Edward Gambier said impatiently. "You believe Langles killed Gage?"

"I am almost certain of it. Tho' the gentleman having fled, he cannot defend himself. I believe he exited The Vyne through an ancient bolt-hole that begins near the Chapel, and ends at the ice house, not a dozen yards from where Gage was found. He used the tunnel to set up his snare the night of Gage's arrival, and again on the morning of his death—to break Gage's neck and steal the Ghent Treaty."

"But why kill Mary?" Edward asked in perplexity. "I thought the fellow had a *tendre* for her."

Raphael West looked at me. "Miss Jane?" he said.

"I overheard Miss Gambier arguing with a man I suspect was Mr. L'Anglois in the passage outside our bedchamber doors, in the early hours of the morning of Lieutenant Gage's death," I supplied. "He demanded something of her; she refused. He parted from her with a threat. You know what ensued."

The Admiral spoke. "But why do my darling violence, if he wanted something from her?"

I lifted my brows. "Because she was adamant in refusing L'Anglois. She chose to betray your secret, my lord, rather than prove the ruin of John Gage and his career."

"What do you mean?"

"Please understand: She tried to shield you for long and long. John Gage told your niece last summer, I suspect, that you had persuaded him to give his name to your child. He probably did so to explain why he could not marry your niece. Perhaps he intended, recklessly, to sue for divorce. He might have exposed your sins in the process. Mary negatived that plan. She would not win John Gage at the expence of your reputation, Admiral. You are everywhere respected as a Christian gentleman, I am told."

Lady Gambier let out a cackle of bitter laughter.

"But how did L'Anglois know what John Gage had told her?" the Admiral demanded.

"He knew," I replied, "because you married John Gage to Aimée L'Anglois—Benedict L'Anglois's sister."

"The Devil you did!" Edward Gambier cried. "Lord, Uncle, you did make a mull of it!"

"How could I know the girl's brother was a spy?" the Admiral spluttered indignantly.

"The wages of sin," Lady Gambier said distantly, "are Death."

This silenced the little murmur of interest that had run round the room.

"His sister, Miss Jane?" Raphael West asked. "Are you certain?"

I nodded. "We might ask her directly now—it is of no consequence.

His wife must have believed Benedict L'Anglois dead, to marry another; but his sister was in communication with Mr. L'Anglois, and he with her. She shall probably admit to the correspondence frankly; it is possible she does not share his treason."

"Mary," Edward Gambier said with dogged despair. "I still do not understand why she had to die."

"It is painful to contemplate, is it not?" I said softly. "A young woman of principle and affection, torn between rival loyalties. Mr. L'Anglois wished her to obtain the Treaty from John Gage—so that he might have his intelligence without violence. He blackmailed Mary with the Admiral's illegitimate child. He expected her to fear publication of the family scandal, and steal the Treaty in exchange for silence. But Mary loved John Gage—and she would not violate his trust. She expected a publick shaming upon her return to Bath—the revelation of Admiral Gambier's *amours*. She could not have known, however, that her refusal to take the document Lieutenant Gage carried, sealed his death."

"Poor woman," Raphael West mourned. "How she must have felt it, when his body was carried into the Chapel that day!"

"And how she spent the ensuing hours on her knees," I added, "in an effort to wring forgiveness from Gage and God."

"So you think L'Anglois gave her laudanum," Edward Gambier said, "because she knew he had murdered Gage and stolen the Treaty? Why in Heaven did she not accuse him, and save herself?"

"She might have done so at the inquest," I suggested. "But first she had to wrestle with her conscience on her knees. To accuse Benedict L'Anglois, she must admit the blackmail—and her family's scandal—to a Coroner and his jury empanelled at the Angel. I believe she had decided to do so. She may even have communicated her decision."

"And so she died."

I walked slowly over to Lady Gambier as she lay upon her couch. "You could not bear to have the truth known, could you, Lady Gambier? In all candour, now—you would rather have Mary die, than have the world know your shame."

She stared at me from her pallid face, her eyes two glittering stones. "I never gave him children," she said. "Never. Tho' I tried. So he went and got them himself. Do you have any notion of the humiliation? The agony of that? To be denied as a mother—and see another woman fill your place?"

"You emptied your laudanum bottle into Mary's coffee, that final night," I said relentlessly, "and when, in her stupor, she had gone down once more to lie by John Gage's bier in the Chapel—you let her lie. You left the empty bottle by her outstretched hand."

Admiral Gambier gave a choking cry, and fell from his chair onto his knees, his head bowed. Edward went to him.

"What life had she, in any case?" her ladyship said indifferently. "The man she loved was dead. She was determined to drag our name through the muck. No one should have offered for her then."

"However empty a spinster's days may be," I said harshly, "she has the right to live them."

"Not at my expence," Lady Gambier retorted. She raised herself on her couch and turned to the Admiral and her nephew. "Look at them. Crying for love. Do they not realise what a cheat it is? There, Miss Austen. A bit of candour for you."

She pulled herself to her feet and walked to the door.

"Lady Gambier!" William Chute said sternly. What did he intend? To charge her with murder?

But she did not even bother to pause in her stride.

"You'll never prove it," she said contemptuously. "Tho' you try the rest of your life long. There is no proof."

EPILOGUE

Thursday, 2nd March 1815
Chawton Cottage

My brother Frank rode north this morning to convey the latest and gravest news from Portsmouth, having just received it of the Signals men over the Admiralty line.[12]

"You will have seen from the London papers that Napoleon escaped his prison at Elba on the twenty-sixth," he said as he threw himself into a chair in our front parlour, "but it is in my power to tell you that he reached Paris yesterday. Other than Provence, which is Royalist, he met no opposition on his journey north. Everywhere the veterans of the Grande Armée have flocked to his sword. I am come to take my leave—for it is certain we shall be at war. I am in momentary expectation of my orders."

I am sure my poor mother's heart sank at this; she rejoiced in the cessation of hostilities only nine months ago, and hoped that Frank might be afforded an interval to know his children better. I felt the

---

[12] The Signals men in Portsmouth conveyed messages between the Navy port and the Admiralty in London through an elaborate semaphore tower line, staffed by naval offices wielding flags. Until the invention of telegraphy, this was the fastest method of transmitting orders or intelligence in England.—Editor's note.

descent once more of a familiar anxiety—I am never easy when my brothers are exposed to the cannon of the Enemy—but I recognised the gleam of excitement in Frank's eyes, and congratulated him. He has never got over missing the Trafalgar action by one unlucky day; I hope this new chance of battle brings him glory.

But as I mounted the stairs to my small bedchamber tonight and took out this journal, I found myself thinking of another set of men: those I had met at The Vyne during Christmas. Benedict L'Anglois—he had never been captured at the Channel ports in his flight two months ago. By the end of February his scheme was complete: Napoleon had broken free of his captors, while the better part of the English army was as yet in America. The Treaty of Ghent, having been lost and delayed in its delivery to Parliament, had only been ratified a fortnight since. No word of peace had yet crossed the Atlantic—where Wellington's crack troops remained. It had been cleverly done. Buonaparte had watched the Congress of Vienna, where the cutting up of his great empire had angered the French; he had awaited his moment—and returned in triumph while no deadly force loomed on the frontiers to stop him.

How had Raphael West greeted this news? Was he even now bound for Paris, on some errand of the Secret Funds? Or was he in disgrace, for having failed in his errand of capturing the French spy?

I have had no real word from him since we parted at The Vyne on the Feast of the Epiphany. A few days after my return from Steventon to Chawton, my brother James forwarded a sheet of paper under cover of a letter of thanks to me, for having effected such an improvement in Caroline's temper and spirits. It was the drawing Raphael West had made of me, crouching in the snow. James enclosed it without comment, and no word from West was scrawled on the picture—only his signature.

I have not shewn it to Cassandra.

Here in Chawton we have whiled away February with reading Mrs. Hawkins's novel, *Rosanne*. It is a collection of sober things and exceedingly silly things, particularly on the subject of Love; she goes on rather better when she takes up Religion. The Authoress herself proclaims at the outset that her purpose is "to point out . . . the inestimable advantages attendant on the practise of pure Christianity." That sentiment cannot help to recall Admiral Lord Gambier—who lost so much through his impure practise. The sacrifice of his niece to his wife's mania for reputation has gone unpunished; as that lady wisely noted, no proof could be found of her guilt. The nephew and husband have abandoned her to chilly solitude in Bath—and have taken lodgings together in Town. Amy Gage and her son, tho' provided for (and not in Bath), remain unacknowledged by the Admiral in all but spiritual ways. Edward Gambier's expectations as heir seem secure.

I have almost come to the end of my work on *Emma*. She is a character I cannot suppose that anyone will very much admire, except for me—but perhaps I am a little weary of frivolity. Close observation of another young lady, of higher principles and dearer sacrifice, has taught me to value the word *heroine*. I only wish that I had achieved Justice—of which I spoke so often, and realised so little—for Mary Gambier in the end.

AFTERWORD

In this, the twelfth of Jane Austen's detective adventures, we find the Georgian author embedded in the north Hampshire countryside she loved so well, and surrounded (with greater or lesser affection) by family and friends. The journal manuscript provides fascinating insights to Austen's life during the period when England was once again at war with her former American colonies; and although Jane's naval brothers, Frank and Charles, were not engaged in the War of 1812, their associates, such as Admiral Gambier, certainly were.

The interest Jane felt in the hostilities, including the negotiation of the Treaty of Ghent, is evident from her comments in a letter to Martha Lloyd dated Friday, September 2, 1814. She was staying with her brother Henry Austen in London at the time; and as Henry was a banker with connections among the Prince of Wales's circle, he shared what he knew of official policy toward the Americans. "The[y] cannot be conquered, & we shall only be teaching them the skill in War which they may now want. We are to make them good Sailors & Soldiers, & [gain] nothing ourselves," Jane writes indignantly.[1] She goes on to assure Martha that she places her faith in the protection of Heaven—which she cannot believe the Americans to possess. Something of this scorn for American life surfaces as well in her early conversations with Raphael West. He earns her mistrust by the simple expedient of having an American father, albeit one whose art Jane admired. In the same letter to Martha, she relates her joy at having seen Benjamin West's "Rejection by the Elders" on this visit to London.

Austen's depiction of Raphael West as an artist-cum-intelligence agent is intriguing. The elder son of Benjamin West has left few traces to history, other than a collection of his sketches from a period of travel in the Catskills of New York, and some studies undertaken on behalf of his father. His remarkable visage is captured, however, in several portraits by Benjamin West. In one, a likeness of Raphael and his younger brother dated 1796, and currently in the Nelson Watkins Museum of Art, he appears as a young man living at the height of European Fashion, with his hair cut in the mode of the French Revolution and his dark eyes full of arrogance and discernment. He may then have been living in Paris, a hotbed of Republican sympathies, and it is as well that Jane did not encounter him at this point in his life; they should not have suited each other.

Finally, it is refreshing to experience what Jane calls "the gaieties" of the Christmas season two hundred years ago. The rituals of the twelve-days between Christmas and January 6, the Feast of the Epiphany, are steeped in the earlier mysticism of Celtic-Roman life in a way that feels uniquely British, and far different from the Germanic celebrations Queen Victoria would introduce some two

---

[1] Letter No. 106, to Martha Lloyd, in Jane Austen's Letters, third edition, Deirdre Le Faye, editor. Oxford, Oxford University Press, 1995.

decades later. Even Jane's enjoyment in the warmth and beauty of The Vyne—which may still be visited today through the National Trust—survives, despite her perilous brush with murder.

Stephanie Barron
Denver, CO
June, 2014